A love
that never died...

"You're so beautiful," Daniel whispered, "more so now than you ever were in your teens." His hand stroked her hair, lingered on the exposed arch of her throat. "You were right then, Gwen: you said you were a woman—and you were. I was just too much of a fool to know it. Too afraid of hurting you, wounding you beyond repair."

The intimacy she'd been fighting descended full force, suffusing her arms and legs with a numbing lethargy. Daniel shifted his weight forward, pressing her against the pillows. His arms were beneath her, cradling her close; his nearness was overwhelming. Tenderly, with infinite finesse, his mouth seared hers, then became gentle, seducing, tempting, until she was light-headed and dizzy. She felt as if she were coming to life again, as if all this time she had been only half existing.

"There's never been anyone in my life to replace you, Gwen. There never will be."

ABOUT THE AUTHOR

Cathy Gillen Thacker is a full-time novelist who once taught piano to children. Born and raised in Ohio, she attended Miami University. After moving cross-country several times, she now resides in Texas with her husband and three children.

Books by Cathy Gillen Thacker

HARLEQUIN AMERICAN ROMANCE

HARLEQUIN TEMPTATION

These books may be available at your local bookseller.

Don't miss any of our special offers. Write to us at the following address for information on our newest releases.

Harlequin Reader Service
P.O. Box 52040, Phoenix, AZ 85072-2040
Canadian address: P.O. Box 2800, Postal Station A,
5170 Yonge St., Willowdale, Ont. M2N 6J3

Heart's Journey
CATHY GILLEN THACKER

Harlequin Books

TORONTO • NEW YORK • LONDON
AMSTERDAM • PARIS • SYDNEY • HAMBURG
STOCKHOLM • ATHENS • TOKYO • MILAN

To Steve, Ruth Ann, John and Beth
All that we are and ever will be,
we owe to each other.

———————————◆—◆———————————

Published May 1985
First printing March 1985
Second printing July 1985

ISBN 0-373-16102-6

Chapter One

Black smoke billowed from the exhaust pipe of the red-and-blue Renegade Jeep as it lurched unreliably up the western Kentucky mountainside. "Come on, baby," Gwen Nolan coaxed the cantankerous machine. "Just one more rise and we'll be home free—or at least in a place where I can phone for a tow truck," she amended with a beleaguered sigh. In response, her Jeep only shook harder, the roar of the engine drowning out the peaceful sounds of the early-summer day. Her hands were wet with perspiration and aching with the effort it took to hold the steering wheel steady, but she didn't dare stop or try to turn around. The incline was too steep, the ditch on either side of the narrow country lane still muddy from the thunderstorm the evening before.

The sound of an approaching vehicle jarred her from her absorption. Simultaneously, a sleek black Cadillac topped the crest. It, too, was hugging the middle of the road, and for a split second the two drivers were face to face. Gwen had a brief impression of an astonished male face. Brakes squealing, the Cadillac swerved toward the opposite shoulder of the road. She gave a sigh of relief as the cars missed colliding only by inches. Then the man and the elegant car were past, streaming behind her like a vanishing bad dream.

Evidently the near-collision after the steep incline had been too much for her ailing Jeep. Before she had a chance to catch her breath, it sputtered once, spewed midnight-hued smoke, and then quit. Instantaneously, the power steering became nearly inoperable, as did the power brakes. "Damn!" Gwen swore. Unmindful of her distress, the Jeep slid backward with escalating and unmanageable force. Gwen stomped on the brake pedal, pushing it all the way to the floor, but the Jeep refused to slow down. Panicking, she shifted into low and tried to control the careening vehicle, but it was almost impossible to steer via the rearview mirror. Still gathering speed, the Jeep zigzagged, brushing first one boundary of the road and then the other. Gwen grabbed blindly for the emergency brake and pulled it into action with all the strength she had. Abruptly, the wheels locked with grinding force, and the Renegade lurched to a halt, slamming Gwen first against the safety straps holding her in, then back against the black vinyl seat.

Seconds later she was still trembling with reaction as she unfastened her shoulder harness and opened the door. Her knees gave way as she stepped down from the interior, and she splayed a palm across the seat to steady herself. In the distance the Cadillac was motionless. Embarrassed, Gwen waved the other driver on. But it was too late. The other driver had already decided to play Good Samaritan. Gwen sighed dispiritedly, watching as he made an arrow-straight, completely controlled path backward.

Her heart lurched as the other driver halted directly across from her and she gazed, mesmerized, at an achingly familiar face. Daniel Kingston surveyed her with suddenly narrowed eyes. Of the many times she'd hoped or imagined she'd see her old beau again, it hadn't been under circumstances such as these. Gwen felt color heating her cheeks.

"Are you all right?" he asked abruptly, calling out from his open window.

She'd grown even more beautiful in the years that had passed, he thought, and judging from her expression, more defiantly independent, too. More, she was furious with him, too, not only for having almost run her down but for having caught her at less than her one-hundred-percent best. He grinned, realizing with an inner happiness that surprised him that nothing essential had changed after all.

"Don't I look all right?" Her voice was goadingly cool as she spoke. She curtsied mockingly and waved her hands as if to demonstrate her ability to stand and prance around on her own.

Daniel's dark brows rose in mocking regard before his gaze fastened with maddening accuracy on the open neckline of her navy-blue-and-white cotton tattersall shirt and the madly beating pulse of her throat. She was still as slender as ever, but softer, more...womanly somehow, her breasts and hips more lush. The response within him was immediate and physically passionate. With effort, he pretended to focus on the casualness of her dress. Had any woman ever looked so good in jeans, he wondered, still mesmerized by the wonder—and delight—of seeing her at all. Her shirt sleeves were rolled to the elbow in a careless fashion that bared freckled lightly tanned skin. She still looked at him with the same I-miss-nothing gaze. But beneath the jaunty exterior she was pale and trembling slightly. It had been a close call. Had her driving skill been less or had he been going just a tad faster she could have been over the side of the ridge, trapped down in a ravine, beneath the Jeep. The thought was sobering and disturbing. His mouth curled derisively at one corner. "As a matter of fact, no, you don't look completely unscathed. You look shaky. In need of a drink." *Or a hug.*

"I'll do without the whiskey, thanks." Her tone was contemptuously droll.

Faintly amused, he wondered if she was a teetotaler now, too. Wordlessly, he switched off the ignition, opened the door and got out. Despite her brave facade he knew she needed comforting, and he intended to give it. If she'd let him. Right now she didn't look as if she'd let him touch her with a ten-foot pole. So for the moment he contented himself with a quick quiz. "What happened? Did you lose control of your vehicle?"

He was dressed casually in jeans and a short-sleeved green polo shirt. As he sauntered closer, she saw that the irises of his eyes were as deep-green as she remembered, like the depths of a spring forest, and rimmed in dark gray-green. His lashes and brows were a shade darker than his golden-brown hair and unfairly thick to boot. Why did he have to be so damned good-looking, she wondered. Why, even now, were her senses reeling, her pulse racing with an excitement she hadn't experienced since he'd left her?

Pretending an ease she didn't feel, Gwen lounged

back against the Jeep, her spine pressed against it for support. If it had been any other old friend she would have hugged that person. She longed to hug Dan, too, but wary of the impulses that it might trigger in either of them, did nothing but maintain a carefully guarded distance. How did one treat an old lover, the only man who had ever mattered in one's life? Moderately faded blue jeans adhered snugly to her long legs, their straight-cut fabric disappearing into soft sand-colored suede Western boots.

"Momentarily, yes, I lost control," she informed him baldly, not bothering to keep the sarcasm from her tone. Her look said she'd be damned if she'd let it happen again. He seemed on the verge of laughter, and she fought the urge to give him a piece of her mind, aware she'd already reacted far too emotionally. With feigned composure, she ran a hand through her hair, smoothing her tousled auburn curls. Needing to break the emotional maelstrom he threatened to draw her into by the very unexpectedness of his presence, she changed the subject, "I never thought I'd see you here again."

He caught the faint disapproval in her voice, the hint that he visited his hometown far too seldom, and his gaze burned into her. His eyes followed the outline of her mouth, lingering unconscionably on the full lower lip. *Admit it,* he thought despite his anger, *you've wanted to see her, too. Hell, it's all you can do not to take her into your arms and hold her tight.* "Undoubtedly, as you're never in town when I'm home."

He wasn't back in his native Kentucky that *often,* she thought resentfully. "Sheer coincidence." She shrugged carelessly, trying not to show what riotous effect he was having on her senses.

Dan shot her a probing look and said, "Happenstance that you visit out-of-state friends every time I come to town? Now who's kidding whom?" He anchored both hands on his waist. To his knowledge, he'd never done anything to make her hate him, except to want a life out of rural Kentucky. Yet she looked at him as if he'd betrayed her. Her attitude hurt and dismayed him. He faced her, bewildered. "Why do you avoid me, Gwen?" His tone was low, coaxing.

She flushed. "I would think that would be obvious, considering the way we parted," she said coldly. His mood soured as he realized there was no going back. Even friendship seemed too much to hope for.

She had no way of breaking the tension that had arisen between them, so she remained silent, concentrating for a moment on his physical makeup. He was eight inches taller than she, and although nearly twelve years had passed, he had not changed much in his overall physical appearance. He was still intensely appealing, though not handsome in the classical sense. His jaw was too angular, his nose a centimeter too broad at the base. His rich golden-brown hair gleamed cleanly in the sunlight and looked silkier than it had been. It looked impossible to rumple seriously, no matter how the wind or rain might go at it. His sideburns were trimmed on the short side. There was a new ruggedness in his expression, new parentheses-shaped lines etched at the outside corners of his eyes and around his mouth.

"Notice anything missing?" Dan drawled, giving her a similar head-to-toe appraisal.

Gwen flushed, hating the mocking sound of his voice. She knew her openly expressed resentment had hurt him, but was powerless to change the way she felt. She'd gone through hell after he left her. And though not all of it was his fault—she had her own share of blame to accept—she still felt that in some aspects he had gotten off easily. Because she had made it easy for him. She had protected him from hurt and, inevitably, in doing so, shouldered more of the dark responsibility herself. At the time it had seemed the most expedient, humane way to proceed. Later, all she felt was hurt and loneliness. But he knew nothing about how she had suffered. And, God willing, he never would.

"Not yet," she shot back tartly, echoing his provoking mood as she reinstated her customary bravado. The teasing gibe was too good to resist. "Except, maybe, a heart."

He laughed at that, but, again, his mouth compressed. She wasn't as pleased as she'd thought she would be to find she had struck a nerve. Daniel sauntered forward with deceptive calm until he stood within touching distance.

She swallowed hard, fighting the abrupt impulse to turn and run. In an effort to break the tremulous silence that had fallen between them, she asked, more calmly, "What are you doing back?"

"I was in Lexington earlier this week for a business meeting. I stopped in to visit my folks." Daniel's eyes lifted to hers. "I'll be here for a few days." His mouth twisted. "In case you want to know what roads *not* to drive in the future."

Gwen blushed again, the flood of rosy color making the light dusting of freckles across her cheeks disappear temporarily. He realized in that instant how much he had missed her and that no other woman would ever so

completely capture his heart or his attention. He even
loved her self-reliance, a trait that had been urged into
prominence after her mother's unexpected death when
she was sixteen. Although her father had loved Gwen
dearly, he had not been capable of giving her the emotional support she had needed at that very difficult
time, and instead had ended up relying on her.

"Very funny," she shot back drolly.

His low laughter enticed her to relax. He wanted her
to warm up to him. He wanted them to be able to talk
again. He wanted them to be friends. "At least you
haven't lost your sense of humor, Nolan. Now, if we
could only teach you how to drive." He glanced at the
hood of her Jeep, wanting to extend their time together. "Look, I've never been much good with cars, but
I'd be willing to give it a try."

Her spine stiffened. She didn't want his help just because he felt that it was the polite action to take. Considering their past, she didn't really want anything from
him—except maybe to be left alone. "You don't have
to be gallant, Dan. I can manage just fine, thanks."
Very aware of his eyes upon her, she climbed defiantly
back into her Renegade. The sooner they ended this
interlude, the better it would be for both of them.

It infuriated him to have her refuse his help when
she so obviously needed it. Neither could he leave her
stranded on the side of the road. To walk into town
from there would take hours. It was a mile to the next
farm. "Right," he answered.

Crossing his arms over his chest, he regarded her
with a stoic ease she found infuriating. Unfortunately,
her Jeep refused to cooperate and wouldn't start.

"Would you like me to wait until it's completely

flooded or venture a look at the engine now?'' he asked calmly.

He was enjoying her discomfiture, she noted, temper rising. He actually wanted her to beg for his help. "Why don't you go home?" Gwen moaned despairingly. He knew she could never manage anything if he were standing beside her, glaring disapprovingly over her shoulder. He probably thought she'd gone haywire. In reality, the last time she had behaved so irrationally had been over a decade before, when they were still dating.

"I'd like to go home," he said dryly. "My code of honor won't allow it." He sent her a level look. "I don't mind helping you. Honestly."

Maybe that was the problem, she thought miserably. Maybe she had always known that deep down inside, and foolishly, she had taken it upon herself to solve her problems and dilemmas on her own. "How gallant," she muttered beneath her breath, though by now her cantankerousness was all for show, what one expected from a redheaded woman by way of temper.

Shooting her a mock indulgent glance, Dan shook his head silently, squared his shoulders, and walked casually toward the hood. Once he'd decided to take over, there was no stopping him. "How's the Jeep been running? Before this afternoon," he qualified as she opened her mouth to reply.

Gwen walked reluctantly over to join him. She supposed, like it or not, she could use his help. Probably that was the fastest way to get rid of him and hence all the tension she was feeling, the anxiety that her darkest secret would somehow be found out. Or revealed in a Freudian slip. She had never been able to lie to Dan—

not effectively, anyway. Hands jammed casually in her back pockets, she admitted, "The darned machine throws out gobs of smoke every time I go uphill. There's also something wrong with my brakes. Or at least I think there is. It should have stopped, stalled or not. But it didn't slow down, not in the slightest, even when I pushed the brake pedal all the way to the floor. In fact, just the opposite happened."

"You knew that it was malfunctioning and were still driving it?" he asked incredulously, his disapproval evident.

There was a perverse pleasure in finding that he still cared what happened to her. "I wasn't joyriding, if that's what you're implying. I'm a nurse practitioner. I have patients in the area, people I have to see." Whether or not her Jeep was running in top form had seemed a moot point earlier. Now, having averted ending up in a ravine, she knew better.

"You ought to get it fixed and not drive it again until it is."

It didn't help her chagrin to have him echo aloud the same sentiments she now had. "As it happens, I've been saving my money to do just that," she informed him in the same mildly exasperated tone. His head lifted, his eyes focusing on her with the intensity of twin laser beams. Sensing a lecture on safety coming, one she wouldn't be able to argue with, she admitted honestly, "At the moment, I can't afford to make the kind of extensive repairs the local mechanic wants me to make."

Dan's mouth tightened with suppressed displeasure. "You can't afford to get yourself killed, either." He spoke as if it mattered to him personally.

A pulse throbbed wildly in her throat as she recalled how gently and tenderly he had loved and comforted her in the past. When her mother had been hospitalized with viral meningitis and later died, he had been the one who had held her while she cried. He had been the one who had listened to her talk about her feelings, her anxieties, for hours on end. The bonds of love and caring were still there, she realized with a start. Not even the years alone could erase what they had once felt.

After a second, he glanced back at the dashboard and the interior of the Jeep, his brow furrowing. "Was the oil or generator light on when it stalled?" His voice was brisk and businesslike.

"No."

Wordlessly, he fiddled some more, apparently finding nothing amiss. Dan straightened up, his muscles rippling across his chest, and sighed in exasperation. Striding back across the road, he removed jumper cables from his trunk and, after backing his car around to face hers, connected them from one engine to the other. Despite his efforts, fifteen minutes later his battery was running low and there was still no luck getting even the faintest sound out of the Jeep. He straightened up, wiping grease off his hands, then shot her a brief commiserating glance after reading the anguish on her face.

He'd never been able to fix anything the least bit mechanical, she remembered fondly. It touched her heart that he'd even been prompted to try.

"It's obvious this isn't going to work. I suggest you hire someone from the garage to come out and look at it." Routinely, he disconnected the cables and tossed them into the back of his car. The breeze stirred his hair, brushing neat one-inch strands across his forehead. "If you can't afford it..." He paused, as if unsure how to proceed.

She couldn't believe he'd have the temerity to offer her a loan. But as he seemed about to do just that, she said, "I'll...find a way. Really. Don't worry about it."

And don't look at me that way, either, she thought. *As if you've just discovered a homeless little kitten in need of tender loving care. Care you'd just love to give.*

She swallowed the surprising rush of tears in her throat, reaction to the knowledge of all they had lost. If only things had been different. But the past wasn't something they could share or discuss. She remained silent.

Eyes narrowing in comtemplation, he said softly, "How will you find a way—if you couldn't afford to get it fixed before this?"

Always the practical person, he'd concentrated solely on what needed to be done, never letting a situation go strictly by chance, as she had been wont to do.

She gestured, uncaring. "I don't know. An advance on my salary. Doc Quarrick is understanding."

"You're sure?" He gave her a searching look. "It would be no problem for me to..." He paused, clearly afraid he would offend. "Gwen, I mean it. If you're short of cash, I could lend you whatever you need. We could have papers drawn up if you like, or leave it informal."

He trusted her. Which, considering how she had betrayed him, made the situation all the more laughable. Gwen felt a bubble of hysteria well up inside her.

"We are old friends, after all," he continued. The situation was as awkward for him as for her.

It hurt, having him know she was cash-poor in comparison. Especially when she knew from his mother and father that Dan was doing so well. Embarrassed, she felt her face flame. "I'll be fine," she murmured, averting her gaze. "But thanks, anyway," she said, her annoyance with him fading at his obvious desire to help. How could she have ever thought him heartless, she wondered, unless it had been in her own defense? To help her do what she had known in her heart had been right.

He nodded, relieved to let the subject drop. "Can I give you a ride?"

Feeling suddenly shy, Gwen nudged a groove in the road with the toe of her shoe. The last place she wanted to be was in the enclosed confines of the car with him, but she had several patients to phone, to tell them she would have to reschedule their appointments with her for the next day. Thankfully, no one was in need of immediate medical care. All the visits were routine. "I do need to get to a phone."

"I'll drive you over to my parents' farm."

"Thanks. I'd appreciate it."

Wordlessly, he escorted her toward the sleek black Cadillac. He held open the driver's door and motioned her in. Had he done it deliberately, she wondered, unable to read the inscrutable expression on his face, evoking the memory of how they used to get in and out of a car when they had traveled anywhere together as teenagers? Or was he insisting she use his door as a precaution, because of the treacherous drop-off on the other side of the unfashionably wide car on the narrow country road?

She was forced to move past him, their bodies close

but not quite touching. He recoiled slightly as she moved past him, his heart pounding in his chest. It came to Dan then how much he still wanted her—physically, emotionally, intellectually.

Her mouth dry, she scooted past the steering wheel. Despite her efforts to play it cool, it was impossible not to be aware of the way his eyes caressed the curve of her thighs and calves and the way her soft, much-laundered jeans hugged both. He slid in nonchalantly after her, slamming the door, and started the car. The air conditioner shot cool air across her fevered brow. He drove much faster than she had remembered. Or maybe it just felt that way because of her jittery nerves. She straightened up focusing her glance on the yards of rusting barbed-wire fence on either side of the country road.

A weathered aluminum mailbox marked the driveway to the Kingston farm. Daniel slowed the car automatically, turning into the driveway. Fifty yards back from the road was a small two-story yellow farmhouse with a wide front porch. Two sun-bleached wooden rockers decorated the cement-floored porch. A huge red tractor stood in front of a weathered gray barn.

Sixty-year-old Miles Kingston was standing in the center of his garden. Tall, broad-shouldered like his son, he was a strikingly robust man with a closely cropped head of hair, now more white than gray. As was customary, he was wearing overalls, heavy boots and a farmer's thin short-sleeved blue chambray cotton shirt. Betty stood on the porch, a puzzled expression on her face. A pink-and-white-striped seersucker dress covered her plump form.

Dan gave his parents no time to jump to conclusions,

saying bluntly, "Gwen had car trouble up the road. She needs to use the phone." He paused, wanting only to escape his mother's scrutiny and avoid what could be a potentially embarrassing situation for both him and Gwen. An assessment of their relationship, past and present, they did not need. "Dad, I got that part you needed for your Rototiller. It's in the trunk of my car. I'll get the toolbox and go try it out."

He couldn't have acted more anxious to leave than had he just discovered she was a carrier of the plague, Gwen though derisively.

"Give me a second to say hello to Gwen and I'll help you," Miles offered. Betty held out her arms warmly and Gwen slid into the plump woman's embrace, grateful for the distraction that covered Dan's retreat.

Seconds later Miles excused himself politely and strode off in the direction of the barns. Betty led Gwen into the kitchen. An oscillating fan above the refrigerator cooled the large country kitchen. Betty waved her toward the large oval table. "Can I get you some iced tea?"

"Please." After her confrontation with her ex-steady, Gwen's mouth and throat felt as dry as the Sahara.

The two women chatted inconsequentially for several minutes. It was clear that Betty was curious about Gwen's meeting with Dan, but she was too polite to ask how the impromptu reunion had gone. Not that she really needed to. Dan's distance was proof enough.

After finishing her tea, Gwen called her patients, then the garage for a tow truck. Betty gave her a ride back to her Jeep. At Gwen's insistence, the older woman left her relaxing against the side of the Jeep, contemplating ways to pass the time until the wrecker arrived. Eventually, Gwen noticed a thicket of black raspberry bushes. Rummaging around the back of her Renegade, she pulled out an old plastic bucket suitable for hauling the garden vegetables her patients generously bestowed upon her. If mechanic Walt Fowler was as long getting there as she suspected he was going to be, she'd be making good use of the time.

Carefully, she climbed the barbed-wire fence and started through the tall, waving green-yellow grass, interspersed with occasional wild flowers and large rocks, to the clump of bushes. They were thick with plump berries, and Gwen began plucking the juicy fruit off and dropping the sweet morsels into her bucket. Unable to resist a taste of the luscious-looking fruit, Gwen tilted her head back and dropped a lone berry into her mouth. The tart juice filled her mouth, covering her tongue with just-picked sweetness.

Without warning came the sound of a car motor. Abruptly it cut off. She glanced up, expecting to see Walt Fowler descending from the cab of his tow truck. Instead, Dan Kingston was back and was striding casually across the country road, his strides purposefully and unnervingly long.

He paused a moment, searching her out. As if realizing abruptly that she was not going to voluntarily close the distance between them, he rested one palm on a splintering gray post and hoisted himself gracefully over the barrier. Once on level ground, he dusted off his hands. His manner was still quite casual, but her heart had begun pounding in her chest. "You needn't look as if I'm about to molest you," he said.

She flushed, angry and embarrassed that he had so

easily read her reluctance to be alone with him. Right hand raised to shield her eyes from the glare of the sun, she remained where she was. The half-filled bucket of berries dangled limply from her perspiring left hand. She used the tip of her tongue to wet her suddenly dry lips. Alone with him now, she could think about nothing else except how it was to kiss him, how securely wonderful it felt to be held in his strong arms.

But his tone was innocent when he spoke after a brief hesitation. "I wanted to ask you about my dad. How does he seem to you?"

"What do you mean?" In an effort to regain her composure, Gwen went back to picking berries. He stalked her quietly step for step, and his nearness made her senses whirl.

"Mom thinks Dad may be having chest pains."

The anxiety in his voice made her stop and pivot toward him.

He continued, "She's been trying to talk him into getting a checkup. So far he won't hear of it."

In the garden, Miles had seemed a picture of health. But looks could be deceiving. "What do you want me to do?" Gwen asked compassionately.

Dan shrugged, for the first time in his life looking uncertain as to how to proceed. "Talk to Dr. Quarrick?"

She nodded agreeably, her concern for his family's well-being evident. "I'll tell him you're worried. Maybe he can stop by, chat with your dad. Sometimes, just the opportunity to speak privately to a physician can spark the need to confide."

"Thanks, I'd appreciate that. Mom will, too." He sighed as if greatly relieved.

They were standing in the shade of a towering hickory tree. The breeze stirred around them languorously, lifting the sticky cloth from Gwen's perspiring form.

"Is that all you needed from me?" There was no hiding the tension in her voice, the agitated way she kept her distance. Being alone with him in a setting so conducive to romance made her nerve endings feel as if they were on fire.

Dan felt a resentment that was deeper and more penetrating than anything he'd ever experienced in his life. The air seemed charged with electricity, a sensual current that neither of them could deny. "Believe me, I wish it were," he murmured softly, his hand lifting to frame her face lightly. His gaze became gentle unexpectedly. "But no, it's not all I want from you."

He glided forward until the fragrance of his breath joined with hers. Her knees weakened as she realized his intent. But it was too late for evading. Maybe, in a sense, for them it always had been. True love did not die in a second, in a decade; it endured forever and ever. As solid and unshakable as the earth. As changeable but as ever-perpetuating as the seasons.

Hands cupping her chin, Dan turned her face up to his. The taste of ripe berry was replaced by the warm insistence of his mouth moving over hers, the tantalizing taste of wintergreen mints, the faint saltiness of his skin as he initiated the chastely tender yet oddly stirring caress. She trembled under the onslaught, desire sweeping through her, alluring and dangerous. His cologne was new, rich, scented expensively with herbs, the clean fragrance of his skin achingly, erotically, familiar. For a time, the years drifted away, as if the separation between them, the disillusionment and heartache, had never been and all that was left was sheer passion, flowing vibrantly, unassuaged.

When she was limp and malleable in his arms, he drew back, his expression just as intrigued as hers, and then his head was lowering again, dipping, caressing, taunting her with his nearness and the soft gentle persuasion of his lips and the fact that nowhere else were either of their bodies touching. She could feel the heat emanating from him, the strength. He had always enjoyed the inherent power of a man over a woman. He enjoyed it now, she thought, mesmerized, as he wielded it to full advantage, convincing her to spiral deeper and deeper into the growing intimacy of his kiss, the potent touching of their mouths, the silent communication of souls. Many things had changed in their lives, but their attraction for one another had remained constant. No one else had ever made her feel that way. She knew deep inside no one else ever would. That intensity of love came only once in a lifetime. But it had ended. As this would end. Must end.

Pressing her hands against his chest, she forced herself to end the kiss. Reluctantly, his face flushed with the heat of their sweet, drugging passion, he drew back. His gaze caressed the light dusting of pale freckles across her nose, the flush of the sun across her ivory skin. He studied her lashes, thick and darkened to advantage with mascara, then the brilliance of her light aquamarine eyes. In the distance, a truck motor sounded, came nearer.

Walt Fowler roared into the clearing and parked his tow truck directly in front of Gwen's Jeep. Dan inclined his head toward the road. He looked both annoyed and relieved at the interruption, indicating to her he was just as mystified, pleased and bewildered by the rebirth of their passion as she. After a moment, he offered curtly, gazing down at her seriously, "If you need me to stay, I will."

To let herself depend on him again would mean eventually to get hurt. "I can manage. Thanks." Her voice trembled slightly with reaction and she straightened up, very conscious of her racing pulse.

Together, they began walking toward the fence. Overhead, the sun beat down from a radiant blue sky. Dan raised a hand to help guide her over the fence. When he'd joined her on the other side of the barbed wire, he said casually, "I want to see you again, Gwen. But I feel it's only fair to warn you that I'm only going to be here a few days."

He wanted to make love to her again. If the thought of his leaving hadn't been so painful, she would have wanted it, too. "I think it would be better if we didn't see each other again," she said quietly, cutting off whatever he'd been about to propose. His glance darkened unhappily. Giving him no chance to dissuade her—which would have been, she thought sadly, very easy to do—she strode off silently to speak to the mechanic. For a moment it appeared that Dan would follow her, anyway, to insist at the very least on taking her back to town. But at the last moment, all too aware of the mechanic's presence, Dan turned and strode back to his car. Determinedly, she told herself it was all for the best, as she watched his car drive off with a spray of loose gravel. She only wished she could have believed it in her heart.

Chapter Two

The Dawson Springs Clinic was nearly deserted by the time Gwen returned at four-thirty. While Dr. Quarrick saw the last four patients, she checked in with the receptionist, returned several calls to patients and phoned in three refills on patient prescriptions to a local pharmacy.

"Trouble with your Jeep again?" her boss asked as he joined her at her desk.

Gwen groaned in mock agony and tossed him a wry smile. The forty-five-year-old physician never passed the opportunity to make a facetious remark about her inherent thriftiness. "You know I never get rid of anything usable," she teased. "And despite its chronic complaints and Walt Fowler's testimony to the contrary, that Jeep's still got a lot of miles left in it."

Bernie laughed, absentmindedly stroking his fluffy red beard and mustache with an open palm. "So you think, anyway. Is Walt going to be able to fix it?" He settled his big-boned frame into a chair. The father of two, Doc Quarrick was devoted to his family and friends. And a godsend to all the patients in the area.

"I didn't give him any choice. I can't afford a new

Jeep, and the prices on resale four-wheel-drive vehicles are astronomical these days."

"True," Doc agreed. Casually, Gwen filled him in on what had happened during afternoon rounds, then ended with Dan Kingston's concern about his dad. "Well, I'll drop in on Miles later in the week," Doc promised, shedding his lab coat and the stethoscope he had laced around his neck. "He's due for a check-up."

"Thanks."

"Don't mention it." Doc paused on his way out the door. "How is Dan Kingston?" His head cocked speculatively as he waited for her reply.

"Polished." Though there were a few rough edges left, enough to let him lose his patience with her. Or had she involuntarily provoked him, as a way of keeping the distance between them, or trying to, Gwen wondered. And the interlude in the meadow. Just what, exactly, had that meant, unless it was strictly for old times' sake? Or was it because he was as curious as she about what had been—memory versus reality— what might have been, had they continued dating? Neither of them had ever married.

Refusing to think about it further, Gwen locked up the clinic, then started toward the parking lot. She was almost to the sidewalk when she saw Dan Kingston, leaning against his parked car. Legs splayed languidly, his feet planted firmly on the pavement, for a long moment he simply stared her way.

"Hi." His voice was a husky whisper.

"Hi." Involuntarily she remembered how warm his breath felt when it sizzled across her bare skin, how gently his hands could caress. And the way he could kiss. Already her defenses were tumbling down like raindrops from the sky.

"Need a lift home?" His tone was pragmatic and helpful, nothing more.

Heat radiated from the blacktop parking lot beneath her, making her want to dance in wary agitation.

As if realizing she needed to know the why behind his action, he said, "I'd like us to be friends again, Gwen."

Her eyes held the promise of his. On some plane, she knew she was behaving like an adolescent. So he was still attracted to her and she to him. So what? *Wasn't it time they buried the hatchet? How much longer could she go on hating him, blaming him for what should have been over for both of them long, long ago.* "I'd like that, too," she said quietly at last. Maybe this was the way to find the acceptance she had so badly needed then, still did in some ways.

His expression inscrutable, he studied the windswept disarray of her hair, the new flush of color in her cheeks. "Good. Then there's no reason why you can't have dinner with me tonight, is there?"

Gwen felt a shiver of uncertainty inside. Many nights she had dreamed of just this happening. But now that the reality was upon her, she wasn't sure she wanted to risk letting her heart be captivated by him again. Did he want to make love to her? Was that the reason behind the invitation? Or was this to be strictly a reunion between friends, a way simply to pass the time while in his home state?

"Please." His eyes held hers.

Caution fled in reaction to the sincerity of his gaze. "All right," she said softly.

Dan smiled his pleasure at her acquiescence.

Defensively, she focused on the old brick buildings and weatherworn awnings that lined the small town's main street. Her voice was casual as she asked, "Where would you like to go?"

"The Old Talbott Tavern in Bardstown is only an hour and a half away by the Western Kentucky Parkway." The restaurant was famous for its fine country cooking.

She nodded her approval. After they'd agreed on a time, Gwen said casually, "I talked to Doc Quarrick. He said he would stop by sometime later this week and look in on your folks."

"Thanks."

Dan dropped her off in front of her house and then, promising to return in a little over an hour, drove off with a casual lift of his hand. Once inside, Gwen headed for the bathroom, stripping off her clothes as she went. She told herself it was curiosity that had prompted her to accept his invitation, but she knew it was more than that. She wanted to go out with him. Crazy as it seemed, she wanted him as part of her life again.

While the tub filled with warm scented water, she thought back to her early days with Daniel. They'd dated on and off through high school, played together as kids. But it had been the summer he turned eighteen when everything had changed, the summer before he'd gone away to college that the passion had flared out of control. It had happened gradually—necking sessions that left them both glowing and aching with desire; explorations, both curious and bold, of one another's bodies, lying together fully clothed, then less protected, until finally kissing was no longer enough and they tested their ardor to the depths. And once that had happened, there had been no turning back. But a month before he was to go to the Eastern university, everything changed. They'd nearly been discovered by a group of hell-raising local boys, and it had brought Dan into keen awareness of what he was asking of her. "This is crazy," he'd said that August night. The moonlight shone down through the trees to illuminate his hair. His features had been tense with anxiety. "Gwen, you're sixteen—"

"I'll be seventeen in a month," she'd argued passionately.

"You're a child." His voice had been rough.

They'd both known that had she been blessed with the parental guidance needed at that point in her life, had her mother still been alive, her father not so busy with work at the mines, their affair never would have happened. Hence, Dan had remained stubborn in his resolve to end their dangerous liaison.

"What we're doing is wrong, not to mention against the law. We're betraying all those who trust us. Your father, my parents..."

Tears had glimmered in her eyes. She'd been all too aware of the consequences of their actions from the beginning. Yet she'd never been afraid of the risk. No, loving Dan had been worth it.

"I'd never accuse you of statutory rape."

"No, but your father might, and he'd be well within his rights," Daniel had countered grimly.

"I'm using birth control." In an agony of embarrassment, she'd bought it in a neighboring town's pharmacy. "I won't get pregnant."

Her pleading voice didn't budge him. His voice was

soft as he reasoned gently, "Don't you see that's not my main concern? It's you. I love you and I don't want to see you hurt. And if we continue, I will be hurting you, more than you know." He'd looked away then, as if unable to go on.

"You're hurting me now," she'd countered softly, tears glistening in her eyes.

He'd had no reply for that, except to say, very low, "I never should have allowed it to go this far." His jaw rigid with resolve, he'd stared at the silvery water rushing over the jutting rocks peppering the mountain stream.

"You wouldn't do this if I were eighteen, too," she'd said harshly. Acutely aware that he was leaving her and going to another part of the country in a month, blindly jealous of the freedom he would have, the access to beautiful, cultured girls, she'd deliberately implied that he was dumping her for less than gallant reasons.

Still, he had refused to let her provoke him, knowing, she now supposed dully, that to fight passionately would also be to love.

Shaking his head, he'd said with wounded resignation, "You're not eighteen, Gwen. Maybe in a few years we'll.... Ah, hell, I don't know. I only know this is wrong. And it has to stop." Swallowing hard, his body rigid with the control he'd been exerting, he'd extricated himself from her arms and strode wearily away, to the other side of the clearing.

Remembering the desolation she had felt then, tears glistened in Gwen's eyes. She'd felt her heart was breaking. She'd followed him into the shadows, hands upraised pleadingly. "Don't go to college," she'd said softly. "Don't leave me."

"I have to." His voice had been coolly implacable. "It's the only way I'll be able to make a decent life for us."

"We could have a decent life here," Gwen had insisted.

"On my dad's farm?" he'd questioned bitterly. "Or in the mines? Is that what you want for us and our children, Gwen, an impoverished existence, living from month to month, always wondering if I'll be laid off or the weather will ruin this year's crop?"

No. It hadn't been. She'd said nothing.

"I want more than that, for me, for us. I thought you did, too."

In the month remaining she'd been silent, hurt, withdrawn, sure she was losing him forever. He hadn't touched her once, had barely even kissed her. But the last night before he'd left for college he'd broken down and said, "Wait for me, Gwen. Promise me you'll wait, that you'll marry me as soon as I'm through school."

Four years had seemed another lifetime away then, a dull promise, a way of assuaging her fears, his conscience. Feeling as if her whole world was slowly shattering, she'd said, "I don't want your promises, Daniel. Not now, not ever." She didn't want him to swear to her anything he wouldn't be able to give. She'd been hurt enough. Nor would she promise her fidelity to him.

He'd left angrily. She told herself she didn't care, that he deserved to be hurt because he'd hurt her, too, spoiled what little time they could have had left.

Months later she'd wondered what would have happened had she relented and made love with him then, that night, or at least promised him she would wait,

write, keep in touch, love only him. But she hadn't.
And weeks after that, her father had been killed in a
mining accident, and her world really had been blasted
apart. Irrevocably.

Gwen dressed for dinner in an off-the-shoulder
peasant dress in softest sky-blue gauze. Trimmed with
frothy blue lace, the full gathered skirt fell to midcalf.

Dan arrived at precisely six-thirty, standing on the
wooden front porch as matter-of-factly as if he'd been
dating her continuously throughout her adult life. He
held a tissue-wrapped bouquet of forget-me-nots in his
hand. The flowers were transferred from his hand to
hers, and then his arms went around her. Unmindful
that they were in full view of the street and the neighbors, he lowered his mouth to hers. The kiss ended as
tenderly as it had begun. "Hello again," he said softly.

"Hi." Gwen led the way shyly inside. The interior of
her century-old brick house was neat as a pin. Braided
rugs covered waxed parquet floors. She'd added cheer-
ful red-and-white floral wallpaper and hand-sewn cur-
tains and slipcovers in the same country print.

While she put the flowers in water, Dan looked
around appraisingly. "You've done a lot with the
house." She nodded, pleased that he liked where she
resided.

They were silent as he escorted her to his car and
expertly navigated their way out of Dawson Springs
and onto the parkway. To lighten the silence, he flicked
on the FM radio, finally settling on a country-and-
western station. "Do you remember that time we got
stuck on Route 62, coming home from a movie in
Princeton?" he said.

"Some first date, wasn't it?" Gwen asked huskily as

the sounds of Kenny Rogers filled the car. Dan was wearing a light-gray sharkskin suit, white shirt and a conservative silver-and-black-striped silk tie. She wasn't sure whether it was her imagination or just the shock of being with him again so intimately, but he seemed even more aggressively fit now—slim of waist and broad of shoulder—than he ever had been in his youth. She laughed. "I remember watching the gas gauge teeter over to a precariously low state. I couldn't believe you were actually going to let us run out of gas. Yet I was too afraid of insulting your intelligence to say anything."

"You should have," Dan moaned, no doubt remembering how far he'd had to walk to call for help, while leaving her stranded alone and terrified in his father's locked car. "I was so nervous about taking you out that I just forgot to look. By the time I got you home, your father was ready to kill me!" he added with a rueful chuckle.

"Your reputation as a heartthrob with the local teenage girls preceded you," she teased, taking pleasure in his chagrined look. He reached over to clasp her hand. "I was sorry to hear about the mining accident that killed your dad, Gwen."

"I know. I got your card." It had been a nice Hallmark. There'd been no inscription except "Dan." And yet she'd carried it around tucked in her address book for months, hoping he would follow it up with a phone call or letter—something, anything, more personal.

"I didn't hear about the accident until it was too late to come back," he said.

"Would you have attended the funeral if you'd known in time when and where it was going to be held?'' Hope sprang eternal within her, but her voice was immeasurably cool.

Dan was too inherently honest to assuage her with false words of comfort. He withdrew his hand, loosely clasping the steering wheel. After a moment, his eyes on the road, he said, ''I probably would have phoned to let you know I was thinking of you if I'd known sooner. As it was, several days had already passed. Frankly, I wasn't sure you would've wanted to talk to me, recalling the way we had parted.'' And it hadn't been that long since they had argued, only a matter of weeks.

''Probably not,'' Gwen agreed unhappily. But if he had come home then, how different both their lives might have been. Dan concentrated pensively on his driving. She shot him a hesitant glance, then looked out the window, watching as miles of Kentucky bluegrass whizzed by. Every mile or so, she saw a beautifully maintained horse farm with sleek-coated thoroughbreds grazing behind sections of immaculately kept fence.

They reached the restaurant he'd suggested. Designed to withstand Indian attack, the Talbott Tavern had been constructed in 1779 and was built with heavy timber and thick stone walls. The original fireplaces and mantels still adorned several rooms. Original Greenough lithographs of famous Indian chiefs hung on the wall.

Gwen and Dan were seated in the oldest section of the building at a heavy antique table near a deep window casing overlooking the quiet Kentucky street. During dinner Dan questioned her quietly about mutual friends and former acquaintances. He wanted to know who had married whom and how many children they had and what they were doing professionally. In addition, he told her a little about his work at IDP, how challenging it was to manage people and resources in the growing field of computer technology.

"You always said you were going to be a success," Gwen commented, not the least bit surprised to discover how well he was doing.

"What happened after you left Dawson Springs?" he asked. Brows furrowing, he leaned toward her slightly. She had changed—that much was apparent— grown more self-reliant, at times pricklier. There was a sorrow in her eyes, a hurt that hadn't been there before. He found himself wishing he could erase that pain, hold her in his arms and never let her go.

She hesitated a moment and looked away, as if she were uncomfortable talking about that time. "I went to live with my cousins in Cincinnati, finished my senior year of high school there and, because I was then an Ohio resident and wanted to attend a state school, applied for acceptance at the University of Cincinnati. By then I'd decided on nursing as a career, so I obtained a partial scholarship to help pay for my tuition. I worked summers and weekends as a nurse's aide in a hospital to earn money for my room and board and books. When I graduated I got a job at Good Samaritan Hospital. I worked there for five years, and then I left to finish work on my master's degree."

Told now, it all sounded so simple and matter-of-fact. Then, she had been going through agony, wrestling with her conscience and her heart, wondering, praying, that she had done the right thing, while all the while trying to keep her immediate past a secret from those who knew her best.

"Why did you come back to Dawson Springs?" he asked.

That she couldn't tell him. She shook her head non-committally, pushing aside her plate as she groped to formulate a reason he would accept unquestioningly. "Because in my heart I guess Kentucky still felt like home to me. And I wanted to try my hand at nursing in a rural environment. I thought it would be good experience." Resting her elbows on the table, she clasped her hands beneath her chin. Inside she was shaking with reaction, realizing how close to being discovered she was now. "What about you? Are you going to be in Chicago indefinitely?" She had to get the conversation onto safer ground.

He watched her quizzically. "Eventually I expect I'll be transferred again, according to the needs of the business. At the moment, I don't much care where."

So he was as rootless as he seemed, she thought, a confirmed bachelor. Her heart sank a little more. When she had know him, he'd been determined to marry and have a family when the time was right. Had that changed? Or had he never found the right woman, the right time? "What, exactly, do you do?" Gwen asked, determined to keep their encounter on a strictly platonic level.

"Currently I oversee all aspects of production, distribution and marketing of the new home computer International Data Processing makes."

"I'm impressed."

Dan lifted one shoulder with the nonchalant ease of a man long used to commanding his own destiny. "I've worked hard to get where I am. As have you." He spoke with quiet acceptance, then reached across the table to cover her hand with his own. He paused, his preoccupation with small talk finally fading. "Are you sorry that we didn't work out our problems and marry as we'd planned?" The question came without warning and there was no emotion in his voice to hint at what he was feeling, only cool calm and the intensely logical side of him that Gwen had sometimes come very close to hating.

She took a tremulous, steadying breath. If only he knew what she'd been through after he left, she thought. If he'd known what that time had cost her in terms of guilt, reproach, personal pain. But he didn't. And she'd promised herself he never would. She glanced out the window at the traffic on the street. Sadness swamped her, colored her words with a dismal undertone. "What point is there in going back?" *Nothing can be changed now, Dan, no matter how much we wish that it could.*

His mouth compressed unhappily. She knew then that it wasn't what he had wanted to hear from her. He regarded her steadily with a cool contemplation and a measured intensity she was unable to fathom. For the first time she had a view of what he might be like in the business world. She wouldn't want to be working against him.

"You've changed," he commented as coffee and home-baked pastries were brought to their table. After the waitress left, he elaborated, "You're not as trusting as you once were."

"I've matured."

"You've been hurt." As her friend and former lover, he wanted to know all the specifics.

But there wasn't any comfort for what she had been

through, so she said nothing as she pushed the crumbs around her plate with the prongs of her fork.

"Is it the kind of work you do?" he asked. "Working in such an impoverished area?" His folks were fine financially now. They always had been fairly well off. Many others were not.

She shook her head. "I enjoy helping people, Dan. True, the money is not as good here as it would be elsewhere. But elsewhere I wouldn't be needed as much."

"And that's all it is?" His eyes met and held hers.

Anxiety, fear of exposure, made her heart pound. "What else could it be?"

"I don't know." His tone was curt and unrelenting.

Gwen pushed her coffee away. "I really should be getting back. I have an early day tomorrow."

After a moment, he nodded reluctantly and rose to help her with her chair. "All right."

On the drive home they were silent. He made no attempt to speak and neither did she. *Too soon he would be leaving Kentucky again,* Gwen thought. Too soon he would be out of her life. Already it hurt.

When he parked at the curb in front of her house, she started to step unassisted from the car. "I'll walk you to the door." He was at her side before she could protest.

Their steps clattered in tandem on the stone walk. Moonlight filtered down through the trees. It was eleven o'clock. Many houses were completely dark, their occupants having already retired for the night. Dan shoved his hands into his pockets and remarked, "I'd forgotten how quiet small towns are at night."

"I'll agree with you there," she said wryly. "Dawson

Springs, with its population of three thousand plus, is not the most exciting place to spend the night." She fumbled in her purse for her key.

Dan had envisioned many times their meeting again. Sometimes in the city, sometimes in their hometown, on the street, in a store. He was always polished and debonair, in city clothes, with a beautiful girl on his arm, someone who would have promised him her soul if he'd asked, who would do anything, give up anything, to be with him. Never, though, did the faceless girl in his fantasy mean anything to him—she was just a way of getting to Gwen and assuaging his hurt, maybe his ego or his pride.

When the actual meeting had come, he'd been prepared for the awkwardness—it had been twelve years, after all. He hadn't been schooled for the change in her. Gwen still had the ability to look right through him as if she saw everything and, more important, understood all too well what drove him. But there was a new guardedness about her. Something that worried him. Even at dinner he hadn't felt that he'd ever gotten her to really open up. He wondered if it was his leaving Kentucky that had hurt her that badly, losing her parents, or something else—something he knew nothing about.

"Offer me a cup of coffee?" he asked hopefully. He couldn't leave her. Not yet.

Since it was put that wistfully, she hadn't the heart to refuse him. "All right." *But no more kissing,* she promised herself silently. *Just...talk.* Tomorrow he would be gone. Her life would resume its even keel. She had to remember that.

Yet a strange contentment flowed through her as

they entered the house together. She wondered at it, decided finally that it was because her memory of Dan had remained largely intact. Dan had matured, become more self-assured, but the essential appealing traits of his character hadn't changed. He was still interested in others, warm, intelligent and soft-spoken, compassionate, incredibly sexy.

She moved forward routinely, switching on several lamps, opening a window. A small box fan on the floor whirred pleasantly. The living room was illuminated with a seductive golden glow. With him in it the room seemed cozier, more inviting.

Dan conversed pleasantly and inconsequentially as she prepared coffee, then carried the tray to the coffee table in the living room. "Why didn't you ever marry?" he asked. "I thought surely by now you'd have a husband, several children."

Her hand shook slightly as she poured his coffee. "I've never found anyone I loved enough to make that kind of commitment," she replied honestly. After a moment she added, "What about you?"

"I came to the conclusion after we broke up I wasn't the marrying kind." His eyes searched her face, lingered, as if memorizing every nuance about her, how she had changed physically, emotionally, how she had not. "Why didn't you ever answer any of the letters I sent you from college?"

Gwen turned away. His scrutiny made her feel vulnerable, completely exposed. It was impossible to make him understand the pain she had felt then, without telling him everything. Even now at times it seemed like some distant memory, as if all of it had happened not to her but to another woman in another lifetime.

"It was over. You'd made that clear before you left. There didn't seem any point in dragging it out."

"I thought there was plenty of reason for us to communicate," he said in a slightly unsteady voice, "the least of which was that I was deeply in love with you. And don't pretend you don't know that."

Was deeply in love with you. Her mind caught on his words and spun them around and around. Past tense. He said he had loved her. Once.

"I never meant to hurt you, Gwen."

But he had.

Dan paused, then began to talk in a mesmerizing but achingly honest tone. "I hate the distance between us. I hate not being able to touch you. Seeing you again today, I felt as if time had stood still for us, as if nothing essential had changed. But at the same time, I don't know you anymore. And I want to if you'll let me."

"It isn't that simple." Tears blurred her eyes.

"Tell me you haven't stopped caring," he urged softly, hoarsely.

She shook her head.

"Is it so wrong to want to go back? To want life to be as simple and uncomplicated as it once was for us?" He seemed as intensely and deeply lonely as she had been.

She felt a melting of the ice around her heart. But she couldn't give in to the love that threatened to overwhelm her, either. Not without getting hurt. "Don't do this to me," she pleaded softly, blinking back hot, bitter tears. "Don't make me think it is possible to go back."

"Isn't it?" To him anything was possible, within reach. He'd always achieved what he set out to do.

"No." She tried to get up, move away. He captured

her wrist with a loose grip and held her on the sofa beside him. The sense of déjà vu that had descended earlier intensified tenfold. True, years had passed, but she still knew the heart of the man and he knew her. He knew what she wanted without her ever having to say it. One by one, Dan removed the pillows she had erected as a barrier between them and slid closer. One arm encircled her shoulders, the other grasped her arm and twirled her to face him. And she knew it was what she wanted—to be swept away by his mastery and his strength, his love. But a tiny thread of common sense and caution remained. "Dan, don't—" Her hands pressed against his chest. Hesitation sounded in her voice. But her body—the best barometer of all—was growing traitorously acquiescent.

Because of the heat Gwen had pinned her hair up in a loose French knot, leaving tendrils to drape against her neck, a feathery fringe of bangs to frame her face. Wordlessly, as familiarly as if they had never really been apart, he deftly located and began removing the pins that kept it neat. As the silky length tumbled to her shoulders he wove his fingers through the curling mass, using his fingers to arrange it, his touch soft and unutterably competent. "I've always loved your hair," he murmured, his lips brushing her lightly. "Today in the sunlight it shone like red gold. Silk fire. I wanted to touch it then, do what I'm doing now."

A wild anticipation flowed through her, sending tremors over her skin. Her face remained uplifted, her thoughts trained on the determination in his gaze, the tantalizing nearness of his mouth and the pleasure she knew deep in her soul he could give. Part of her wanted to protest, move away. And yet, wasn't this the sensual whimsy her dreams had been composed of these many long years? Mistaking her silence for complete acquiescence, his fingertips slid beneath the elastic neckline of her dress, coasting over her skin, the upper swell of both breasts. Common sense returned. "No," she whispered frantically, trying unsuccessfully to free herself from his grasp.

He had done that purposefully, to shock her into awareness, as deliberately as he would kiss her now. "Yes. I want you, Gwen. And you want me."

He spoke as if everything were so simple. "Yes, I want you," she whispered back fiercely. "But I don't need you anymore, not the way I did. And I can choose now not to have you as part of my life."

Anger flared briefly in his eyes, then the contemplation of a man taking up a challenge. Too late, she realized she had said the worst possible thing. He was determined to win now at all costs, and physically at least, she was powerless to stop him. In some part of her, still despite all the heartache that had passed, she was shocked to discover she didn't really want to stop him. He lowered his head, fingertips lacing in the ends of her hair, and cupped the back of her neck so that she had no choice but to submit to his possession. His lips brushed hers once, then again and again. Having starved for love for so long, she gave in to the passion and took what she needed, giving him back caress for smoldering caress.

He drew back as fire consumed her, rendering her helpless in his arms. "You're so beautiful," he whispered, his anger abated, "more so now than you ever were in your teens." His hand stroked her hair, lingered on the exposed arch of her throat and the U of her collarbone. His eyes darkened with a desire she knew must be mirrored in her own. "You were right then, Gwen. You were a woman. I was just too much a fool to know it. Too afraid of hurting you, wounding you beyond repair." He had loved her more than he had thought it possible to love.

The intimacy she'd been fighting descended full force, weighting her arms and legs with an ardent lethargy. Both of his hands cupped her chin. He held her lightly as his mouth descended, as if again afraid she would bolt, but she was no more capable of movement then than had she been shackled hand and foot. One of his hands coasted down over the bare skin of her back. Where flesh touched flesh heat sparked. He shifted his weight forward, pressing her back against the pillows. His arms were beneath her, cradling her close, his nearness overwhelming. He pushed the neckline of her dress aside, his arched fingertips tracing the uppermost swell of her breasts. Her nipples tautened. He leaned forward and touched them with his lips through the cloth. Pleasure shot through her—wild, unprecedented pleasure. Her eyes shut against the warm, rough suction of the dress as his lips pressed against her. Softly, he teased the hollow between her breasts first with his teeth, then with his tongue. His eyes studied the damp cloth and silken globes.

Involuntarily Gwen murmured her need of him, of love, then drew his head back to hers. Tenderly, with infinite finesse, his mouth seared hers, then became gentle, seducing, tempting, until she was lightheaded and dizzy, gasping between subsequent kisses. His heart pounded in cadence to hers, his arms cradled rather than restrained. She felt as if she were coming to life again, as if all this time she had only been half existing.

"There's never been anyone in my life to replace you, Gwen. There never will be."

The harshly whispered confession brought her swiftly back to reality. And her doubts, about their future, then and now. She paused, then pushed free of him, swinging to a seated position, her feet flat on the floor. "Then why didn't you ever get in touch with me deliberately?" she asked quietly. At any given time, he could have found her through the web of their mutual acquaintances. He hadn't. He'd never even tried.

A muscle worked convulsively in Dan's jaw at the accusation mirrored on her face. "I didn't contact you because you made it perfectly clear how you felt when you didn't reply to that last letter I sent — uninterested." His tone became gentle, resigned. His hand covered hers warmly. "It wasn't until I saw you today that I realized you still felt as deeply about me as I did about you. I never stopped caring for you, Gwen." He looked directly into her eyes, meaning every word.

Yet certain doubts remained. "It didn't take you long to get engaged to that Boston heiress." Despite her effort to remain coolly impassive, she sounded bitchy. Gwen winced. His engagement had been in all the local papers, she recalled bitterly. His parents had been aghast at the match. She'd been devastated, knowing that while she was suffering the most tragic loss of her life, he was out partying.

"I was on the rebound from you. It didn't last."

Then again, neither had *their* affair. She sat down on the sofa, feeling very weary. She raked a hand through her hair. What before had been gloriously seductive now felt merely rumpled. "It's too late, Dan. We can't go back to where we were, even if we wanted to." He wouldn't be around long enough. And even if he were to return periodically from his job, it would never be the same. They were grasping at straws, relying on memories for love. Maybe it was better to let it end now, painful as that would be.

He shot her a sharp look. "Is that really what you want—do you want me to leave?"

"I don't want to be hurt again." Beyond that, she just didn't know.

The phone rang, cutting into the silence of the room. She bolted to answer it, glad for the opportunity to escape him. After a moment she handed the receiver over quietly. "It's Doc Quarrick. He wants to speak to you."

Dan strode into the kitchen to take the call. When he returned moments later, his face was pale and drawn. There were lines etched tautly around his mouth. "It's Dad," he informed Gwen. Moisture glistened in his eyes, but his voice was composed. "He's having chest pains. They're taking him to Bowling Green Medical Center by ambulance. A cardiologist will be there to greet them in the emergency room. I've got to go."

Chapter Three

"If you're free for lunch I really could use a friend."

Gwen glanced up to see Dan Kingston silhouetted in the clinic doorway. His features were taut. Nearly a week had passed since his father had been admitted to the hospital. On the surface Dan looked just as self-possessed as ever, but she knew from her talks with him that the experience of nearly losing his father had changed him. It had made everything seem more precious, including her, she supposed dimly.

"Sure." Elation at seeing him again made her smile. "Just let me tell Doc where I'm going. Elyse Dalton, our licensed vocational nurse, who runs the day-to-day operation of the clinic, didn't come in this morning, so we're shorthanded. I'm substituting for her here." She was chatting too much, trying to fill the void of silence between them. He didn't seem to mind.

Moments later, her responsibilities taken care of, they walked across the street to the small park across from the town square. Her white skirt swirled in the wind. Dan glanced down at the shirtwaist dress with its three-quarter sleeves. He grinned approvingly. "That's the first time I've seen you in a uniform." He paused long enough to extract a blanket from his car. Together they selected a nice shady spot and spread out the patchwork quilt.

With a wry laugh Gwen admitted, "Doc Quarrick thinks it looks more professional. I like to humor him in regard to his quirks. But when I make rounds on my own, I've found a lab coat will do just as well. And jeans are vastly more practical when climbing across mud puddles or broken-down wooden gates." Which she often did.

Dan had sandwiches, fruit and a thermos of icy lemonade, which they shared. He looked haggard and tired, as if he'd lost weight. She knew that the past few days had been a very rough time for his family.

"How's your dad?" Gwen asked softly. To her disappointment, he hadn't let her go with him to the hospital that night. He had called her near dawn to let her know his dad's condition had stabilized and had checked in with her every night since then. Their conversations were short and punctuated with pauses, but she'd come to look forward to them. It was a way of regaining their past intimacy, and though they were no longer lovers, she was beginning to see that the years of deep friendship would never be erased. In some ways now they were as close as ever.

Dan stretched out on the quilt, his back and head resting against the roughened bark of an old hickory tree. "Dad's much better, thank God. He's been moved from the cardiac care unit and can have visitors now. All the tests have been completed. They found no permanent damage, nothing that would keep him from living the next twenty years of a fairly normal life. His cardiologist diagnosed the problem as premyocardial infarction syndrome."

"A warning that prefaces a heart attack." Gwen reflexively translated the medical jargon into simpler terms.

Dan nodded. "Yes. Although this felt much like one to Dad, it wasn't a real heart attack." Frowning, he continued, "Dad was very frightened at first. We all were. Once he was given the test results, his mood lightened. Now, I don't know. It's almost as if he's trying to pretend nothing out of the ordinary happened, as if he's trying to deny the seriousness of the situation entirely." Dan shook his head, perplexed. He rested his hand on his bent knee.

"Depression and denial are fairly normal reactions to any illness, Dan. He'll come to accept it eventually. And go on from there."

"I know." He turned to her as if for moral support "It's the recovery period that I worry about. So does Mom. Some of the contributing habits, like smoking and ingesting too much cholesterol, have taken a life time to develop. It isn't going to be easy for Dad to make all the changes his doctors are insisting he make. I want to help him, Gwen. I thought, since you're a nurse, you might have some suggestions on how to make the transition easier. Is there anything I can do?"

So now they were down to the real reason for his visit. Disappointment flooded her, but she kept her tone carefully light. "You mean other than just being there and offering encouragement?"

He nodded. "I was thinking along the lines of education, physical therapists to help develop his exercise

regimen. If we could let Dad know that he's not alone
in this, if he had someone to talk with who'd been
through it or dealt with the resultant depression it
would be easier.''

Gwen understood. Heart attacks were common in
Dan's executive world. So the victims had plenty of
peers to commiserate with. But in rural areas, farm accidents and black lung were more prevalent causes of
illness and in some respects, because they did happen
so commonly, were easier to deal with. The support
systems were better. "There's a clinic in Richmond,"
she said finally. "It's expensive. It's set up like a resort.
They specialize in treating people who are recovering
from heart attacks. They have all sorts of physical activities supervised by physical therapists. There's joint
education and a counseling program for spouses. They
even teach cooking the no-salt, low-cholesterol way.
One of Doc's patients went there a year ago with good
results. You might check into it."

Dan withdrew a small notebook from his shirt
pocket. She watched as he scribbled down the name
and address. "Thanks."

As they finished their lunch, a self-consciousness
sprang up between them.

"So, how are you getting along?" Gwen asked.

He cast her a puzzled glance. "Having your dad hospitalized was quite a shock for your family. You've
been through a severe trauma yourself." He hadn't
been eating much. Had he been going without sleep,
too?

He lifted his shoulders inconsequentially. "I'm recu-
perating."

Aware of his eyes upon her, Gwen sipped her lemonade. "Will you be going back to Chicago soon?" she asked.

"It all depends on Dad, on how he progresses."

Damn it, she thought, *why does he have to be so sure of himself, so self-sufficient?* His message was that either way, he would cope, without her, as he had always coped. Across the square the church bells chimed once. Gwen glanced at her watch.

"Time to go?" His hand closed over hers as he helped her to her feet, making her feel simultaneously cherished and protected.

Gwen nodded, bending to clear the remains of their picnic away. Together they packed the hamper, then folded the vibrantly colored patchwork quilt. "Afternoon office hours start in another half hour." She had phone calls to return before the patients arrived.

"I'll let you know what happens with Dad," Dan promised, walking her to the clinic door.

"I'd appreciate that. In the meantime, give my best to your folks."

Giving her one last lingering glance, he promised, "I will."

To Gwen's surprise, Elyse was in the clinic preparing for the afternoon patients when Gwen arrived. She faced the vocational nurse worriedly. "I thought you were sick," she remarked. Indeed, the normally well-groomed younger woman looked as if she hadn't slept all night. Her thick blond hair lacked its usual cared-for luster and was pulled back severely from her face. "Are you sure you're well enough to be here?" Gwen asked, concerned that Elyse was pushing herself too hard.

"I feel all right. The problem isn't physical, anyway." Without warning, a tear slid down Elyse's cheek.

Sensing that something was very wrong, Gwen word-lessly touched her friend's arm and directed her into a nearby lounge and shut the door. Now that she looked closely, she could see behind the tortoiseshell glasses, beneath the deceptive coating of foundation, that Elyse's eyes were puffy and swollen, as if she'd been sobbing her heart out most of the night. "What is it?"

"Buddy and I have split up."

Nervously, Elyse walked to the staff refrigerator and aimlessly studied the contents inside. Another trouble sign, Gwen thought. Although possessing an enviable figure, Elyse always ate voraciously when upset. Fortu-nately for Elyse, she never had any trouble working the extra calories off when her anxiety passed. Gwen only wished she could say the same about herself.

"Are you sure it isn't just a fight?" Gwen watched as, after a lengthy pause, Elyse sighed and shut the re-frigerator door without extracting anything to snack on. The Daltons had only been married a year. And though Buddy was over a decade older than the pretty twenty-year-old Elyse, they had seemed genuinely in love.

"Buddy packed his bags and moved out last night." Elyse paced to the window, her hands stuffed into the pockets of her white pants suit, her blue-green eyes glittering, her jaw clenched. "He's staying in a trailer next to his construction site. When I talked to him this morning—well, let's just say he has no plans to come back. Not until I come to my senses. Frankly, I think he's the one who's being unreasonable." She stopped and bit her lip.

"Why?" Gwen pulled up a chair and sat opposite her.

Elyse whirled to face her. "He wants me to have a

child. I've tried to tell him I'm just not ready, but he won't listen to me." She pressed a palm to her sternum, her voice lowering compassionately as she talked. "It's not that I don't understand how he feels. I do. I know he wants to have children while he's still young enough to enjoy them, but I just can't commit myself to that. When I do have a family, I want the time to be right."

"Maybe everything will cool down in a few days," Gwen encouraged. She hated to see the two break up. "In the meantime, I'm always here to listen."

"I know. Thanks." Standing up, Elyse removed her glasses and wiped the rest of her tears away with the back of her hand. She glanced at her watch and took a deep bolstering breath. "We'd better get with it. The patients will be coming in any minute, and you've got several nonurgent calls to return before you leave on afternoon rounds. I'll get your messages now."

Gwen was busy the rest of the day, fending off calls and questions about a minor epidemic of chicken pox.

Dan stopped by about nine o'clock that evening. At his suggestion, he and Gwen walked the six blocks to the neighborhood Dairy Queen. The fact that he'd sought her out specifically lifted her spirits. But physically, except for an occasional guiding touch of his hand to her elbow, he was remote. More disturbing still was his extremely down mood.

"Do you want to tell me what's on your mind?" Gwen asked finally, unable to bear any more silence, after five minutes and nearly three blocks had passed.

Dan shoved his hands into the pockets of his trousers. His teeth were clenched as if in distaste. "Dad says he'll go to the Richmond clinic if, and only if, I

come home and run the farm for him," Dan reported
shortly. "And you know as well as I that we're not talking days, but a matter of weeks, depending on his progress. Even when he does come home, I won't be able
to just take off. Not until I'm sure he's settled in prop-
erly, that he has someone he trusts to help him, to do
the heavy work on the farm full-time. Anything less
and Dad will be back out there before you know it,
running the tractor and baling hay himself."

"Would that be so terrible? Would staying in Kentucky for a few months be so terrible?" Gwen faced
him. She couldn't help but see how trapped he felt.
Was she part of the prison, too?

Dan shrugged, pretending for a second that it didn't
matter to him what happened to his career. "I've been
gone almost ten days now. I can't rely on my subordi-
nates to keep covering for me indefinitely." They
reached the Dairy Queen window. After studying the
menu, Gwen selected a fresh strawberry sundae. He
chose a chocolate cone, then paid for both.

"Could you get a leave of absence from IDP?" she
asked moments later, savoring the sweet berry topping
on the white plastic spoon as they strolled languidly
back in the general direction of her home.

"Yes, but not without some cost to my career." He
was as emotionally distant as if he were a million miles
away. "But that's not what's bothering me, Gwen.
Dad's always had this dream of my returning someday
to take over the running of the farm and make it my
home, my life's work. After all he's been through, I
don't want to raise his hopes, only to dash them again
in that respect. Yet I can't let him down, either. He's
asked me for so little. And I know he'll never be com-

fortable going to the clinic in Richmond unless I am here, overseeing the tobacco crop, which, by the way, promises to be a banner one this year."

Any sort of stress for the elder Kingston could be harmful, Gwen knew. "So what are you going to do?" she asked softly, finishing the rest of her sundae. Dan tossed his unfinished cone in the trash, then cupped a hand possessively beneath her elbow.

"Stay and run the farm." He forced a tight smile, but happiness was not reflected in his eyes. Dan sighed deeply and ran a hand wearily through his hair. "Maybe in the interim I'll be able to find someone to take over the heavy work, someone Dad would like and trust and get along with."

"And if not?" Gwen asked. In her heart she wanted him to say that he would stay there in Kentucky with her if he had to.

His mouth set with grim determination, Dan said only, "I'll find someone."

They walked in silence for the next few minutes. The streetlights illuminated the way. A warm damp breeze wafted through the trees, hazily blurring the sounds of the small-town night. As they reached her house and Gwen prepared to mount the steps, Dan caught her arm, reeling her back to his side. His eyes searched her face. "You're disappointed in me, too, aren't you?" There was an underlying bitterness in his low tone that sent a knife blade of pain into her heart. She didn't want him to resent her, too.

"The country's never been as bad as you make it out to be," she admitted finally, unable to tell the lie that would have temporarily soothed them both.

"Neither is wanting a different kind of life, Gwen."

And by all appearances he had made a very good one for himself, one that for all practical aspects might have been a whole other world away. Gwen's spirits plummeted even more as she realized how far apart they had really grown. The time they had spent together, getting to know one another again, was really no more than a port in a storm. Like everything else, this interim, too, would pass, no matter how pleasurable she found it, or how much she longed to have him back in her life.

Her mood cooled considerably as they moved up onto her front porch. "It's still early," he commented. She said nothing in response. She couldn't. "Aren't you going to invite me in?" he asked, when she turned as if to say good night. His tone was incredulous.

She hedged, not wanting to hurt him, but not able to bear intimacy at that moment, either. "It's late, Dan."

"And you're angry." More than his father's demands, he resented her lack of support.

She lowered her eyes from his accusing ones, concentrating on the geraniums growing in the window boxes on the sill. "I don't want to be your consolation prize during your enforced stay in Kentucky, Dan."

Shock etched his features into rigid lines. "You think that little of me?" He was astonished and angry.

Feeling the rip cord of tension that shot through his body, she exhaled a wavering breath. "You're in need of comfort. I'm here. I'm available, and you know in some strangely sentimental way that I still care for you." She swallowed hard. "But that's all a renewed liaison between us would ever be, Dan, a temporary fling." Gwen had chosen her words carefully, not wanting to reveal the depth of her feeling. Judging by the harsh, hurt look on his face she had succeeded. But it was too late to go back, make amends—not without endangering herself to further pain.

After a moment he relented, with an exasperated shake of his head. He released his grip on her arm to stare down at her. "Would a fling, as you put it, be so terrible?"

"Yes." It would break her heart, and she couldn't bear it.

Ever so softly, Dan said, "You'd really prefer it if I'd never made anything of myself, if I'd stayed here and worked the land. If I had, you'd be in bed with me right now."

If he had they would have been married. They weren't. She ducked her head away from his steady gaze. "Maybe. Maybe not. What difference does it make?" *Why did he insist on playing this absurd guessing game of love?* In reality she knew he'd done what he had to, to survive. As she was about to now. Because already he was seeing too much, making demands on her that she couldn't possibly meet and remain intact. He was probing into emotional areas better left unexplored.

He grasped her shoulders lightly. His touch burned her skin and she pulled away. His mouth tightened reflexively. A muscle throbbed involuntarily in his jaw. "Would it help if I put some good Kentucky dirt under my nails? Would that make you feel more at home? Or do I just need that down-home-boy demeanor—you know, the one with a lot of 'ain'ts' and 'aw shucks' and 'yes ma'ms.'"

He didn't have to be that rude. Anger haughtily straightened her spine. "Good night, Dan." Her tone was icy.

"Just like that," he said.

"Just like that." She slammed the door in his face. Part of her thought—hoped—he might pound on the portal and demand entrance. He didn't. She leaned against the door long after he'd gone, tears of bitterest regret streaming down her face.

"AND I THOUGHT I WAS MISERABLE," Elyse said, early the next day. Her luxuriant blond hair was once again freshly washed and curled, her uniform nicely ironed.

"What have you got there?" Gwen peered into the aluminum can. Although she had to leave to start her calls in a few minutes, her stomach growled hungrily. She'd gotten up too late to have breakfast.

"Peanut brittle. Want some?" Elyse offered, pouring herself another cup of coffee.

Considering the disastrous way her world was going, Gwen replied, "Why not?" She propped her feet up on a nearby chair. There were times when the staff lounge was a refuge from the world. And right now she needed a friend.

"So how's Dan's dad?" Elyse asked.

Gwen relayed what Doc had told her. She hadn't seen or heard from Dan since their fight several days before. "Miles is better. He's going to that clinic in Richmond I told you about. Leaves today, as a matter of fact."

Elyse studied her curiously, then reached for another small section of brittle, savoring the caramel flavor. "Does that mean Dan will be staying in the area?"

Gwen laughed bitterly. "Only under fire. To him, I'm afraid, it's a fate worse than death to be here, even temporarily."

"And that bothers you?"

Gwen waved a finger. "I'm part of the package, or punishment, however you want to look at it."

"Sure you're not being too hard on him?" Elyse got up to pour them both some more coffee.

Gwen handed back the peanut brittle can. Lately, nothing tasted good. Her nights were spent tossing and turning and dreaming of Dan. *Sweet heaven, why couldn't she just let go?*

"Are you going to see him?" Elyse asked.

Dusting off her hands, Gwen swallowed a last bit of candy and reached for her lab coat and bag. The sooner she got to work the better. "Not if I can help it. He left me in the lurch once, Elyse. I'm not going to give him the chance to do it again."

Elyse studied Gwen with knowing eyes. "Will Dan let it go at that? I know from what you've told me how persistent he can be when he gets his mind set on something."

"He's going to have to," Gwen said grimly. Because she had no intention of ever changing her mind.

IT WAS A WORLD MADE FOR COUPLES, and she was a cog out of place, Gwen concluded, leaving the theater and stepping out into the balmy darkness later that same evening. She was almost to the door of her Jeep when she saw him, leaning against the back fender.

Straightening lazily, Dan strode toward her, his eyes drifting over her, taking in the swirling sundress—the same aquamarine as her eyes—the spike-heeled sandals and bare suntanned legs. She thought he saw too much, that she was lonely and at loose ends, that she needed to feel attractive and ultrafeminine again, that

in just two short weeks he'd made her miss the un-
equaled intimacy of a mutually nurturing man-woman
relationship.

"How did you find me?" Inside she was a fluttering
mass of nerves, but her voice was calm, slightly challenging.

"You weren't home. This is your Jeep. I knew all I
had to do was wait." That sooner or later she would
appear.

She was embarrassed, humiliated, angered that he'd
checked up on her. Their gazes touched. She lowered
her regard, concentrating for a moment on the other
couples leaving the theater and getting into their cars.
Young and old, all were holding hands, talking, laughing. One woman walked past, a stray tear spiraling
down her cheek. Gwen knew how she felt. Happy endings made her want to cry, too, perhaps because they
were so seldom imitated in real life.

"How long is this going to go on?" Dan wanted to
know, his tone low and faintly exasperated, angry.

Gwen faced him, careful not to show what riotous
effect his unexpected appearance was having on her
senses. "I don't know what you mean." He placed a
staying hand on her arm, blocking her entrance into the
Jeep. She stepped back, free, a flash of resentment
lighting her eyes.

"Like hell you don't. You've refused all my calls at
work. At home, you're not answering your phone. You
won't see me or even agree to go on a date."

"We've been through this, Dan. And I told you, I
don't want to get involved." She shrugged her shoulders
expansively and, after unlocking the door, climbed up
into her Jeep. The near slam of the door was emphatic.

The outdoors might have been cool, but the interior of her Jeep was stifling. Gwen rolled down her window. She tried to start the engine. It rumbled once, coughed weakly, then quit. Out of the corner of her eye, she saw his car parked across the street.

Dan heaved a sigh with the force of a gale wind. "If you want the truth, neither do I." When he had her attention, he continued in an irritatingly pragmatic tone. "That's never stopped us before. For once in your life, face the truth, Gwen." He lowered his tone persuasively. "We've always been drawn to each other."

She had proved to herself that she could resist him. She needn't come running every time he beckoned. No doubt that was partially responsible for his frustration now. He felt like a man scorned. *Well, let him discover what it felt like to be jilted.* She had.

She turned the ignition key. Again the engine refused to kick over. His brow furrowed worriedly. He inclined his head in the direction of the hood. "Still having trouble with it?" he asked.

"It's cantankerous." Always had been. Always would be.

"Let me give you a lift."

"It'll start in a minute."

"Then I'll follow you home," he said quietly. "We'll talk."

Talk or make love, she wondered, unsure of what he wanted from her other than the physical satiation. Her hands on the steering wheel were trembling, and not all from anger, she knew. Where he had touched her earlier in an effort to delay her, a white heat had started. Minutes later, it still ran riot over her skin. Had he read her desire? Either way, her decision was final. "No."

New, deeper resentment flared in his eyes. Before Dan could say anything else, she started her Jeep and pulled out of her space. Two blocks later, the sleek car was behind her. It stayed there for the duration. Once home, she parked in her driveway and slammed down from her Jeep. He was at her side, waiting casually, almost as if invited, before she could speak. Just one dissecting look was enough to set her own irascibility—where he was concerned—skyrocketing out of control. The air fairly crackled with tension. It was as if, Gwen thought emotionally, all the resentments they had been harboring the past ten years had been pushed to the fore. She sensed he knew that he was behaving irrationally. She was not exactly in control. Yet there seemed no going back, once the peace between them had been dissolved. It was now or never. The end or the new beginning of their affair.

BELLIGERENTLY, she told herself she wouldn't let him disrupt her life again. Wordlessly, she brushed past him toward the porch. He followed her to the door, making no effort to keep up with her decisive, long strides.

"I'd invite you in—"

"I'd like that." Dan parodied her mock-smile.

"But it's late," she finished coldly.

He thrust his hands into his pockets and leaned against the jamb, towering over her, his eyes tracing the lines of her lips, the slope of her throat. "Not that late."

Her pulses pounded anew. Wordlessly, she opened the door, then turned to face him. The dusky shadows camouflaged his intent.

"You're not making this easy on me." Despite

everything, she didn't want to be cruel. It was not in her nature.

He straightened indolently from his post. "I don't intend to make it easy." It was obvious that he hated having to pursue her so avidly. She wondered how long it had been since a woman had told him no. Had anyone? And yet, despite that, he wasn't leaving until he'd gotten what he'd come after—time alone with her, presumably, she thought on a fresh burst of feminine outrage, in bed.

Her temper skyrocketed out of control. "What's the matter, Dan? Does it bother you that you can't control me any longer, that I do what I damn well please, regardless of what you might want from me?" He took a warning step toward her. Gwen threw up her hands in dramatic dismay, equally as much for the mocking effect as to ward him off.

Lips compressed, he agreed mildly, "You are a damn sight more irascible in the years since I dated you. I don't know why." His tone said that he intended to find out.

A shiver of fear went through her. Determined to drive him away in anger, she taunted softly, "That's right, isn't it. You always did want everything to be just so, all nice and tidy. Your women of legal age. Sex after marriage." He took another step forward, less cautious now, and she continued brazenly, unafraid, blinded by the anger and pain she'd felt when he had first told her he was breaking off their affair. "Well, I'm available now, Dan," she purred provokingly. "And I'm of legal age, too."

She never knew there could be such satisfaction in getting even.

There was an unexpected elation in raising his temper. It made her know she still counted in his life. Despite everything. "Well over the age," he affirmed in a lazy, insulting drawl. Resolutely, he clasped a hand around her waist and backed her forcibly through the screen door and into the house. He shut the door behind him, his eyes sweeping over her in a dangerous, brazen manner. She flushed as his glance dwelled on her breasts. She had gone too far. But she knew how to end it.

Stepping forward, she raised her hand to slap his face. He caught her hand in midmotion and held it there, raised, impotent. All the feelings he'd repressed were concentrated in the pressure flowing down her arm to her shoulder. Part of her was glad he was reacting. She wanted to get the air cleared between them.

His breath was ragged. "Is this the way you act with all your beaus?" he taunted softly. "A little tease, a little denial, then the final chase? What's the usual speech, Gwen? 'I'm here. I'm available. Take me.'"

He was deliberately misinterpreting her confusion where he was concerned, twisting the same weakness around to apply to other men, when she was sure he knew that could never ever be true. Fury blinded her. Again she tried to slap him, but he held her wrist in an iron grasp. "Damn you." She struggled, trying unsuccessfully to wrest free of his grasp.

"Damn us both," he uttered softly. Suddenly, she was aware that there were only the two of them there, that she had pushed him beyond his endurance and that she herself was teetering close to the edge of pure, unadulterated passion. He read the apprehension in her eyes; there was an answering satisfaction in his deliberately goading appraisal. "I'm not afraid of you!" she whispered. Yet her breasts were rising and falling with each breath.

"Maybe you should be," he said roughly. His eyes focused on the movement, tore away. Gwen felt the strain of his muscles as he held himself tautly in check. Clearly, he wanted her. But he wouldn't take her in anger; he would never force her. He would never deliberately hurt her. And it was that concern of his, that gentleness so much a part of him even when pushed to the brink, that tumbled the last of her defenses. And in that instant she wanted him, too, unbearably.

Realizing this, Dan released her, almost as if he'd been burned, pivoted quickly and with a negative, self-censuring shake of his head, strode wordlessly toward the door. His pang of conscience at that late moment infuriated her. What a horrible way to evoke a sense of déjà vu. Could he really leave her again that easily? Tears pricked her eyes. To cover her hurt, she adapted the tact that would wound him the most. "Afraid of what will happen if you do stay?" She sauntered toward him. Her high heels showed her long slim legs to best advantage. He studied them in a long, slow caress, his dark intent almost enough to make her turn and run.

"Still throwing down the gauntlet, Gwen? Your temper's showing." His voice was ultracool, but a dangerous light flared in his eyes.

It occurred to her then that he was in no shape emotionally to have such a confrontation with her. "I'm sorry." With effort she choked out the words.

"I'm not. I accept your oh-so-gracious invitation." Dan turned and walked to the door. He bolted it, then turned to face her, began loosening his tie. There was no room for compromise in his gaze.

Gwen swallowed hard. She hadn't meant...she'd never really thought he'd... "I think you'd better go." She sidestepped past him.

He caught her arm and whirled her toward the stairs at the end of the hall. "I just got here." Agitation flared in his eyes. When she didn't reply, he took charge of the situation, "The bedroom it is, then."

"Dan..." She dug her shoes into the floor, pulling back, refusing to go any farther.

In a retaliation as stubbornly insistent as her own, he trapped her against the wall before she had a chance to react, both arms coming up on either side of her. "I thought this was what you wanted," he said roughly, his warm breath fanning her face. "What you always wanted, even when it was foolish and dangerous as hell."

"I did. I don't now." Her pulse beat madly in her throat. She felt hot and cold, scared and exhilarated, all at once. The passion was still there, but this wasn't what she wanted—a raw, calculated sexual encounter. She wanted love. She wanted what they'd had.

But he had no understanding of that, and she wouldn't explain. "Funny, isn't it, that when you exhibit the trait you most hate in me—the human condition of having second thoughts about the wisdom of an action, especially one that is inclined to hurt someone you love very much—I'm supposed to just forgive and forget. When you, lady, have done neither."

For the first time Gwen sensed how angry he really was, how hurt. "Dan, please..." He was beginning to scare her. Not because she was afraid he would hurt

her, but because she was afraid he would make love to
her in anger and for all the wrong reasons, and that
would destroy her more easily than any physical blow
he could wield.

"Please what?" he said roughly. "Please make love
to you, or please leave? Make up your mind, Gwen.
And do it now."

Chapter Four

Gwen's heart was pounding so hard she felt she could hear it. *Did she want Dan to leave?*

"Tell me to leave, Gwen," he whispered. "Tell me that you want me to go now and I will."

If she didn't he would stay and make love to her. The question was, what did she want? The darkness of the hallway was overwhelmingly seductive, as was the primeval desire in his gaze, the fleeting sense that they were not really beginning again, but simply taking up where they had left off, where perhaps they had always been in their hearts.

"Tell me," he insisted raggedly.

She couldn't. She needed this; she needed him as she needed life. Wreathing her arms around his neck, she murmured, "I don't want you to go." Not from Kentucky, not from her house or from her arms. Not ever.

With a groan of capitulation, Dan nudged his knee between her thighs, stepping closer. She felt his hard male contours evoke an answering fluttering sensation in her lower midriff and a dampness between her thighs. Her knees weakened treacherously. She swayed against him, her body yielding to his demands. Wordlessly, he edged the back zipper of her dress down past her waist, while holding her firmly against his chest. His motions were tantalizingly slow, like white heat shocking her senses.

His palm ghosted over her shoulder blades, down her spine, pausing to caress every vertebra with soft circular motions. The silence between them was interrupted only by the raggedness of her breath, the harsh, steady sounds of his. Shadowed concern passed over his face, fled when she offered no resistance. His palm drifted lower past her waist over the swell of her hips, to encounter the lacy uppermost edge of her bikini panties. He molded her against him, aligning the hardness of his hips to the soft flat plane of hers. "I've wanted you so long," he said.

And I you, she thought. She could feel the tautness of his muscles, as if he were deliberately holding back, watching, waiting. And it was that control, the deliberateness of his actions, that got to her. Realization of what was happening sliced through the sensual fog. She struggled against him, only to further their awareness of each other's bodies.

With a determined movement, he trapped her against the wall. As if he had known all along that she wouldn't go through with it unless the timing, the reasons, were right. "No more evading, Gwen. We're going to have this out, once and for all. And only then will we be able to go forward. If you resent me, say it. If you hate me, say it. But no more of this holding all your feelings in check, looking at me as if I were part devil, part god." The plaster was cool and smooth against her back. His lips pressed against her temple.

"All right. I hate you."

"What else?"

I love you. She wouldn't say it. "Why are you doing this to me, pursuing me, when you know you're only going to leave again?"

"Because I want to make love to you. I want you to remember how it was."

Doubts made her wary. Her jaw edged out truculently. "Memories can be deceiving." She was afraid that, as before, once they had experienced the bonding that came with lovemaking, there would be no turning back. Only this time, knowing by rote what pain and loneliness stretched ahead, that no other man would ever make her feel as good or want as much as he did, she wasn't sure she could recover. When his look demanded an explanation, she said, "We're different people now, with different hopes and dreams, different life-styles." Were they setting themselves up for an even larger hurt by even entertaining the faint hope of a reconciliation?

He didn't think so. "Is this deceiving?" He touched her breast lightly, circled the swelling globe and cupped it warmly, watching as she responded tremblingly. "This isn't fear that's making you quiver, that's making your eyes dilate and your mouth part in sweet invitation to mine. It's desire, Gwen. Passion, pure and simple."

And love, she thought, knowing well the territory of her own heart. But her love for Dan had left her hurting and crying. It had kept her alone all these years. She didn't want to go through that again. She didn't want any more heartache.

"I'm not going to be part of your chemistry experiment, Dan. Not ever." She pushed against his chest. He caught both hands in one strong grasp and ever so slowly lifted them above her head, pinned them to the wall, so that she was completely vulnerable to his touch, his gaze. And it hit her then that she was dealing not with a teenage boy caught up in the throes of first love and physical discovery, but with a man who knew exactly what he wanted and who for the past eleven years had been accustomed to getting it. She turned her head sharply to the side. She wouldn't let him bulldoze her into an involvement. She wouldn't.

"Go ahead and fight," Dan whispered softly, "if it's what you want. But it won't change the outcome." He lifted her chin to his as his grip intensified possessively on her wrists. "What we've shared in the past and will share again is inevitable."

His mouth lowered to hers. She'd expected, despite his uncharacteristically macho tactics and speech, gentleness, a probing but utterly seductive kiss. He was rough, overwhelmingly passionate, demanding a response. And that was a first, too. She fought against him, against herself and her own burgeoning response. Because, God help her, despite everything that had gone on between them she still wanted him as ardently as she had years before. She still craved his touch and felt half-alive when he was not with her. Memories swamped her. His kiss became gentle as he felt her response. Her mouth opened farther under the evocative encouragement of his tongue, the pressure of his soft, firm lips. And then all was lost in the searching, tantalizing quality of his kiss. When at last he released her moments later, she was trembling so badly she could barely stand.

Her hands fell to rest against his chest, as limp and as malleable as clay. Satisfaction swept him, softening his features, doing nothing to mask the male triumph in his eyes. There was no denying her reaction to his kisses. His intensity unnerved her. "Let me love you the way I used to," he said, holding her close and weaving his fingers through her hair.

Reminded of how he'd left her, refused her when she'd felt a similar need, Gwen pushed him away. "I can't." Her voice was ragged, reflecting her discomfiture. "Don't you see? Nothing's changed. We were wrong for each other then; we're wrong for each other now. Our lives couldn't be more diverse."

"That could be changed."

"How? By my giving up my career?" she wondered aloud on a burst of renewed resentment.

Agitation had brought color to Dan's cheeks. He reached behind her, silently doing up the back zipper of her dress. "Nothing important has changed, Gwen," he said finally. His voice was a throaty caress, threatening provocatively to stir her senses all over again.

She said nothing, merely lowered her head, studied the glossy parquet of the floor.

"Would it make a difference if I were living here again full-time instead of just staying here temporarily?" he asked. There was a speculative light in his eyes that she couldn't fathom.

Sensing a trap, she resisted answering.

"If I made this my home permanently, would you let me court you?" he repeated.

About that much she had nothing to lose by answering. He'd never leave his high-powered job. He had made that abundantly clear even as he'd decided to stay on in Kentucky through the summer while his father recovered his health. "I suppose."

"Still stubborn as a mule, aren't you?" Amusement tugged at the corners of his mouth.

Prickles of resentment sent her head up. Her expression was drolly acknowledging. "As I said, Dan, nothing's changed."

He stepped away from her, and sighed with exaggerated patience. Shaking his head lightly in derision, he pivoted and strode toward the door. He let himself unceremoniously out into the quiet duskiness of the street. She stood leaning against the screen long after he departed, wondering why she felt so let down. She'd gotten what she wanted—an end to the evening without renewing the physical intimacy that had caused her so much heartbreak in the past. Yet still she felt more hurt than relief. Was Dan right to wait until she could freely admit and accept what she needed—time alone with him and no one else? Or were they once again headed on a collision course of love, passion and, ultimately, denial?

SOMEHOW, GWEN WAS NOT AS ANNOYED or surprised as she would initially have expected to be when Dan showed up unannounced on her doorstep at one o'clock Saturday afternoon. Dressed in cutoff jeans and a shirt, he looked more relaxed than she had seen him in days. And more Kentucky-casual. She stepped out onto the porch. "How are things on the farm?"

"As well as can be expected, considering who's in charge," he remarked wryly, a thumb pointing facetiously at his sternum.

"And your parents?" Gwen asked.

"Both are adjusting to the clinic routine with ease, last I heard. Unfortunately, in order to get them to go away, I had to make a lot of promises other than that I'd take care of the tobacco and see to the care and the feeding of the livestock." Dan sighed heavily. There was a new hint of tan to his features. "I also promised to can the vegetables from Mom's garden."

"You're going to do the canning?" She gaped at him in amazement.

"Mom suggested you might be persuaded to help if I asked nicely," he said dryly, rubbing his jaw.

So Betty Kingston had turned matchmaker, Gwen thought, not entirely unamused. "I suppose you're here to beg for assistance."

"On bended knee, if necessary. So, about those vegetables? Are you game?"

Gwen smiled. Even if she could have refused Dan, which was doubtful, she could never have denied to lend a hand to a neighbor in need. "When do we start?"

"As soon as we can get there."

He hadn't been kidding when he said his mother had left produce to can. There were three bushels of Kentucky runner string beans and a similar quantity of cucumbers to pickle, and cabbage to turn into sauerkraut. Knowing that it would be impossible to get it all done in one day, they decided to work only on the green beans. Dan washed and snapped the crisp vegetables while she sterilized the mason jars and filled the pressure-cooker-style canner.

"Tell me more about your work," he said. "How is a nurse practitioner different from a regular registered nurse?"

"First of all, there's the level of education. I completed a master's degree in community health. Before getting certified by the American Nurses Association, I had to meet the requirements for the advanced training and experience and pass their certification exam."

Gwen bent to pick up a stray string bean. As she did her camisole top gaped open, revealing her lacy semi-transparent bra to his frankly assessing gaze. She straightened up, flushing, her hand moving automatically to adjust the neckline. He grinned unabashedly, not at all sorry.

Dan reached behind her for a bowl, his legs accidently brushing up against hers momentarily in the process. The feel of his hair-roughened skin pressing so lightly against hers sent a shiver of sensual awareness down her spine and started another more intense spurt of longing that was as much emotional as physical. She needed to be held by him. She needed to be loved.

He sat back in his chair.

Gwen's voice was composed as she continued. "Basically, as an N.P. I get to take a more active role in the care of a patient. I can now perform physical exams, do some lab tests, make some diagnoses and prescribe medication according to protocols of state law."

He paused to rest his chin on his upturned palm. His eyes glittered with interest as he surveyed her leisurely, from the tousled disarray of her upswept hair to her tennis shoes and sweat socks. "How does your work here in a rural environment compare with hospital work?" he asked.

She turned back to her task and doled out snapped and washed beans into sterilized jars. She sighed her resignation. "There were times in the hospital when I felt like more of a technician than anything else. We were chronically understaffed. Most hospitals are. There was never enough time to spend with the patients or their families. Some physicians cared what we thought. Others wanted no input from the staff nurses, no matter what the situation. I found it very frustrating." She paused to wipe a bead of perspiration from her upper lip. His eyes focused on the movement and held, igniting a new, deeper fire within her. She flushed and brushed back a stray tendril of auburn hair. "Here, at least, I know the people and something about their history. Dr. Quarrick respects my abilities and enables me to work closely with him in all aspects of patient care. I feel as though I make a difference," she concluded softly.

With effort Gwen lifted the filled canner and started toward the stove. When filled, the large stainless steel pot was heavier than she had imagined, and she staggered slightly beneath its weight. Before she could rethink her decision or even start to turn back and put the heavy pot down, her wet hands slipped, precariously loosening her hold. Dan was behind her in an instant, his hands coming up beneath hers, the flat of his palms squarely beneath the heavy pot.

"Thanks." Gwen's breath was ragged. She tremulously sighed her relief. She was acutely aware of the warmth of his body, spooning hers.

"Where did you want to put the canner?" His warm, fragrant breath billowed softly past her ear. The slightly abrasive surface of his jaw rubbed her cheek.

"On the stove." She sounded as winded as if she had run a mile. Her pulse was pounding so hard she could hear it as a roaring in her ears.

"I'll help you carry it." There was no way they could transfer the canner from him to her without risking the loss of several valuable hours of work. "Just go slowly, one step at a time," he ordered.

Close together, they moved that way toward the stove. She was acutely aware of the strength of his arms nestled firmly beneath hers, the warm pressure of his chest, the stirrings of his immediate arousal, the purposeful strides of his legs. Wordlessly, he helped her lower the stainless steel canner onto the burner. She was flushing, unable to meet his gaze. Busying herself adjusting the temperature of the stove, she pushed a tendril of hair from her cheekbone.

"Could you work as an N.P. somewhere else, or is it just done in rural areas where there's a shortage of physicians and medical help?"

He strode across the kitchen, carrying another batch of unsnapped beans to the counter. As she watched he ran fresh water in the sink, began methodically rinsing the vegetables. She thought, but wasn't sure, that his concentration seemed a little too complete.

She shrugged. "If I could find a physician willing to employ me as an N.P., I could. Unfortunately, in many cities the idea of handing over some of the routine responsibilities to a nurse has not really been accepted."

She watched him covertly under half-lowered lashes, but he did not turn around. Why was he asking, she wondered. Could it be that he was already thinking ahead to their future, trying to find a way for them to be together? Or was he just making conversation to distract them from what had been an uncomfortably sexual moment for both of them? His expression gave no clue.

Dusk was upon them when they finally finished and the last dish had been dried, the canner put away, the jars of canned beans all sealed and lined up neatly on the pantry shelves.

"Well, how about dinner?" he asked.

Although they'd stopped for a sandwich and a Coke at midafternoon, she was ravenous. She shot him a warning glare, playing off his helpless-male look, and teased audaciously, "I know what you're thinking, and I'm too tired to cook." So if it was a hot meal he was after, prepared by her bone-tired hands...

He shot her a mock sympathetic look and shook his head in facetious dismay. "They sure don't make women like they used to. Why, I can remember a time..." He stopped, ducking the pot holder she sailed at his head. Laughter rumbled deep in his chest as he straightened up. On a serious level, he just wanted the pleasure of her company. "How about a picnic?" he asked affably, tossing the pot holder back, his expression as innocent as that of a newborn babe's. "We could take a basket out to the pond."

Tension stiffened her posture. He was talking about going back to their favorite former trysting place. "I don't know, Dan." He couldn't have forgotten what had happened there, she thought.

"I'll behave myself, I promise." He held up his palms in a gesture of open surrender. Abruptly, he seemed serious about keeping his physical distance. And he hadn't so much as kissed her all afternoon.

Gwen bit the inside corner of her lip. She didn't know if she wanted to risk falling nostalgically under his spell.

"Please," he said softly. "It would be my way of repaying you for all your help."

She couldn't refuse him when he turned on the charm. She never had been able to.

Compared to the heat of the Kingston kitchen the evening was briskly cool, the air unusually springlike and clean-smelling. They took the family's pickup truck to the center of the Kingston property, then carried the wicker basket to a grassy area next to the pond, spread out a canvas drop cloth and then over that a multicolored hand-sewn quilt.

Gwen had never felt as contented simply to be with someone as she did with Dan, either before or now. Oh, she'd known deep in her heart that eventually she would become involved with someone again; it wasn't in her nature to live out her days alone. And she did want a family eventually. But she'd also known that whatever she found would be a lesser relationship, more a marriage of convenience than anything else—a platonic love, a way to have a family. Even with those low standards, every male she had met had been sorely lacking.

Face it, she thought as they opened and shared a bottle of chilled white wine, *compared to Daniel and how he can make you feel, there isn't a man alive today who could even hope to take his place.* She knew just by being there with him in their old trysting place that she was treading on dangerous ground. But then, her attraction for Daniel had always been dangerous. Perhaps that had been part of the allure. The knowledge that she never had been able to control him. Still, her attraction to him scared her. She could lose herself so willingly in him. There had been a time when she would have sacrificed everything for him. And in a way, she had. She could grow to depend on talking to and being with him every day, every night. And to do that would mean to sacrifice the serenity she had fought so hard to attain after the tumult of his leaving.

"Why so quiet?" Dan broke into her thoughts softly at length.

The hard warmth of his body next to hers called up the past, made the memories of their love affair achingly real, made her want to love him unreservedly again. "I was just thinking how lovely it is to be here with you again."

He studied her, as if experiencing the same warm drift of pleasure. "You don't feel pressured by the fact we're seeing each other in such an evocative place?" He obviously had intentions of loving her again, if she were to judge by the dark, half-shuttered gaze.

There was a sudden frantic clutching at her heart. Nervously, she sat up and tucked her knees half beneath her. Her laugh floated over the stillness, breaking the sensual tension between them. "If you're talking about that time you talked me into skinny-dipping in the pond..."

He smiled, remembering, but made no move to sit up. Plucking a blade of grass, he ran it through his teeth. "It didn't start out that way. We were just going to wade in the stream."

She nodded, watching water ripple over the rocks. "But then the hem of my dress got wet. And you talked me into taking it off entirely." Not that she'd been that naive. No, just abandoned and young and eager to please and be pleased. If only they could go back to that carefree innocence, she thought. But they couldn't. She knew now what heartbreak that could cause.

"I can still remember that slip you wore—all lacy and

white." He grinned and tossed the blade of grass aside. "It was strapless, because of the cut of your dress." His eyes roved approvingly over her breasts. She flushed as her nipples peaked beneath the thin cloth. Could he tell? He could.

She drew her knees up to her chest and clasped her hands about them. Too late, she realized the alluring view the new position gave of her tanned legs, bared to upper thigh by the brief white cotton shorts. She continued reminiscing, her voice as steady and elusive as she could make it. "It was an Empire gown." She'd been wearing a pink organdy dress trimmed with ribbons and lace. It had been her one formal dress, worn to the prom and every wedding and special occasion thereafter, and Dan's mother had helped her sew it. "We were very badly behaved adolescents."

"Wild," he corrected. "Though, as I recall, you didn't seem to mind." His shoulders lifted in an expressive shrug, drawing the fabric of his shirt taut across his chest. "Sometimes I used to think if we'd just gone to the party that night as we were supposed to..."

His parents had been off visiting relatives. And the promise of the mountain pond had loomed like a gift from the heavens. They'd known no one would disturb them or intrude. And it had been such a lovely summer night, so much like the one they were now sharing. "I remember we were only going to stay a minute," she said softly. And they had ended up staying past midnight. And after that, there had been no going back. Their lives and their love had been changed irrevocably. Her eyes traced the rounded pectoral muscles, the flatter plane of his abdomen and rib cage.

He studied her with heavy, half-hooded eyes, as if knowing full well the emotions whirling inside her, then leaned over and gently touched her cheek. It was just one movement, and yet a thousand reassurances. They finished their wine in silence, staring out at the swirls of mist rising like steam toward the sky as they both mulled what had been.

"How's the farm work going?" she asked eventually, when they'd finished their hastily packed dinner and most of the thermos of coffee. She attempted a lighter, more impersonal note. "Think you're going to be able to handle running your dad's tractor?" Big, red and spanking new, it was Miles Kingston's pride and joy. And also, upon occasion, something of a toy as well. He treated it as some men treated their Jeeps, always testing its capabilities over the roughest, most dangerous terrain. Though she supposed now, with his new restrictions, that, too, would have to stop.

"I won't be driving the thing up and down the hollows like Dad, that's for sure," Dan joked. There was a second when he looked worried, his thoughts once again on his father and the momentarily precarious state of Miles's health. Gwen started to touch him, to offer comfort, but he cut off the words in her throat with the touch of his index fingers to her lips. "I know Dad's going to be fine, Gwen. I don't need any reassurances on that score. I do need you. I need this. Maybe, in reality, it's all I've ever really needed."

"Then you don't resent being back here so much," she asserted quietly. "Having to stay on to help out?"

He frowned, staring out at the stream. Around them, the night grew chill. "I could never stay here permanently. But for the moment it's all right, mostly because I've been able to spend time with you again—time we both needed to have." He turned toward her beseechingly. "Gwen, I want you to think about returning to Chicago with me when I leave."

Stunned, she faced him. What, exactly, was he proposing? His watchful expression gave no clue.

"There's work for you there," he continued. "Plenty of it. People in need."

The thought of leaving Kentucky, her home, the people she thought of as family, was painful. Tenderly, Dan reached for her hand and laced his fingers through hers. His touch was comforting. There was a rough edge to his voice, "I wouldn't pressure you unduly about becoming sexually involved. But neither would I hide the way I feel." He sent her a probing look. "I do want to make love to you again. Very much." She swallowed hard. He continued pragmatically, "You'd have your own apartment, or you could live with me." His thumb leisurely stroked the inside of her wrist. Her thighs were slippery with need.

Gwen withdrew her hand and turned away. He wasn't offering marriage, wasn't even entertaining the hope. Her heart sank like a stone toward the bottom of the lake.

Dan read her disappointment. "We made a lot of promises before, Gwen, promises in regard to our future that we were unable to keep. And you're right. We don't know each other now, not nearly well enough to make commitments of any kind with even a prayer of seeing them through. I don't want that for us this time," he said softly, "the disappointment and the hurt. I just want to take it one day at a time."

It was a reasonable solution, a sensible approach to

the difficult situation between them. Why was she feeling so crushed? "I don't belong there, Dan," she said finally. "I enjoy the rhythm of the country, the slow pace, the fact that everyone knows everyone else and automatically considers them family."

"I enjoy it, too, Gwen. Occasionally. But we both know my work is there, and eventually I have to go back to Chicago. I want you with me."

"Why is it so important to you?" She shivered and he pulled her close, wrapping his arm around her shoulders for warmth. She could feel the steady pounding of his heart beneath her cheek.

"Because when you're not with me I feel more like a corporate machine than a man." She studied the expression on his face. He was serious. "I'm not saying I can't do my job fairly and competently. I do. It's just that without you I have no personal life, no reason to come home or go out or do anything other than work. And I've lived this way for too long. Having Dad ill— being afraid for a while that he would die—I realized I wanted more out of life. I wanted you and I wanted your child—our child." His voice caught emotionally, but he didn't look away.

Tears of regret blurred her eyes.

He caught her wrist when she would have risen, walked away. "I've upset you." He hadn't meant to.

"No." But a lone tear had started a zigzagging pattern down her cheek. Wordlessly, he wiped it away.

"I never should have left you, Gwen. I should have never let you go. Forgive me? Give me a second chance? Let us do it right this time."

"I want that," she murmured around the clot of tears in her throat. But not with the lies between them.

And to tell him now, when she was just regaining his love, that she had deceived and betrayed him more than he could ever imagine—oh God, what a mess. What a terrible mess.

"But not in Chicago." He misread the depth of her fears.

Gwen wiped her cheek with the back of her hand and composed herself with effort. "I just think it's too soon to be deciding about something as important as my relocating," she said tremulously.

Not for him it wasn't. "I'm committed to you, Gwen. I have been since the first day I saw you again. I've never been more certain of anything in my life."

Would it continue if he knew the truth, she wondered.

Chapter Five

Dan was just coming in from the fields when Buddy Dalton's beat-up pickup roared into the Kingston driveway. His throat was dry and parched. Sweat poured into his eyes, rolled down his back and face. Dan hopped down from the tractor and met him midyard. Seeing his weary state, Buddy grinned impertinently, then whistled insultingly through his teeth. He never had been able to resist the opportunity to razz someone, Dan noted, not entirely unamused by his old friend's antics.

"Hey, there, Kingston, looking a mite tired, aren't you?" Buddy called. "This country life wearing you out?"

With comical insolence, Dan looked his former colleague up and down, focusing at length on the stained, rumpled shirt and jeans, the dust-encrusted baseball cap stuck on the top of his head. "Looked in a mirror lately, Dalton? You aren't exactly dressed to kill yourself!"

Buddy grimaced, and mimed a sloughing-off gesture toward his grimy clothes. "Yeah, well, you can blame that on Elyse. As in most marital separations, not only does she have the house, but the washer and dryer, too. I'd go over there and use both if I thought she'd let me in the house without a fight." He grinned. "In her current frame of mind, she'd probably shoot me on sight."

Dan shot back dryly, "There are Laundromats in Dawson Springs."

Buddy looked contemplative for a long moment before he shot back with his usual air of overblown machismo, "Now, Dan, we all know a woman's got her responsibilities. And part of that means taking care of her man. Besides," he finished drolly, with a conspiratorial wink, "I'm hoping she'll see me and feel sorry for me. Heaven knows I couldn't feel much worse." The last was spoken honestly.

Feeling sorry for Buddy would be hard not to do, Dan noted. His pal had all the come-hold-me-save-me charm of an abandoned mutt. "Interesting strategy." Beneath the happy-go-lucky exterior, he did look more down than Dan could ever remember seeing him.

"Listen," Buddy continued more seriously, "the reason I stopped by is that there's a fund-raising drive under way for emergency care facilities here in Dawson Springs. We want to add on to the present clinic. Doc Quarrick said you might be interested in helping. There's a meeting at his place tomorrow night. Seven o'clock. We thought that maybe with your business connections and all, you might be able to give us a hand. Gwen Nolan is going to be there, as well as my wife, Elyse."

"I'll be there."

"Great, I knew you'd come through." Buddy paused, looking reluctant to go. Dan was anxious to get caught up on old times, yet apprehensive about where to begin. Razzing Buddy was one matter. Teasing him about something close to his heart was another. Buddy was clearly capable of violence where his women were concerned. Yet he couldn't just ignore what was happening in his friend's personal life, not when Buddy had just brought it up. Dan finally decided to say it straight out.

"I'm sorry to hear about the trouble between you and Elyse," Dan said.

"Yeah." Buddy sighed, taking advantage of the audience Dan had granted. "Women—who can figure them out? I provide her with a nice home, everything she could want. You'd think she'd be glad to stay home for a few years and have a couple of kids. She doesn't make one tenth what I do in salary. We rarely even spend any of the money she makes, so that can't be it. Worse, she comes home every night exhausted."

"You don't approve of her working?" The idea seemed antiquated to Dan. Yet he knew from his experience in counseling employees that many men felt the same, regardless of all the sociological changes the last decade had wrought.

Buddy removed his baseball cap and ran a hand through his short white-blond hair. "It was okay when we started out," he said. "I didn't want her to get bored. I assumed she intended to work at her job at the clinic only until she got pregnant. Now, she tells me she doesn't want children, not now, maybe not ever." He waved his hands wildly at his sides. "Who knows? She certainly doesn't. She just keeps saying the time has to be right and it isn't right now."

"Maybe it's not such a bad idea to wait."

"I've been telling myself that for the past eighteen months, but I'm running out of patience, Dan. I'm not getting any younger. I want to be able to enjoy my kids. Frankly, I think deep down she equates having kids with getting old and losing her looks. I don't think she is ever going to want that. Add to that, she's gained several pounds the past six weeks because she eats whenever she gets nervous or upset. Naturally, I got blamed for that, too. So, being the good guy that I am, thinking I'd help her out, I suggested she go to this behavior modification class on how not to overeat." His mouth twisted in a rueful grimace. "That was the fight that got me thrown out of the house."

"Wait a minute," Dan interrupted. "I thought you walked out on her."

"Only after I'd suffered more abuse than any man ought to have to endure. Not only did she call me an insensitive male chauvinist pig but she said from now on I could wash my own clothes, cook my own meals and make my own bed, after which I could lie in it— alone. Yeah, imagine that," Buddy said, shaking his head in stupefied disgust before Dan could comment. "I said hell, if that's the way it was going to be, I'd rather live alone anyway, so I grabbed a suitcase and she swung open the front door, and the rest you know."

Sounded like himself and Gwen, Dan thought. "Must have been some fight."

"Believe me, it was." Buddy was silent, staring pensively off into space. "I don't know, Dan. I love Elyse dearly despite all this and I want to be with her, but I just don't know if it's ever going to work out."

"Why do you say that?"

"She's changed. I don't know how or if I'll ever be able to make her happy. Before we got married all she ever wanted was to be with me. I felt the same. Now, she's even talking about going back to school and getting her B.S.N. She'd have to start from scratch, go full-time, and it would take her three or four years. Then, after that, I suppose she'd want to work some more. It would be silly to go through all that and not take advantage of her education, if you think about it. Either way, where does that leave me?"

Dan had no easy answers to give. His problems with Gwen, in comparison, seemed much easier to work out. "Give Elyse time. Maybe she'll come around. Maybe if you compromise the two of you can still work things out."

"I don't know. I hope so. This time apart from each other was supposed to give us time to think. Instead, we seem to be drifting further and further apart. Frankly, I was hoping the time alone would force her to make a decision. One in my favor."

"And has she?" Dan wiped the sweat off his brow with the back of his hand.

"Yeah. She temporarily hates my guts." With feigned indifference, Buddy chuckled nonchalantly and shrugged off his melancholy mood. Hitching up his pants, he adopted his usual cocky manner. "But we all know that'll pass."

Would it? Normally, Dan didn't give personal advice. He didn't feel that it was any of his business. But recalling what had happened to his relationship with Gwen, he relented. "Push her too hard and you'll lose her for sure."

Buddy sent him a quizzical look. "There was a time

when you would have come off sounding as macho as me. Working at IDP must have really changed you."

"I suppose it has. I've learned it's a big world out there. Women want to be with men who are sensitive to their needs, and like it or not, there are now plenty of guys out there who are only too willing to comply."

Buddy looked momentarily disconcerted, as if it had never occurred to him that Elyse might find someone else. Someone who might not pressure her with demands she couldn't or didn't want to meet. He shrugged. "Be that as it may, I know what I want and I'm not giving in until I get it. Not this time." He clenched his jaw stubbornly.

"I wish you luck," Dan answered, thinking of all he'd lost when he'd broken up with Gwen—what he would be able to give his soul to recover.

Buddy grimaced and rolled his eyes skyward. "Thanks. No doubt, knowing Elyse, I'm going to need every bit of help I can get. See you tomorrow night."

"Right." Dan watched pensively as Buddy stalked back to his pickup, hopped up into the cab, and drove off in a cloud of dust.

DAN WENT IN to get a drink and then upstairs for a shower. It was a little after five when he heard another car in the driveway. He glanced out the upstairs window, saw Gwen Nolan pulling up next to the house. He stood for a moment, watching her get out of the Jeep.

As she approached the house he noticed she looked tired and warm. He found himself wishing that she didn't have to work so hard and that he could do something to ease the pain she kept suppressed inside and at the very least that he could get her to confide in him a little more. He never seemed to know what she was thinking anymore, a fact that both mystified and annoyed him.

Swiftly, he grabbed a shirt as old and comfortably worn as his jeans and, shrugging into it, went down to answer the door.

She stopped when she saw him, awkwardly cradling the casserole dish in her hands. Her hair had been swept up off her neck and was curling erratically in response to the high humidity. Her cheeks were flushed, whether from the heat or embarrassment he couldn't tell; her freckles stood out against the luminescent glow of her skin.

He opened the door, stood sideways so she could slip by him. "Come on in."

"Hi."

Gwen moved past him gracefully. He'd been listening to albums he'd had when he was in high school. She started at the sound of Jim Croce's "Photographs and Memories." It had always been one of her favorites, he recalled. If it helped her recall what they'd shared together, he was glad it was playing.

She glanced over and saw the ironing board and stacks of folded clothes and towels. One of his business suits was out, wrapped in plastic and obviously just back from the dry cleaners. She sent him a quizzical look.

Dan explained, "The Lexington plant has a problem with controls. Specifically, they don't have adequate information coming back on the products they're shipping out. They've assembled a task force to help solve the problems, write a new system. Since I'm in the area and have expertise, I've volunteered to help."

As well as continue his work running his father's farm. So the superachiever she'd known in high school still lived, Gwen thought. How could she ever have imagined he would give up his success in the business world? Even temporarily. It was as much a part of him as being a nurse practioner was to her.

"Then you'll be working out of the Lexington plant now?" She seemed hopeful that the move was to be a permanent assignment.

Unfortunately, he could offer her no such news, neither now nor in the future. "On an informal basis," he affirmed, answering her question with effort. "Most of the work I have to do, studying the design of their systems and the input and output for the past six months, can be done right here at home. Considering all the work I've done the past two weeks, the tobacco crop isn't going to need much of my time until harvest. And by then I'm hoping to have employed one of the neighbors to help with hauling in the crop." His father would also be back, to supervise and lend his own expertise.

"Then you're not really even on leave of absence?" She looked crushed.

He frowned, irritated that she resented his devotion to his work. Any other woman would have admired it. "IDP knows the major priority in my life right now is my father—his health and the continued prosperity of this farm. So technically, yes, I am on leave—at least in the sense of my normal responsibilities in Chicago. However, that doesn't mean I have to quit working for the company completely, Gwen. So in the meantime, if I'm able to lend a hand with the problem here at this branch and still get paid for it I will."

"I see." She swallowed hard, looking almost ready to cry.

Another guilty rush tore through him, followed swiftly by irritation. That additional pressure he didn't need. But he supposed she couldn't help her feelings any more than he could help his—wanting her and his job, too.

Dan looked down, saw there was a covered Pyrex dish in her hands.

Looking grateful for the diversion, Gwen explained, "Your mom called last night. She's worried that you're not eating right. So I promised to bring a casserole over, just in case she was right and you weren't. There's enough for several nights. I hope you still like lasagna."

"Love it." He took the dish and ushered her into the kitchen. "It's been a while since I had any, though."

"Why don't you cook it yourself? It's not hard."

"So you are liberated!" he teased back.

"Mm," she agreed on a definitive note. Whirling to face him, she observed, "I also think you're more than old enough to fend for yourself."

"But you wouldn't dare tell my mother that."

She blushed again. "No." She sighed. "Some things never change, and around here—right or wrong— women seem to cater to their men." *Except for Elyse. And maybe herself.*

"No chance you'll join the crowd, is there?" he asked hopefully. She could tell from the glint in his eyes he was still joshing.

She shook her head, confirming lightly, "Not a one."

They'd spent the previous day canning, too, and though he'd suggested another picnic Sunday evening, she'd begged off, saying she had to work, and then had left in a rush before he could do so much as issue a good-bye kiss. He'd let her go, figuring she needed some time to herself. But now, he didn't know. She looked as wary of him as she had on his first day back. And he'd be damned if he could figure out what he'd done, other than try to make love to her again, and she hadn't minded at the time. Did she think he was trying to take advantage of her, he wondered. That he was out for what he could get? Had she never had another affair? Or had she had one and been similarly hurt? Was she in love with someone else? None of the thoughts were comforting. He pushed them from his mind.

"Can you stay for a cold drink?" he asked, sliding the casserole into the refrigerator.

She paused. There was no denying the heat had parched her throat and left her clothes sticking damply to her skin.

"I've got lemonade already made, iced tea, beer," he tempted, wondering what was her pleasure. He wished it was himself.

"Lemonade would be nice," she said finally with a shy smile.

She watched as he poured the lemonade, standing so that her back was against the refrigerator. "Want to sit out on the porch? It's cooler out there," she suggested softly.

"Sure." As they passed through the living room, he righted a stack of unironed shirts. The action stretched muscles that were already overworked. He cringed as he brought his arm back to his side.

Gwen frowned. "What is it? What's wrong?" Concern radiated from her eyes.

He grimaced. Feeling foolish, he admitted reluctantly, "I'm beginning to feel a little stiff. I'm not used to the steering on that tractor It's always been difficult. The fact that I've been away from it so long makes it more so. I don't use that particular set of muscles playing racket-ball—at least not that way." Her palm, lightly brushing his shoulder, felt cool against his heated skin.

She was suddenly all professional nurse—or loving woman. He preferred to think her concern stemmed from the second approach as she counseled seriously, "Have you got any muscle relaxants around?"

He shook his head. "No, not that I'd take them if I had them."

She smiled. "I hate them, too. About all they ever seem to do is make me sleepy."

"You've had to take them?" He was curious.

"I got carried away chopping firewood for the winter last fall. Several years previously my car was hit from behind in city traffic. I had my seat belt on, but had a little whiplash anyway."

"Anyone else hurt?"

"No."

"I wish I'd been there to take care of you." He hadn't meant to voice his thoughts. Seeing her flush with pleasure made him glad he had.

She changed the subject adroitly. "Have you got anything to put on it? Any liniment or arthritis cream?"

He groaned. "Don't make me out to be any older than I am, woman. And, no, I don't have any of that, either. For your information I left it all in the city."

"Hm."

He liked the tenderness he read on her face.

"I might have something in my bag that'll do. Wait here." Finishing her lemonade in a single gulp, she handed him the empty glass and darted down the steps. Several moments later, she returned, triumphantly waving a tube of first-aid cream, as distant as if he'd been just any patient on her medical route. "Just put a little on."

"Sure." Already aching more than he had been, Dan shrugged out of his shirt and started to rub the cream in, then winced at the pain that that slight motion caused.

"Here, let me." Her touch was soothing, heavenly, and he closed his eyes, savoring every tender loving sensation. Her palm was flat and secure against his bare skin, massaging gently. Idly she tried to make conversation, and her voice quavered slightly with the effort it was costing her. "You really ought to be careful not to overdo. You know you're not used to it."

"Yes, ma'am."

She flushed at the faint note of sarcasm in his tone. "I'm nagging, aren't I?"

"You sound like a wife." His hand gently touched her cheek. He smiled. "I like it."

Swallowing hard, she held his gaze for a long moment, then looked away. Wordlessly, she capped the tube and handed it over for him to keep. He shrugged back into his shirt, again leaving it unbuttoned to midchest in deference to the heat of the day and of his skin.

"Stay and have dinner with me," he urged softly.

She looked crestfallen and then relieved. "I'm sorry. I already promised Elyse."

He nodded, with effort masking his disappointment.

He had promised not to push her. He had to honor that. "Are you going to be at the fund-raiser tomorrow night?"

"Elyse and I both will be." Her tone was noncommittal.

"I could pick you up." He felt like a high school boy trying to ask a girl for a first date, only then, he had to admit ruefully, he'd been a lot more successful.

The guarded look was back. She weighed her options and finally declined. "Thanks, but I don't think so."

"Still keeping your distance?" Frustration made him clench his teeth. He was unable to keep the taunting edge from his voice.

Her eyes darkened resentfully, and he could have kicked himself for pushing too hard too soon. "I think it's the best course. I've got to be going." She sped gracefully down the steps, then turned hesitantly, wanting to end their encounter on a pleasant note. "Thanks for the lemonade."

"You're welcome." He stood, watching her drive away, wondering what was bothering her the most—the fact he was still working for IDP and hence would not be staying on in Kentucky or the knowledge that he still wanted her as part of his life.

"Thanks for hanging out with me tonight," Elyse said.

They were at Gwen's place, sitting cross-legged on the floor, splitting a pizza, drinking icy beer. Unfortunately, there was no respite from the heat. Gwen's air conditioner was out of commission, and though they were clad in just halters and shorts and the box fan was swirling continually, both were perspiring freely.

"I half expected you to be with Dan."

"He expected that, too," Gwen said wryly, making no effort to hide her irritation.

"You say that as if you're mad at him."

"I guess I am, in a way." *For past injustices he knew nothing about and hence could do nothing to correct. Not now, not then.* Gwen sighed.

"You're still in love with him, aren't you?" Elyse sent her a penetrating glance.

Gwen blushed despite her effort not to. "Does it show?"

"Are you kidding? You haven't looked this vulnerable and edgy since I've known you. Not ever. He's the reason you never date much, isn't he?"

Gwen nodded. "I feel as though I've been through an emotional whirlpool. Damn it, Elyse, it's as if he walked in expecting everything to be the same as it was ten years ago, just because he wants it that way, for now."

"Is it?" Elyse queried, not put off by Gwen's anger or her denial.

Gwen lifted both palms noncommittally. "Yes and no. He says he's never stopped caring about me. He says he's never gotten over me. He's even asked me to return to Chicago with him when he goes."

"Then what's the problem?"

"If his dad hadn't gotten sick, this never would have happened. Dan wouldn't have been so determined to seek me out, at least not on any permanent basis. He's here temporarily, but that's all. Even now, he's already working for IDP. On a casual basis, he says. The truth is that he can't bear to be away from his work, out of the center of activity. Even his leisure reading material is business-oriented now. You should have seen the books on his coffee table when I was over at his house. They were all excruciatingly technical. I keep thinking that if I give in to my heart's desire and do go to bed with him again, let him into my life, that I'm in for a big fall. Only this time I'm not sure I could recover." She wasn't sure she could survive his leaving. She wasn't sure she would want to. "Does this make sense?" She sent her friend a penetrating glance.

"Only to fools and people in love." Elyse's mouth twisted wryly. "Fortunately, I've been there. When Buddy and I first got married, it was just wonderful. He'd come home at night glowing with reports of what his construction company was up to. I had just started at the clinic, and though he never really took my work as seriously as he took his, he was proud of me. As time passed, we started taking each other for granted. He stopped talking to me, and I stopped trying to communicate with him about everything but the most mundane matters. You know—like the sink doesn't work or the stove needs adjusting, the grass needs cutting again, the hedges need trimming."

"With Dan," Gwen lamented, "the distance goes much deeper." And there were secrets she'd kept hidden for years, facts she lived in terror she would somehow inadvertently reveal. To him, to anyone. Part of her wanted that, wanted him to know what she'd been through after he left, and the other part was terrified that if he did find out he'd further dishevel her life.

Elyse studied her dismay, adding finally, "Then do something about it. Go and see him."

Gwen contemplated that briefly. "I can't. We'd just end up sleeping together and that wouldn't help. That would only confuse matters." It would make her want to confide in him all the more.

"Then tell him that."

"Are you going to see Buddy?"

Elyse nodded. "But I want him to have a few more days to cool off without me first. I want him to realize what he's missing. Then, when he's ready to compromise, we'll talk."

"Don't wait too long," Gwen advised. Yet she envied Elyse's confidence. The younger woman knew that she was attractive. And she played on it.

"I won't," Elyse promised. "But don't you, either."

They finished the pizza in silence. Once again, their talk turned to their men.

"Do you think you'll ever find your way back to each other?" Gwen asked curiously at last.

"I don't know." Elyse shrugged, stretching out on the floor. "But I'm beginning to see that life isn't worth much without him. I don't like being alone, Gwen." She rested her chin on her hands. "But at the same time, I want him to respect me. To be perfectly honest, right now, I don't think he does. I think he sees me as a glorified servant, someone to take over where his mother left off. I don't want that for myself, Gwen. I'm just beginning to realize how much. Which is why I've decided to go after my bachelor's degree and become a registered nurse."

"That's great!" Gwen said.

Elyse sat up wearily, stretching her arms above her head. "Buddy doesn't think so."

Now they were getting down to the heart of the matter, Gwen realized. "When did you decide this, before or after your separation?"

"Before. It's one of the many reasons we're now living apart."

"What prompted your decision? Was it the difference in salary and responsibility?" Although an L.V.N. could change bandages and give some medications, she could not assume administrative positions or act as charge nurse or team leader.

"No, it's much deeper than that," Elyse confided, tracing patterns on the rug. "When I started out, I was just interested in obtaining a job skill. I chose the L.V.N. program because it would be completed in a year's time. I did it as a way to satisfy my folks and bide time until my marriage. I was already engaged to Buddy. But once I got into the program, I really enjoyed my studies. Now, I'm frustrated. There's not enough for me to do. Frankly, I'm bored. And lately I've been taking my job dissatisfaction out on Buddy."

Gwen said cautiously. "Maybe you should try talking to him."

"I've tried, but he just completely shuts me out. His mind is set on having children, now. That's all he wants to hear. He won't accept the idea of my going back to school. He feels threatened by it. Frankly, I think he suspects I am doing this because I eventually plan to leave him."

"So he left you first," Gwen quipped, shaking her head.

"Only after issuing all sorts of macho ultimatums first. Honestly, you should have heard him. He ran around like a bull with a burr in his foot. Oh, I know he didn't mean half of what he said but..."

If she was waiting for an apology, she could wait forever, Gwen knew. Buddy hated to admit he'd been wrong, particularly to his wife or anyone of the female persuasion.

"I just want him to meet me halfway," Elyse continued. "In the meantime, he can continue wearing his half-washed rumpled clothes and sad-puppy look."

"You've seen him?" Gwen asked.

"Who in this town hasn't?" she asked dryly. "Believe me, his disheveled appearance is not going to budge me an inch. He's going to have to raise his consciousness first. Then and only then will we see."

Chapter Six

The Quarrick farm was located in Caldwell County, north of Dawson Springs. Complete with chickens, horses, beef cattle, kittens and a pet lamb, the two-story white stone Georgian was centered at the top of a heavily treed hill and bordered by white fence on all sides. Gwen was last to arrive, and understandably nervous, knowing that Dan would be there, too. Phyllis Quarrick fanned herself agitatedly as she met Gwen at the door. "How do you like this heat?" Fortunately for the Quarricks, their house was fully air-conditioned.

Gwen moaned. "I'm dying."

"You don't have an air conditioner?" Phyllis asked with a commiserating sigh. Clearly, she wondered how Gwen was managing.

"I bought a window unit secondhand last year, which kept the whole house pretty cool. But it quit on me several weeks ago. I had a repairman out to look at it the other day, and he said it would cost more to repair it than to replace it. So, for the moment, I'm relying on a fan." Though, to be truthful, all that did was blow the warm air around.

"Are you going to buy another one?" Phyllis asked,

gracefully leading the way to the dining room where the others were gathered.

Gwen grimaced. "I don't know. I really can't afford it right now, and I hate to purchase anything on time payments, so I think I'll just wait this hot spell out." Sooner or later it would pass.

"From all accounts, it could be a wickedly hot summer," Doc cautioned, picking up the tail end of the conversation. "If you want an advance on your salary..." He was perfectly serious, she knew.

"I'll be fine." Gwen looked up and saw Dan standing there. Her heart turned over.

His sunburn had lost its pink hue, and was now a deep golden-brown. His hair had several new coppery-gold streaks in it. Against the tan of his face and the luminous white of his eyes, his irises seemed even greener. "Hi," he said softly.

"Hi." She flushed. Everyone noticed. She glanced away.

In the adjacent living room, ten-year-old Robyn Quarrick was seated cross-legged in front of the television. She had her Barbie doll case in front of her and was busy arranging the doll's long blond hair with a minuscule brush. Her brother, Andrew, was some distance away from her, quietly engrossed with a pile of plastic, easily assembled building blocks. Gwen felt a pang of envy for the family scene.

"Well, shall we get started?" Doc rubbed his hands together and led them toward the huge bleached-oak table where a work place had been set up. "Gwen and Elyse have made up a list of supplies, along with approximate projected costs for the first year. I've tallied figures for the services of another physician, specially trained in emergency medicine. We'll also need an X-ray machine and more lab equipment, as well as salaries for two technicans. Buddy has agreed to build the facility for cost.''

"I talked to the people at IDP when I went to the plant in Lexington this morning," Dan said quietly. "In accordance with company policy, they've agreed to match every dollar I put up for the building. I've also spoken to the people at United Way. They've promised to get back to me with a definite financial commitment, assuming they're able to make one, by the end of the month.''

"The community church has agreed to sponsor an ice cream social and white sale," Phyllis added as she served iced tea and freshly baked cookies.

"We're off to a good start," Doc said.

Before he could go into detail on what needed to be done next, Robyn came crashing into the room, followed briskly by Andrew. The baby was screaming at the top of his lungs. Robyn was also crying, holding up evidence of a headless, legless brand-new Barbie doll with a torn dress. "Mom!" she shouted agitatedly. "Look what he's done now!"

At that Andrew screamed louder, toddled and fell down on the floor.

"Oh, for heaven's sake!" Doc exclaimed, moving forward to pick up his son. Phyllis wrapped daughter Robyn in a consoling hug. "Honey, I'm sorry. I know Andrew can be a pest!''

Robyn sniffled louder. Although the previous year she had been inclined to dress in pretty dresses and ribbons, she now wore preppy oxford cloth shirts, fashionable khaki shorts and knee socks and powder-blue running shoes. Her hair, though long and thick, was drawn back in a single braid.

"You'll excuse us while we restore equilibrium in the living room," Doc said, motioning his entourage out of the room.

"Help yourselves to more refreshments," Phyllis added. "There are extra cookies and lemonade in the kitchen."

Buddy and Elyse exchanged a glare. There was no mistaking the tension between them, and although Buddy looked nicer than he had in weeks, all spruced up in what appeared to be a new sport shirt and slacks, his jaw freshly shaven, his hair combed to one side, Elyse looked as though she wanted to kill him. Dan caught Gwen's glance and lifted his shoulders in an expressive shrug. He had no idea what was going on, either.

"Anyone for more tea?" Gwen asked brightly. She didn't know what was sparking the feud between the estranged Daltons, but she did not want to witness a quarrel, and it looked as if they were about to start.

"I'll take some," Dan said.

"Me, too," Buddy joined in.

"I'll help you," Elyse said, getting up and following Gwen into the kitchen.

"What's gotten in to you?" Gwen hissed as soon as they were alone.

"Isn't it obvious?" Elyse whispered back agitatedly, slapping her arms defiantly across her chest. Jaw clenched, she glared straight ahead. "Buddy's seeing someone else!"

Buddy *was* wearing enough after-shave to kill a horse, Gwen had noted. But that could mean any number of things. "Hold it," Gwen urged, nicely arranging gingersnaps on a plate. "Don't you think you're jumping to conclusions?"

"No, I don't," Elyse said seriously. She munched absently on a cookie, forgetting for a moment the extra calories she didn't need to ingest. "The more I think about it, the more I know I'm right. He didn't leave me because I wouldn't have a child. He left because he's in love with someone else. And his new clothes prove it! He hasn't been that dressed up since before we were married. In fact—" she waved her index finger emphatically "—the only time I've ever known him to look that nice was when we were dating, and that stopped soon enough after we tied the knot."

From Gwen's view at the sidelines, that happened to many wives. And husbands, too. Their spouses just stopped trying to look nice once the wedding ceremony was over. Gwen searched mentally for a way to cheer Elyse up and at the same time calm her down. "Maybe he wanted to look nice for you," Gwen said hopefully.

"I wish." Tears moistened Elyse's eyes. She picked up another gingersnap and broke it in half. "There's a suitcase in the back of his car. Try to explain that." While she waited for Gwen to ingest the importance of that, she compulsively munched on her cookie. "It's a small one, just perfect for overnight. I saw it on the way in. He didn't have that when we were married, either."

Heaven help them, Gwen thought. Buddy couldn't be cheating on her, could he? And yet who would be in a better position to know? If Elyse thought . . . no, it just wasn't possible, she decided sternly. In keeping with that conservative opinion, Gwen suggested, "Maybe he's going out of town for a night. On business."

"To do what?" Tears welled up in Elyse's eyes, spilling over her lower lashes and onto her cheeks. Defiantly, she brushed the tears away. Gwen handed her a tissue from the box on the counter. Elyse continued as she dabbed at her eyes. "All his construction business is right here in this county. And besides, if he were bidding on a new property he would have said something about it to Doc or to Dan or to me. You know how proud Buddy is of his construction company!"

"Well, I still think you're jumping to conclusions," Gwen said.

"Am I?" Defiantly, Elyse placed both fists on her hips. "I called his trailer at five this morning, Gwen. There was no answer. And I let it ring at least twenty times every five minutes for an hour."

Gwen pretended to savor her gingersnap thoughtfully. In reality, the sugary confection tasted like dust in her throat. Finally, she shrugged. "Maybe he wanted to get an early start at the site."

Elyse stomped her foot, agitated. "He never leaves the house before first light, never! Unless of course he's not there to begin with." Tears glistening in her eyes, she slammed her hand down on the kitchen counter, saying finally in a much lower, more dejected voice, "That's not even the worst part. Today I ran into a friend of mine who lives in Princeton. She said Buddy's been spending an awful lot of time over there now. She's seen him driving through town at all times of the night and day. What's worse, I've just noticed there's a new key on his chain. And before you say anything to dispute that, it's not the big key ring he keeps all of his work keys on, Gwen, the one he wears on his belt, but his personal key chain, the one with the keys to his truck, our house, the trailer, and now..."

"Now what?" Gwen asked, exasperated by the young woman's melodrama and yet scared for her all the same. Elyse was right, Buddy was acting peculiarly. In all the time she had known him he'd never dressed the part of a single man on the make, yet that was exactly how he looked now. Could it be true? Was Buddy taking advantage of the nightlife in a neighboring town? Perhaps in an effort to reprove his desirability after experiencing his faltering marriage?

Dan stuck his head in the kitchen door. "Need some help?" He gave Gwen a strange glance, taking in Elyse's furious tears.

Gwen shook her head and picked up the platter of home-baked cookies. "No, we'll be right there."

Phyllis and Doc rejoined them in the dining room several minutes later. "All's calm for the moment!" Phyllis held up her hand, fingers crossed. "Robyn's agreed to entertain Andrew for another half hour."

Gwen shot both her and the physician an envious look. She'd been around the Quarricks enough to know that a fracas was an infrequent occurrence. "You're very lucky to have two such wonderful children."

Phyllis poured them all some more tea. "Yes, we are. Though I'll be the first to admit Robyn has had a difficult time of it the past two summers. Andrew takes up a lot of our time. And she was used to having us all to herself."

"She'll adjust," Doc said confidently. He absent-mindedly stroked his closely trimmed auburn beard.

"I know. Still, there are times when I wish I didn't

have to divide my time between the two of them."
Phyllis sighed. In hostess skirt and organdy blouse, she
looked very attractive. It was clear to Gwen she loved
both children very much.

"Back to business," Doc said. "About the building
supplies. Buddy, you want to check into that?"

An hour later they were nearly finished. Buddy kept
glancing at his watch surreptitiously. Dan was less obvious, but also concerned about the time. At eight
o'clock Doc said finally, "If you all have got to be
someplace—"

"As a matter of fact, I do have to run in to Princeton
tonight," Buddy said. Elyse sent Gwen a glittering I-
told-you-so look. Buddy averted his eyes from all at the
table, barely suppressed a guilty flush.

Dan came to the rescue, rising easily, "As a matter
of fact, I've got to be going, too. I promised to be at the
Lexington plant first thing tomorrow morning." He
sent a questioning look toward Gwen. "If I can drop
you . . ."

"Thanks, I've got my Jeep." Her throat was con-
stricted with emotion. Part was sympathy for Elyse,
horror at the thought that Buddy might actually be
stepping out on her friend, separated or not, and part
reluctance to see Dan go, even for one night.

From the living room came the sounds of unexpected hilarity from Robyn and Andrew. Gwen realized that it had been quiet for a long time—too long.
The group found them playing peekaboo with Robyn
and Andrew's cat. Strung around the family room was a
mass of unraveling Ace bandages, beige cotton strips
draped haphazardly over lampshades, sofa and end
tables. Robyn's black-and-white kitten was sniffing the

bandages individually, standing on his hind legs. Andrew was giggling riotously, his laughter as infectious, it seemed, as the mess.

"All right, you two scoundrels," Phyllis scolded good-naturedly. "Enough of this! Robyn, put the cat out, please."

Doc shook his head at the freeway-interchange-like mess. "Where did they get all of these?"

"From the box in the hall. The bandages are for the First-Aid Marathon for Robyn's scout troop." Phyllis Quarrick sent her daughter a mock stern look. "Which, young lady, you very well know."

"I know, Mommy, but Andy got into them when I wasn't looking. And then Buttons—my kitty—joined in." She giggled again, and Gwen felt a rush of affection for the pleasant-natured child. How quickly she had recuperated from the mangling of her cherished Barbie doll.

While Doc retrieved the box from the hall, Phyllis picked up Andrew and deposited him in the nearby playpen for momentary safekeeping. The remaining adults began untangling flesh-colored Ace bandages, one strip at a time. "Just put those in the laundry room," Phyllis directed her husband when they'd finished. "I'll have to run them through the wash." Robyn assisted her father.

"You've got enough bandages there to minister to an army," Buddy commented as Phyllis showed them affably to the door.

"Which is about what it'll be when we get through. My junior girl scout troop and several other troops from our district are getting together for mass work on their first-aid badges Saturday in the high school gym.

Gwen, Elyse and other members of the medical community here have all volunteered their services, so it should be a lot of fun as well as educational. We're in need of more victims, though, so if either of you men would like to volunteer..."

Buddy and Dan both cheerfully volunteered.

"You men don't know what you're letting yourself in for," Doc cautioned laughingly, rejoining the group. "Last I heard Phyllis even planned to use fake blood for the senior scout groups."

"Catsup," Phyllis corrected, shooting her husband an affectionate look. "And how else could we effectively stage a mock major emergency on a par with those responded to by the Red Cross?"

Buddy left first, then Elyse. When their cars had departed, Dan gave Gwen an unasked-for lift up into her Jeep.

"You know, I'd be happy to stop by and look at your air conditioner," he said quietly. Outside, the humidity was stifling.

"Thanks, but I think the only thing that's going to help there is a new unit, and as you heard me tell Doc, I can't afford it."

For once, Dan didn't argue. His eyes traveled up and down her, apparently liking very much what he saw and sending an answering response spiraling hotly through her limbs. "I'll see you in a day or so, then," he said quietly. He thrust a piece of paper into her hand. "If you need to reach me for any reason, here's the number in Lexington where I'll be working. If you want to talk, you can call or stop by nights at the farm."

He was gone before she had a chance to comment or protest.

GWEN SPENT A HECTIC DAY at the clinic and out making calls and returned home at seven, wanting only a cool bath and an icy drink. As the heat wave and high humidity continued, her house was unbearably hot after being closed up all day. She walked listlessly through the dwelling, opening windows and turning on the downstairs fan. It only served to swirl the warm air around and around. She sat down on the sofa and fanned herself wearily with an old magazine. Through the screen she saw the Kingstons' farm pickup truck pull up in front of her curb.

Dan appeared moments later. Beside him on the porch was a large cardboard carton. "It's a window air conditioner," he explained, in response to her stupefied glance. "I picked it up in Lexington for you."

Opening the door, Gwen came out onto the porch. Her throat closed tightly. Seeing the trouble he'd gone to made her want to cry. Only the practical streak in her nature kept her from bursting into tears. "I can't afford that," she warned. "So there's no reason to even take it out of the carton."

He grinned, not put off in the least. "Sure you can. My terms are very easy. Just a kind word, a friendly smile, a few minutes of your time now and then."

And a toss in the hay, she thought cynically. Surely Dan wouldn't try to buy her affections... would he? "It's very thoughtful of you, but I can't accept such an expensive item, even temporarily. It wouldn't be proper."

An exasperated sound whistled through his teeth. But his manner remained calm and nonchalant. "Then think of it as a gift, repayment for the canning you did for my folks."

Her spine stiffened regally; her chin shot up better to survey him. His hair was combed neatly in a side part and brushed back away from his face. His upper lip was thin in comparison to his full lower lip. Both were exquisitely soft, talented when it came to caressing. "I never expected anything for that." Quietly she studied the oval lines of his face, the distinct lines of his jaw. To her dismay, a warm blush of embarrassment colored her cheeks.

He faced her firmly. "So much the better, then. The air conditioner stays. Now, are you going to keep me out here on the porch all evening or ask me in graciously and offer me a cold drink?" His teasing tone penetrated what was left of her armor. "Some supper would be nice, too. I haven't eaten."

He did look tired. And she knew he'd been in Lexington on business all day. Despite her determination to stay angry, a little of her reserve melted at his cajoling smile. "I can't believe how much you take for granted. You make yourself right at home, don't you?" She crossed her arms defiantly over her breasts. How could she have forgotten the strong unpredictable streak in his character. Just when she thought she had gotten him all figured out, he liked to turn around and surprise her.

"I intend to, yes. Got a wrench?" He cast her a side-long glance as he ushered her through her front door, his hand cupping her elbow possessively, his touch warm and thrillingly tender. She had no choice. She gave in. Moments later they had wrestled the heavy carton into her living room and had removed the new air conditioner from its protective shell. "This model cools approximately seventeen hundred square feet, so it should work on cooling your entire house. It's also energy-efficient." Dan paused to remove his tie and unbutton his shirt several notches. He glanced toward the half bath on the lower floor, then out toward his truck. He hadn't even gone home first, but apparently had come straight from work and the store. "Would you mind if I changed into jeans?" he asked, gesturing toward the suit pants he still wore. It thrilled her to know he had been so anxious to see her that he hadn't even wanted to take the time to change.

"You do plan ahead, don't you?" she shot back reflexively, secretly admiring his gumption. Only a thoroughly secure male could do what he had done and hope to get away with it.

"I sure try." His eyes held hers and refused to let her look away.

Gwen felt as though she had a vise on her throat. Her voice was husky as she consented, "Go ahead and change. I'd hate to see you ruin your suit." Which looked like a designer suit from the cut and quality of the fabric.

"That's what I like, a woman who's all heart," he murmured, lightly tweaking her beneath the chin. Moments later he had retrieved what he'd needed and disappeared into the bath.

While he was occupied, she studied the unit he had selected. The only drawback was the price. The unit easily cost upward of a thousand dollars, Gwen knew. She had priced them just the previous week. On her salary and budget, with all the costs that went along with maintaining a mortgage payment alone, it would take years for her to repay him.

Dan emerged from the bath. Clad in a white short-sleeved polo shirt, jeans and running shoes, he looked much more relaxed. Reading the anxiety on her face, knowing intuitively her concern had to be financially oriented, he stressed softly, "Let me do this for you. Please."

She shook her head. "It's too much." She turned away.

In two swift steps he had closed the distance between them. His arm resting lightly on her shoulders, he turned her to face him. "No, it's not, Gwen." His mouth touched the tip of her nose, stirring her every cell into ardent wakefulness. The scent of his aftershave clung to his skin, further enticing her into his magically protective spell. "It's just the beginning of what I want to do for you."

Abruptly it sounded like a payoff to her, a way of bartering his way into her bed. "You can't buy me, Daniel." The angry words were ground out like shards of metal. She shrugged free of his grasp and stalked toward the door, intending to usher him out. *Damn the air conditioner, anyway! Damn her for wanting him in her life!*

Perspiration beaded on his upper lip and brow. He stalked closer, hands splayed defiantly on his hips. "Is that what you think I'm trying to do?" Incredulity made him vulnerable. And in that second she knew she had misjudged him and his motives badly. Maybe she had subconsciously even wanted to find an excuse to kick him out, to keep him from intruding on her life.

"No. I don't know." Gwen ran a hand through her hair. She was so confused. And his open generosity wasn't helping.

"You accept vegetables from my family's farm," he

pointed out. "I know from the possessions scattered around your house that you've had embroidered pillows given to you, several paintings by local artists, wood carvings, as gifts."

"That's different."

"Not really. Those people want you to be happy. So do I. I can afford to do this for you, Gwen, very easily."

She took a deep breath; it was her turn to be amazed. "You make that much?" She had assumed he was well off. Not having dated any corporate career men, she had no idea how financially comfortable he was. His implication stymied her.

He nodded. "I'm an executive. As of last year, my salary is well into the six-figure range, complete with stock options and full company benefits." The chasm between them seemed wider than ever. He studied her speculatively. "That bothers you, doesn't it?"

She hated the indulgence in his face. Never had she asked him to pity her. "Why should it?" She tossed her curls.

Very gently, he responded, "You tell me."

Avoiding his probing gaze, she said, "I'll fix you supper. It's the least I can do after all the trouble you've gone to, misguided as your actions were. But I can't accept the air conditioner."

He grabbed her arm and twirled her around. He rested his hands on her shoulders and drew her to him, so that they were standing toe to toe. "I can't sleep nights, knowing you're alone in this heat. And I don't like the idea of your sleeping with windows open and being alone. I worry about whether you're safe from criminal intrusion and whether you're physically miserable." His honest words, unsteadily spoken, affected her like no demands ever could have. She felt herself weakening, swaying toward the strength and refuge he offered. "Let me do this for you, Gwen. Please. We'll set up payment terms, anything you like."

He took advantage of her shock to lower his mouth to hers. Softly, seductively, he teased her mouth open, sweetly savoring every soft lingering caress. Weak-kneed, she leaned against him. What little had been left of her will to fight him was gone, completely out of reach. She faced him in pliant resignation.

Dan seized victory while her spirit was less, his attitude once again brisk and businesslike. "Where are your tools?" He unlaced her arms from around his neck and jubilantly towed her along behind him as he strode toward the appointed window. First the old unit would have to be removed.

"I'll get them. And I'll pay you back for this if it takes me ten years," she vowed. "I also want to see the receipt." She didn't want him lessening the retail price or omitting taxes, just so she could better afford it. And if she didn't insist on the paperwork, she knew he would. Darn him anyway! How hard it was to fight someone so chivalrous!

"As you wish," he said wryly, kneeling to begin his task.

While he worked, Gwen fixed dinner, slicing a ham, preparing a crips vegetable medley. When Dan joined her for the meal, there was also potato salad, and a fresh-baked apple pie cooling on the stove. The new air conditioner whirred wonderfully, robbing the humidity from the air, cooling her house in a matter of minutes. Over glasses of iced tea, they basked in the controlled comfort.

"Have you given any thought to returning to Chicago with me?" Dan asked. They sat side by side on her sofa, feet propped up comfortably on the low coffee table. He'd long since removed his shoes. His stocking-clad feet nestled next to hers.

She glanced down at her tea. Chicago, with Dan. About this much she could be truthful. "I don't belong there, Dan." Not as his... steady. It was too much in limbo, and she'd already been living that way for the past decade. The only difference was that lately she had been minus the day-to-day pain. She'd had her work. She'd known she was needed, at least on a professional level. And in some respects, personally, too. To be with him again, never knowing if it would work out, always fearing he would again decide to leave her... Cold chills slid down her spine. She sat up, feeling the hurt anew. He mistook her unease.

"Is there some place else you'd rather live?" Idly his thumb and forefinger encircled his glass. "IDP has plants all over the world. I'll be up for reassignment when I return. Because I'm on leave of absence, I can't promise first choice, but I do have some input into where I go."

"But you could probably go back to Chicago if you wanted to."

"I had planned to request that location, yes. But if there is somewhere else you'd rather live, Gwen, I'll do my best to try to get assigned there. I don't think I'll ever live permanently in Kentucky again, not as long as I'm with IDP. Not unless they open another plant, and at this moment they have no plans to. The Lexington facility is fully staffed on an executive level. On the other hand, Chicago has a variety of positions, any number of them I could fill."

Yes, Gwen thought, in Chicago she could imagine there would be many more openings for a man of Dan's caliber. "You'd do that for me?" She observed him wonderingly. His hair rumpled, looking slightly worse-for-wear after an agonizingly long day, he was still delectable. And so sweet, thoughtful. But his career had always come first. She had to remind herself that hadn't and wouldn't change. Could she live her life second to his work?

"Yes." His hand twined with hers. Though she made no effort to pull back or disengage his grip, he felt the reserve, the stiffness in her limbs. "I'm rushing you again, aren't I?" He rubbed her wrist with forefinger and thumb. The action sent shivers up and down her spine.

"Yes." Her voice was tremulous, unsteady. He was standing so close that she was achingly aware of the rich herbal scent of his cologne. "I want us to get to know each other again. I don't want to rush into anything physical, the way we did before." She didn't want to endanger what emotional closeness they had found. And she was afraid that the pressures of an affair begun too soon would do just that.

"Okay." He dropped his hand and placed it squarely on his knee. There was a determined set to his jaw. He stared straight ahead at the new darkness of the night. "I can go slower." He cast her a sideways glance. An unsteady shudder of need swept through him. "I don't want to. But I will." Without warning, he was on his feet, gathering up the neatly folded stack of his business clothing, his black wing-tip shoes. "I'll see you at the first-aid session at the high school tomorrow night?" His eyes held hers, the intensity of his regard caressing her like velvet.

She nodded. Then swiftly he was gone, his steps echoing on the porch and then the walk, to the car parked at the curb. For the first time in a long while, she held out hope for the future, his and hers.

Chapter Seven

Gwen paused for a moment in the middle of the high school gymnasium, both amused and awed at the scene around her. Scout chairman Phyllis Quarrick stood in the middle of the gymnasium, organizing chaos like a traffic cop in the middle of a busy intersection. Girls in pine-green uniforms crowded around her attentively, their youthful faces upturned as they waited for their scout leader's instructions, their diagonal sashes ribboned across their torsos from shoulder to waist. Elyse informed high school students and adults where they were expected to be.

Gwen put a stack of poster boards emblazoned with step-by-step instructions on the table set up for instruction reference for bandaging sprains. For easier identification she'd worn a dressy white uniform left over from her hospital days. In Gwen's estimation there were easily five hundred people now milling about, maybe more.

What had started out simply to be an instructional session for Phyllis Quarrick's scout troop had turned into an event that involved the whole community. Not that anyone who knew Phyllis Quarrick was all that surprised. If ever there'd been a born organizer, she was it. The first to see moneymaking potential in the venture, she'd conferred with Gwen and others on the committee and then invited several of the local women's clubs to sponsor refreshments and a bake sale later in the evening. Proceeds would benefit the new Dawson Springs Clinic. The other scout leaders involved had followed suit and done the same. They were all setting up in the cafeteria.

As soon as she had a minute, Elyse came over to confer with Gwen. Two seconds later Buddy and Dan walked in simultaneously, followed by a group of construction workers from Buddy's firm. Elyse stiffened reflexively and turned away from her estranged mate. Buddy did the same.

"Go talk to him," Gwen encouraged Elyse in a low voice.

"Not if he were fighting for his life," Elyse replied haughtily.

After another glaringly tense moment Elyse departed to organize "accident victims" on the school's front lawn for the senior scouts to work on. Reporters from several local papers followed, there to capture the moment and help publicize their fund-raising efforts and the improvement of community health skills. In another corner of the gym Doc was explaining to a television news reporter what was needed at the clinic specifically, and what they hoped to accomplish by providing better emergency care.

Gwen gathered Phyllis's elementary-school-age troop around her. As per Gwen's instructions, Robyn importantly passed out an Ace bandage to each child.

"Need some help?" Dan asked, angling in at Gwen's

side. As he stood beside her, his thigh accidentally brushed hers.

"Shouldn't you be with the other accident victims?" Gwen asked, all too aware of the blood storming madly through her veins.

He sat on the edge of the table, his arms crossed casually over his chest. His gaze roved her face as if he were mesmerized. "I was. Elyse said that they had far too many casualties and sent me in here to assist."

Phyllis agreed as she breezed by with a reporter in tow. "And besides, Gwen, you need someone to demonstrate on." At Phyllis's choice of words, Dan sparkled. Gwen successfully fought down a flush. Knowing there was no way gracefully to get rid of him and aware of the attentive circle of little girls, she gave in.

Whirling back to the girls, she began, "Okay, we're going to talk about sprains. A sprain is an injury to the ligaments that support the joints in the body. The usual symptoms will be pain upon moving the injured part. Swelling. The skin will look puffy. Tenderness. The injured area will hurt when you touch it. There may also be discoloration of the skin or black-and-blue bruises around the injury." Aware of Dan's interested, admiring gaze upon her, Gwen went on to explain how to apply supporting bandages such as a pillow or blanket splint, how to elevate the injured part and apply ice to reduce swelling.

Dan was a model victim, sitting quietly as she demonstrated on his arm, but her hands trembled ever so slightly every time she touched him. Noticing, his mouth lifted a fraction of an inch. She tried to glare him into behaving, but succeeded only in capturing his attention even more.

"The easiest way to splint a broken wrist or forearm is to wrap a towel around it, then a magazine or folded newspaper." Gwen demonstrated on Dan's arm, while, to the girls' giddy amusement, he made comically pained, anxious faces. Gwen couldn't help herself; she smiled, too. "Then we secure it with strips of cloth, several neckties or string. And we're done, we're ready to go to the hospital or doctor's office to have it x-rayed."

At Gwen's urging the girls repeated the first-aid procedure. Because there was one girl left over, the vivacious Robyn volunteered to practice on Dan.

Doc Quarrick approached, pausing for a moment to watch his little girl. "Everything all right?" He lifted his gaze to Gwen.

Feeling a lump in her throat the size of an apple, she nodded. Moments later, when all had mastered and had a chance to practice the first lesson, she began instructing them in the use of a figure-eight bandage. Again, Dan was the test vehicle, watching as she wrapped his sweat-sock-clad foot and ankle in the stretchy cloth bandage. Many giggles and mix-ups later, all the girls had mastered it.

When the session ended, Robyn came up to Gwen. "That was fun." She smiled, tugging nervously on one long red-brown braid.

Gwen smiled. "I'm glad you enjoyed yourself."

"Will you come back sometime and teach us some more?" she asked.

Gwen glowed in the wake of the little girl's admiration and affection. "Yes."

"I've never seen them so enraptured," Phyllis remarked pleasantly as she joined them. She paused to place an arm affably around her daughter's shoulder. Robyn responded by linking her arm about her mother's waist. Phyllis laughed, confessing, "I didn't know they could be that quiet and well-behaved for so long. Thanks for coming. We all appreciate it."

Dan stayed to help Gwen clean up and put all the bandages in the box. "You were good." He slanted her an admiring glance.

Gwen watched Phyllis and Doc depart with their daughter toward the cafeteria, envying their close-knit family unit. "Thank you."

When Dan and Gwen entered the cafeteria, Buddy and Elyse were standing together wordlessly, unhappiness etched on their faces. After a moment Buddy pivoted and stalked off.

Watching him converse animatedly with a male employee of his, Gwen said, "Doesn't look much like a reconciliation, does it?"

"No, it doesn't," Dan concurred with her appraisal curtly. "And it's a damn shame."

They spent the next half an hour socializing with others from the community. Dan walked her to her Jeep, then followed her home—to make sure she arrived safely, he said. She felt that it was just because he was reluctant to see the evening end.

He paused, watching her fit her key in the front door. She deliberately hadn't asked him in. Mainly because she didn't trust herself to behave responsibly.

"I guess this is good night then." He leaned an arm across the doorframe, towering over her with an evocative sensuality that set her every nerve ending quivering.

Gwen wanted to make love to him. But she was feeling too vulnerable now to let him into her life. His hand captured hers. He leaned forward and brushed a light lingering kiss across her lips. "I'm not giving up on you, Gwen," he promised softly, watching her steadily. "I'll be back."

Yes, she thought. He would. "For as long as you're here in Kentucky, anyway," she finished with a wistful sigh. She hadn't meant to say the words aloud.

"So that's what's bothering you," he said. He moved away, not disputing what she was thinking— that one day soon he would be leaving her without so much as a backward glance. He stepped back from her and regarded her with an intense longing that made her heart race. Reverently, his voice lowered. "Watching you with those girls tonight, I realized how much love you had to give. Those girls adored you. Almost as much as I do." He paused. Tension showed in the tiny lines bracketing his mouth. "Do you really want to spend the rest of your life alone?"

He would never physically force her to have an affair, Gwen knew. He wouldn't take unfair advantage in the physical sense. But he would use every possible means to sway her toward his way of thinking, and at the moment it was the dictate of her own heart.

Gwen lowered her eyes, feeling suddenly, inexplicably near tears. "I've never wanted that," Gwen said. "But it is the way my life has worked out. Our lives don't always go according to plan." She couldn't forget that he had been the one who had left her, the one who had walked away, the one who in the final analysis would probably still walk away.

He sighed, but surprisingly made no effort to argue the point. "Have dinner with me tomorrow night." He made no effort to mask the need in his eyes.

The emotion affected her like no words ever could have. But she had promised Elyse that she would drive in to Lexington with her for the day. And maybe, just maybe, her unavailability was for the best. "I can't. I've got... other plans," she said finally.

"Monday, then." Impatience simmered in his pose. He straightened up, fists splayed on his hips. "I'll pick you up at seven," he said, not giving her a chance to think up an excuse.

At that moment she could have no more refused him than she could have denied herself life. "All right." He leaned forward for one last gentle kiss.

"I still wish you'd invite me in."

She couldn't, not as susceptible to his charms as she was feeling. "Good night, Dan." She turned and disappeared wordlessly into the house.

He did absolutely nothing to stop her, but just the same it was several moments before he finally walked away.

GWEN WAS LOCKING UP the clinic Monday evening, when she spotted the teenage girl standing against a battered pickup truck several decades older than Gwen's Jeep and rusted through in several places. Wearing faded and threadbare cutoff jeans and a cotton T-shirt, she was staring with a peculiarly anguished expression at the Dawson Springs Clinic sign. On impulse, Gwen strode over to join the young woman. She was jiggling a one-year-old baby, clad in a diaper and faded sunsuit, on her hip. Up close, she looked exhausted, as if she'd been under tremendous strain, and Gwen's heart went out to her. She was so young.

"May I help you?" It was nearly five-thirty, but

Gwen still had plenty of time before meeting Daniel for their evening dinner date.

The young girl bit into her lower lip tremulously. She glanced back toward the clinic door, the white lab coat and the keys Gwen still held in her hand. "Do you work here?" she asked softly.

Obviously impoverished, the girl was nonetheless extremely well groomed. Her long dark hair, pulled away from her face, gleamed cleanly and was fastened in a ponytail at the nape of her neck.

"Yes. I'm Gwen Nolan. I'm a nurse here." She smiled, extending her hand. The girl's palm felt cold and clammy as they briefly clasped hands in introduction. The girl was very pale beneath her tan. Noticing Gwen's concerned regard, a dark stain colored her cheeks. "Officially, the clinic's closed for the day, but if it's an emergency..." Gwen offered. Was she worried about her baby? Sucking energetically on a pacifier, he looked extremely healthy.

"I—" Without warning, the girl faltered, swaying uncertainly on her feet. Gwen caught her in her arms, steadying her and the baby both. After a second her color began to return, but she still swayed unsteadily. "I'm sorry," the girl gasped, putting a trembling hand to her face. "The heat..." Weakly, she allowed Gwen to take the baby from her arms.

"Don't faint on me. I'm not licensed to do stitches." With one hand, Gwen extracted an ammonia capsule from her pocket and waved it in front of the girl's nose. She started, coughed. "Better?" Gwen said, watching her closely. Tears in her eyes, the girl nodded. "What's your name?" Gwen asked.

After a moment's hesitation she said softly, reluctantly, "Nicki Kaufman." Gwen knew then that whatever was wrong could not be discussed on the street. Nor, from the cautious way Nicki was looking over her shoulder, did she want anyone to see her there with Gwen. With her permission, Gwen got her into the clinic and helped her lie down on one of the cots. The baby played nearby with a box of infant's toys extracted from the office waiting room.

"Dr. Quarrick, our physician, has gone home for the day," Gwen said, shaking down a thermometer. "But if you want me to, I can call him. I'm sure he'll be glad to come back."

Nicki shook her head. She waved the thermometer away. "No. No doctor. I can't afford it. I know what's wrong, anyway. Or at least I think I do." She sighed wearily and shielded her face with her palm. On her cheek a lone tear had begun to fall. "I'm pregnant again."

Gwen sat down beside her. Compassionately she took the young girl's hand. Though obviously old enough to be married and have a baby, in many ways the eighteen- or nineteen-year-old girl was still very much a child in need of comforting herself. The role of counselor and mother-substitute was one Gwen had played many times. "Have you had any tests done?" she asked quietly.

Nicki shook her head. "No." Panicked, she went on, "And I can't pay for them, either. Money's really tight now." She stifled a sob. "My husband just lost his job. I don't know when or where he'll be able to get another one, and we c-can't afford to move."

"Don't worry about that," Gwen said softly. "We have funds to absorb incidentals like this." And both

Gwen and Dr. Quarrick would render their services free of charge if need be. "When was your last period?" she asked. To her relief, Nicki's son looked healthy and happy, with no signs of neglect or abuse. In such cases that wasn't always true, she knew sadly.

"Six weeks ago." Nicki sighed. "I'm usually so regular. My breasts are tender. I can't keep anything down. Mornings are usually okay, but evenings—evenings are terrible."

"Have you been using any form of birth control?" Despite her anxious, overwrought state, the girl seemed intelligent, informed.

Nicki nodded. "My husband was. But then one night, he didn't. And now—we didn't think the risk would be that great because I'm still nursing Cade." She began to sob again, heartbreakingly.

Gwen waited until she had gained control, then handed her a tissue from the box on the counter. Then, in an effort to make certain Nicki's fears were justified, she suggested, "Let's run a test to make sure you are pregnant." She handed Nicki a plastic cup. "If you'll give me a urine sample, we'll know in about half an hour or so."

When the test was under way, Gwen held the baby and they chatted some more—about Gwen, the clinic in general and how it was run, and finally, when Gwen felt she was up to talking about it, they got back to Nicki's situation. Gwen learned that the girl was from a neighboring county and had driven to Dawson Springs because she'd heard Doc Quarrick sometimes took charity cases. Once there, she'd nearly lost her nerve.

"Does your husband know you're here?"

Nicki shook her head sadly. "I couldn't tell him. He has so much to worry about as it is. We can barely afford to feed Cade. And now to have another child so soon—it's so unfair." She gulped, continuing, "You see, we're both from large families. And we promised each other we'd wait to have more children until we'd bought a place of our own. Tim, my husband, wants to own a farm. But that takes money for a down payment, and we haven't got enough even to pay the rent, come the first of the month. Oh, Ms Nolan, if they evict us I don't know what we'll do."

"There's always welfare, unemployment."

"No." Nicki shook her head vehemently. "Tim won't hear of it."

"Your families, then," Gwen suggested.

"Neither are in a position to help us. And they disapproved of our marrying anyway, because we were so young. We eloped as soon as we turned eighteen. They said this would happen. I guess they were right."

Gwen returned with the results of the test after the lab timer had sounded. "It's positive." Nicki was silent, her face white and strained. "I know what it's like to feel like your whole world's crashing down around you," Gwen sympathized readily. "But given time, solutions can usually be found for even the toughest problems."

"I know what you're getting at, but my husband doesn't believe in handouts, no matter what," Nicki confessed shakily, sitting up and sipping the glass of juice Gwen had fixed for her. "Normally, I wouldn't either, but . . ." Her voice trembled. She paused, unable to finish.

"Then you do want this baby," Gwen ascertained.

"Oh, yes," Nicki affirmed. She reached for her baby boy, smiling as he stood on wobbly legs and accepted a lift up into his mama's lap. "I couldn't think of doing otherwise."

"And your husband," Gwen asked gently, "how do you think he will feel?" Would this split them up, or in the end, only bind them closer together? From her experience she knew it could go either way, depending on the parties involved.

"He'll want the baby," Nicki said solemnly. She stared glumly at the drawn clinic shades. "But that won't help us feed either child." She sighed. "Tim's been talking about going to work in the mines. He's had his name on a waiting list for over two years. But I don't want him to do that. I don't want him to give up his dream of owning his own farm."

"Does your husband have experience in that regard?" Gwen asked, thinking of the help Miles Kingston was going to need. "Does he know how to run a tractor or mend a fence?"

"Oh, yes," Nicki said. She sighed. "But with the economy so bad, nobody's hiring this summer. They're all getting by the best that they can."

"I may know of a job," Gwen said. "I'll check into it and let you know." Gwen made an appointment for Nicki to see Doc Quarrick early the next day. "You'll need a complete exam, some blood work. He'll probably also start you on some prenatal vitamins and discuss whether or not you want to continue nursing your child."

Subdued but much happier, Nicki rose to leave, slinging her shoulder bag over her arm. She lifted Cade with the other, then suddenly swayed again and with

Gwen's help sat down abruptly. "Do you feel well enough to drive?" Gwen asked, recalling the battered old pickup.

"Actually, no—" Handing the baby over, the girl rushed off to be sick in the closest bath. That settled it as far as Gwen was concerned. "I'm driving you home," she said firmly.

"But my truck..." Nicki protested weakly.

"Your husband can come back and get it today or tomorrow. At the moment you're in no condition to drive."

As it turned out, it was nearly nine o'clock when Gwen returned home. Only then, seeing her dress laid out over the bed, did she remember her dinner date with Dan. Aghast, she tried to phone him. When there was still no answer half an hour later, she drove out to the Kingston farm, hoping to catch him outside or en route home. No such luck. The house was empty. His car was gone. She knew he must be furious with her. She couldn't blame him. Regardless of the circumstances, she had stood him up. She only hoped he wouldn't be too angry to listen to her explanation and to accept her heartfelt apology.

Wearily, she pinned a note inside his screen door, explaining she'd been held up at work, asking him to call, then drove home. She spent the rest of the night wondering, worrying, waiting for him to telephone her or answer the phone at the farm. He did neither. Worse, she was unable to reach him the next day or the next.

On the third day she got nothing but a busy signal when she dialed the Kingston number. On impulse she stopped by the Kingston farm on her way back from

morning calls. Dan's car was in the driveway. Everything looked normal on the surface. Yet no one
answered the bell. She tried the door, found it open
and after another moment's hesitation, feeling more
than ever like a jealously intruding female, walked in,
calling, "Dan?" *Please don't let him be too angry,* she
prayed.

A second later footsteps sounded on the stairs. Dan
tromped halfway down. Seeing that it was Gwen, his
expression didn't alter. His mouth was thin, his eyes
hard as cut jade.

"I'm sorry for barging in like this," she began nervously. He gave her no encouragement whatsoever. "I
didn't know if you heard me."

From his expression she knew he had. "If you want
to talk to me, you'll have to come up here," he said
curtly and started lightly back up the stairs. She started
after him slowly, nonplussed, then, determined to get
the tension worked out between them, followed at a
more rapid pace. He was headquartered at the far end
of the Kingston house. Gwen paused in the doorway of
the guest room, gaping at the personal computer and
high-speed IDP printer he'd set up. It was hooked into
the phone. "Make it fast," Dan said coldly. "I'm working." Although he didn't appear to be going anywhere,
he had shaved and showered, dressed neatly in casual
ivory slacks and a boysenberry-color cotton pullover.
More mesmerizing than his appearance was the grim,
newly weary look around his eyes.

"For IDP?" The computer screen was momentarily
blank, though the printer was merrily typing away.

He nodded stiffly, explaining, "I'm hooked into
their Lexington computer via the phone line."

Which explained where he had been and why she hadn't been able to get through all day. Relief poured through her. At least he hadn't been with another woman, had he? No, he didn't look the least bit social toward anyone. When confronted with the dangerously impatient look on his face, she trod carefully. Attempting a joke to break the tension between them, she said, "That'll cost a fortune in long distance."

He faced her stonily. "I'll make it worth IDP's while. You wanted to see me? Get to the point."

She swallowed. He was as difficult and unforgiving as he had been a decade ago. "I wanted to explain about the other night."

He crossed his arms over his waist and leaned back in his chair. He lifted the coffee cup at his side and stared at her over the rim. "Go ahead."

She met his treacherous gaze levelly. "I had a patient emergency."

The corners of his mouth twitched mirthlessly. He put his coffee aside and pushed out of the chair, whirling to face her, his hands splayed defiantly on his hips. "Funny, Doc Quarrick had no record of sending you on a call." His jaw jutted forward. His teeth were clenched.

She paused, biting into her lower lip, slightly taken aback by the fact that he'd contacted her boss. And worse, Doc Quarrick had said nothing to her. Males siding together, she wondered, against the fickleness of the female species? Or just Dan's carefulness, his ability to elicit information from an unsuspecting person. The latter was probably more likely, she concluded, knowing the straightforward nature of her boss. "You phoned Doc?" She choked out the words.

She felt like a fly who'd just fallen into the spider's web. What else had they discussed? Anything?

He grimaced, pivoting toward the window, staring out, over the fifty-five acres of tobacco, evidently embarrassed that he'd gone to such lengths to discern her whereabouts. "I was worried when you didn't show up. I thought your Jeep might have broken down. Doc reassured me you were fine, probably just forgot we had a date, but fool that I am, I insisted upon combing the countryside for you. I trailed over every damn road in three counties. Nothing, Gwen. Not a thing."

Well, honestly, she thought, had he expected to find her that way? He had. It pleased her on some level to know he was capable of reacting just as irrationally as she at times. "I left you a note," she pointed out calmly. It still didn't explain where *he'd* been the rest of the night.

"Oh, I found it." He whirled toward her, stalking closer with slow, measured steps. He stopped when they were toe-to-toe, and towered over her, mocking her with his strength. She could see the muscles straining beneath the thin fabric of his shirt. He qualified the time tautly, "When I got back to the house the next morning, close to dawn."

"You were out all night looking for me?" Her heart lifted with hope.

"Unfortunately, yes." Although he tried to suppress it, she saw the first hint of self-deprecating humor gleaming in his eyes. He relaxed. She sighed, wanting to step back, but not about to give him the satisfaction of knowing she was the least bit uncomfortable. Yet with every breath he took she was tantalizingly aware of the shampoo-fresh scent of his hair, the newly soaped fragrance of his skin mingling with his cologne. "Why didn't you call me?" she said finally, feeling all the more ridiculous. What a comedy of errors they had created!

His brows lowered like thunderclouds over his eyes. "Because I had a flat! And no spare tire! About five miles from the nearest phone. Ever try to get help at three in the morning when the people don't know you from Adam? No one wanted to help me, Gwen. It took three farms before I found someone to let me in. And of course, out this way there aren't any garages open, either." Clearly he had no humor about the situation. She successfully suppressed a giggle, but could do nothing about the lopsided slant of her mouth.

"I'm sorry."

"So was I, Gwen." Abruptly, he seemed as distant and indifferent to her as when she had first arrived. He walked back to retrieve his coffee cup. Though she guessed the liquid was cold, he sipped it thirstily. His eyes swept over her, assessing the quality of her casual clothing, the white lab coat she hadn't yet bothered to take off.

"I'm sorry about what happened. But before you get totally bent out of shape, there's more you need to know, about what happened that night, why I was late." She told him what she could about the patient without revealing identity. "The young woman was upset, sick, impoverished. I knew if I didn't run a pregnancy test right away that she probably wouldn't come back, and I couldn't just leave her." *Or risk her having a baby that had not, due to circumstances, had the benefit of adequate prenatal care.*

He had mellowed slightly, but his voice, though low,

was still unforgiving. "I don't know why not. You evidently had no qualms about leaving me in the lurch."

That was different. He could take care of himself. Nicki couldn't. Not manage her baby and pregnancy, too. "Why didn't you call right away and let me know?" he said quietly. "I was home."

That she had no excuse for. She hadn't even remembered her date with him until she'd gotten home hours later. "I'm sorry. I would have called had I remembered we were going to go out." She lifted her shoulders in an apologetic shrug and saw his lips compress. "I got so caught up in her plight—"

"That you forgot all about me," he finished grimly.

"I forgot everything," she corrected. "The girl was desperate, Dan."

He faced her motionlessly. For a moment, he seemed very close to calling a halt to the argument. Again, his disappointment in her took precedence. "You know how little time I have to spend here, Gwen. You know every minute counts. Whatever you were doing could have waited until the following day."

Normally, Gwen would have agreed with him. But he hadn't seen the anguished look on Nicki's face, the baby that needed care, too, or the place where they lived—with no phone, no electricity, nothing but the bare necessities. It had broken her heart, and she'd stayed long past the time she had needed to, getting groceries in for both mother and child, talking to the husband about the possibility of interviewing for a job with Dan Kingston's dad, or the tender loving care and understanding his wife was going to need. By the time she had driven Tim Kaufman back to the clinic to pick up the battered pickup truck his wife had been forced to leave behind, it had been all she could do to go home, anticipating a hot bath and all the comforts she was blessed with but very seldom really appreciated. Only then had she thought about Dan, their date. And even that had seemed ridiculously unimportant.

"I can't help but wonder if you stood me up deliberately," he said quietly for a moment. "as a way of avoiding me. Making me angry so I would stay away."

His words struck a nerve. Gwen turned away. Had she been unconsciously looking for an excuse not to be with him? She'd known in her heart when he'd left the night before that it was just a matter of time before they made love again. She'd also known she wasn't ready for that. Had Nicki's plight just served as a reminder of the past, what might have happened to her had she and Dan married right out of high school? Why hadn't she worked harder at trying to get hold of Dan?

Dan stalked closer. She'd hurt him terribly. She could see it on his face. His eyes were oddly possessive, searing her as he moved even closer. "If you wanted to discourage me, why not say so straight out?" he said in a very low voice. His hands rested lightly on her shoulders. Involuntarily, her face lifted to his and, once hypnotized by his searching glance, stayed. "Why the games, Gwen? Are you still trying to get back at me for the way we parted before?"

Wordlessly, she shook her head. It was difficult to breathe. She couldn't swallow. "No." But in her heart she wasn't sure of that, either. A long time ago she had wanted him to suffer.

"And yet you'll let any little thing come between us." Gently, he turned her to face him.

"It wasn't unimportant, Dan. The girl *was* desperate." And would remain so until her husband found work.

His brows rose. For a second he almost seemed inclined to agree with her, then his jaw tautened. "It could have waited until the following day."

She wrenched free of him, her temper raging uncontrollably. Words flowed from the heart before she could censor or stop them, or consider what her uttering them would mean. "Oh, what would you know about being pregnant with an unplanned child, with no one to turn to, no one to confide in or trust, with no way to support either yourself or the child!" And Nicki's problems had been compounded by the baby she already cared for.

"And you do know what it's like?" he snapped back, just as angrily. "You've been there, I suppose?"

She turned white, then red in realization of what she had just said. Dan studied her wordlessly, alert to everything about her.

Flushing, Gwen said swiftly, not about to reveal any more than she already had, "I've got to go."

He caught her arm, his grasp as implacable as the questioning look on his face. "That girl's plight really got to you, didn't it?" As he waited for her answer he barely seemed to breathe.

She swallowed. Her heart was beating triple-time. "Yes." She'd meant her voice to sound cold and unyielding. It was thick with unshed tears and unspent emotion she had repressed for years.

"Why?" His grasp gentled. He turned her completely around to face him.

Gwen knew if she let his tenderness penetrate her emotional armor, she'd collapse. She remained silent.

He continued watching her pensively, seeing, she thought, so much more than she had ever wanted him to.

Quietly he observed, "Just now, you looked not only as if you understood her pain, Gwen, but as if you felt it, really felt it. How is that possible, unless...?" Perplexed, he left the thought hanging.

She struggled to be free of him. "Let me go!"

His hands laced around her waist, holding her torso to his. He was all muscle and bone. When she averted her head, he forced it back, as if suddenly understanding what had hurt and changed her in the time they'd been apart. "You've been there, haven't you?" he said softly, savagely. "Pregnant with a child you didn't plan, maybe had no way to care for. You know firsthand what it's like!"

She twisted free of him, panting, made it across the room. He beat her to the door, his strides purposeful, and stood, arms crossed, blocking her exit from both the room and his house. "Tell me, Gwen."

Tears glimmered in her eyes and spilled down her cheeks. Her lower lip trembled as helplessly as her voice. "Leave me alone." Which was, she thought in retrospect, almost as good as admitting his accusation was right on target.

His brow cocked. "You're saying that the child you carried wasn't mine?" She knew then that if she had aborted his child he would never have forgiven her, even if she could have forgiven herself. But the truth was not much better, not to him.

"Please..." To her mortification, a new wave of tears veiled her lashes.

"Answer me, damn it, have you been pregnant?"

He closed the distance between them swiftly, taking her by both arms.

The lie she needed so badly to tell wouldn't come. He thrust her away from him, reading his own truth. His voice was laced with bitterness. "You had an abortion, didn't you?" he grated in a tone aching and numb with hurt and disbelief.

She couldn't bear to see him hurt like that, to let him think she would have been part of destroying the child they had created. "No," she said softly, fiercely. "I didn't have an abortion." Tears coursed down her cheeks. With the back of her hand, she brushed them away.

He faced her warily, his eyes dark with his suspicions.

She'd never meant to tell him that much. But now that she had, she had no choice but to continue. "I gave the child up for adoption." There, it was out.

Silence spanned between them, deeper than the years that they had passed apart, deeper than any of the hurts they had previously inflicted. "Was it mine?" he said finally. "Was the child you gave away mine?"

The possessive note in his voice said he knew it had been. But she realized, looking at the anger and betrayal on his face, the dangers inherent in her answer. She couldn't risk hurting their child, not now, when so much time had passed, when Gwen had already suffered so much. The child must be left alone, she decided, at whatever cost to herself in Dan's esteem. "The child was mine—briefly," Gwen said. "A very long time ago."

Exhausted, she fled the room, then the house. Later, she thought, that it was only because he was still so much in shock that he did absolutely nothing to stop her.

The drive home took forever. When she reached her house, she shut the door behind her, then slumped into a chair, exhausted, weeping. There were so many things she wished she could change, that she wished she had the power to undo now. She wished she had mustered her courage and gone to see him, told him she was pregnant, demanded that he marry her or at the very least financially support his child. She wished he'd been there when the baby was born, that he'd held her hand and coached her through her labor. She wished that rather than a standard delivery she'd had a Lamaze birth and that they'd taken the classes together. She would have liked to see her first baby being born. She would have liked to experience their child's birth with joy and love rather than with trepidation and sorrow.

More than that, she wished she had not cut Dan out of her life at such a crucial point. She wished they had shared the baby's sleepless nights and teething and first tottering yet blissful steps. She wished they'd had other children. She yearned for the impossible. Because what she wanted would never come to pass. Their child had weathered the first decade of life without them. The child would, God willing, continue to do the same.

She wanted to tell Dan everything that had happened to her, how lonely and anguished the days of her pregnancy had been. She wanted to tell him of the minor bleeding she had suffered during the first trimester and how it had terrified her, but ultimately, thankfully, turned out to be nothing more than the result of a slight malformation of her cervix. She yearned to tell him of the nightmares and heartbreak that had followed the birth, the way she'd searched the face of every baby she met or saw, in hopes she would somehow recognize or regain admittance into her child's life. How, later, she'd worked relentlessly in school and out, in an effort to put the whole traumatic episode from her mind. How she'd tried to forget Dan by dating other men, and how lacking they had been as suitors in comparison.

She wanted him to know how difficult it had been for her to work in the obstetrics section of the hospital during her nurse's training, and that the first live birth she had attended had reduced her to helpless tears, and that for weeks and months after—remembering, suffering—she had cried herself to sleep every night. She wanted him to know how much it had hurt her, and yet how driven she had been. First to protect her child, and then, later, simply to find out what had happened to the baby.

IT HADN'T BEEN EASY, however. Disclosing that kind of information was strictly against the law. So she'd gone back to the Welby Home for Unwed Mothers as a registered nurse, volunteering to teach nutrition and birth control methods twice weekly to the already pregnant teenage girls. Luckily, the staff there had changed over the years. No one knew she had attended the home some seven years before. Or so she had initially thought, anyway.

The first weeks there had been agonizing as, one by one, she got to know the current residents, their problems, their fears. In many ways it had been like reliving the past all over again, but the days had served their purpose, too. Because they had shown her sharply why it was best that Gwen had not kept her child. The girls there were children, emotionally, intellectually. Yes, they had bodies that were remarkably in tune with nature and its resulting desires, but they were in no way equipped to handle the care and raising of a child. What set them apart in most cases was the fact that the girls knew this, accepted it, and were noble and unselfish enough to do what was ultimately best for their unborn children. Yet none of them would walk away unscathed. And it was in that sense that they needed Gwen most and that she felt most ill-equipped to help. Because she couldn't in reality tell them that it would get better. Because for her in many respects it had only gotten worse.

But Gwen kept working because she knew she had to come to grips with what she had done. She also befriended the home's chief social worker, Beverly Melvin, the woman who screened all the adoptive parents as well as the girls who applied to live at the home. Several years older than Gwen and raised in a tough biracial neighborhood, Beverly was married and sterile, with adopted small children of her own.

As if sensing something was amiss, she had watched Gwen closely from the start. But it wasn't until late one Monday evening, after the first of the year, when they were trying to get their records straight for routine auditing by state and local government agencies, that Beverly questioned Gwen's interest in the Welby Home.

Feet up on the desk, a carton of yogurt in her hand, she'd asked casually, "What is it with you, anyway? And don't tell me it's nothing. I saw you crying today when the Fredericks girl had to give her child away."

"It's just that they're so young. I'm not entirely sure they know what they're doing when they sign those papers," Gwen had argued tiredly. Or how they would feel five or ten years from now looking back—at a time when they probably would, in contrast, be capable of rearing and loving a child the way he or she should be loved. Would they forgive themselves then? Gwen hadn't. Days spent working in the local hospital had made the print blur before her eyes. She told herself she was not crying again, she wasn't.

"Uh-huh," Bev said wisely. "And the way you look at the newborn infants when the parents come to collect them. Like someone is personally tearing out your heart."

Beverly had a heart. But she was also quite capable of doing what had to be done, bulldozer-style if necessary. And apparently she thought exorcising Gwen of her grief and guilt was essential.

Defensive and angry, Gwen had stood up and walked over to replace a file in the cabinet drawer. "So what of it?" Her tone was curt as she felt a lecture coming on.

Beverly's tone had become gentle. "This work is obviously getting to you. Why continue?"

Gwen shrugged. "Because I want to help those girls. I want them to have someone to talk to."

"Do you think talking to you makes them feel better?" Doubt permeated Beverly's voice. Gwen recalled that Beverly's life hadn't been easy, either. Both her parents were alcoholic, and she had singlehandedly— and illegally—raised a brood of seven more children when she herself was little more than fifteen.

Gwen refused to let Beverly's knowing gaze get to

her. She had known hard times, too, both before and after her father had died. "I know what the girls are going through," Gwen had shot back calmly.

Beverly nodded, taking everything in. She put her yogurt down and faced Gwen as if she were an angel greeting her on Judgment Day. "And how is that? How do you know so much, Gwen? Why do you feel so much more than the rest of us—and don't give me any flak. You know how caring the rest of the staff here is. Sure, giving up a baby is hard work, but it needn't tear you apart every time. It doesn't tear everyone else up."

"Lay off," Gwen had warned, feeling tears of frustration and hurt well up in her eyes.

But she'd worn her heart on her sleeve too long.

"You'd better start telling me the truth, helping me to understand where you're coming from and what, exactly, it is you want." When Gwen shot her a bewildered look, she said, "You can start with your own stay here at the Welby Home. Six years ago, wasn't it?"

Gwen had paled dramatically. Her knees buckled beneath her. Weakly, she found her way into the chair. "How did you find out?"

"Too many pieces didn't fit. I did some checking of our files. I'm only surprised someone else on staff didn't put two and two together and come up with four instead of five. You know the rules, Gwen Nolan. The Welby Home does not divulge to the unwed mother where or with whom it places the child."

"Have I asked?" Gwen had shot back defiantly, terrified and furious at having her motives found out so quickly and easily. She hadn't had nearly enough time

or the opportunity even to get a look at the back files or
to discern the whereabouts of her child.

"No, but it's occurred to me that, working here, you
might try to find out. If you're caught breaking into the
files, the director will have you put in jail, Gwen. You
know that. Legally, she has no choice if she's to offer
any of the people involved in the adoptions any protec-
tion or confidentiality at all."

"What are you going to do?" she said quietly, in a
voice that trembled. Every hope of finding her child
vanished. Gwen was more despondent than she ever
had been in her life.

"Ask you to resign, before I have to turn you in."

"You'd do that?" Gwen asked. She'd thought Beverly was her friend, or well on her way to becoming
one. But she was also a woman who had adopted a
child, and because of that, she had her own interests to
protect and those of others in her situation. Gwen
couldn't blame her, nor could she quite forgive her for
being unsympathetic. She did understand. In Beverly's
situation, she would be overprotective, too. She was
overprotective now.

Beverly had answered stalwartly. "I have no choice."

Gwen was silent, reflective. Desperately, she tried to
make Beverly understand how she felt. "It's tearing me
up inside, knowing my child is out there somewhere."

"You've got to go on, get married again. You're one
of the lucky ones, girl! You can have a family of your
own."

"I don't want another child."

"You will when you have one," Beverly counseled
wisely. "That will make all the difference. You'll see."

"Just tell me what happened to my baby."

"No."

"Please." Gwen started to cry.

"I can't." Beverly sighed, then swore. Gwen cut her off when she reached for the phone. "Please, just tell me about her parents, what kind of town she lives in. If she has any brothers or sisters."

But Beverly had remained adamantly against it. "No I'll expect your resignation in the morning, Gwen. You can tell the director anything you like. I won't divulge your secret if you go quietly. But don't come back again. Don't torture yourself. Don't put the whole program at risk."

Gwen had tried to do as Beverly advised. Honestly, she had. But two months later she'd still been haunted by the knowledge that her child was out there somewhere, alone, maybe needing her, maybe not. She only knew she had to find out. And so, waiting until the home was almost shut down for the day, she'd gone back, on the pretext that she had left an old uniform in one of the lockers in the staff lounge.

The custodian had known her, of course, from her days of working there and had been glad to let her in. Gwen had gone down to the lounge, returned moments later, a spare uniform over her arm. Saying good-bye to the custodian, she'd promised to let herself out. He'd agreed, and gone to his work. Instead, she'd hidden out in the ladies' lounge on another floor. After two that morning, when all was quiet, she'd gone down to the records room, and shaking, flashlight in hand, had personally gone through their files.

Locating and opening the one marked "Gwen Nolan," she had been relieved to discover her child was well taken care of after all. Tears of joy streaming down her face, she had copied the name and address of the adopting parents. Somehow, she knew she would find a way to insert herself into their lives. Because, one way or another, she was going to watch her child grow up. If it had to be from a distance, so be it.

Yet, always in her mind, was the thought that she had to be careful, that she mustn't let anyone see how she really felt. That same decision held firm years later. And regardless of her emotional allegiance to Dan, that much of her thinking had not changed. She must protect her child at any cost. And for the moment, she rationalized sadly, that meant continuing to deceive Dan, too.

CONSIDERABLY CALMED OUTWARDLY, Gwen returned to work. She went through the rest of the day glancing over her shoulder, expecting to see Dan at every turn. He wasn't there. After work she went to a movie in Princeton, then shopping and out to eat, driving around endlessly, killing time, not returning home until midnight. The house was dark and silent. Flicking on the air conditioner as she entered, she walked slowly upstairs, not bothering to turn on the hall light. She was halfway through the portal when she saw Dan sitting in her bedroom chair, his feet propped up lazily on the bed. Momentarily her heart seemed to stop, then resumed pounding full force.

Chapter Eight

"You didn't really think I'd let it go at that, did you?" He was in a dangerous, quiet mood. She watched, paralyzed with dread, as he rose stealthily to his feet. Why had she imagined she would be able to put this off? Or that no matter how long she stayed away he would give up or desist? Wasn't the outcome inevitable?

"Dan, it's late. I'm tired." And most of all, she didn't want to talk.

She might as well have been throwing sand at a 727 for all the good it did her and the staving-off effect it had on him. "I want to know the details, Gwen. I want to know how it happened, who the father was."

He looked as miserable as she felt. The charade was over. Prolonging the mystery would just create agony for both of them. "The child was yours, Dan."

The color left his face swiftly. He looked numb with shock. Filled with joy and a terrible sense of dread and loss. "Ours?" His normally steely voice was barely above a whisper.

She swallowed hard. "Yes. The baby was ours. Was. No more." The words were cold and concise. But it was the only way she could handle a discussion, by reciting the facts of their life as dispassionately as she would have read statistics off a page.

It took him a moment to recover, and even then she sensed he was still reeling from shock, that maybe he hadn't really expected her to tell him anything at all. Either that or he'd expected the news to be worse, to be that the child hadn't been his after all.

He strode closer. "I want to know everything about the child. I want to know why you kept knowledge of the pregnancy from me." Softly, persuasively, he finished, "I have a right to know, Gwen." She opened her mouth to protest and he cut her off firmly, his eyes steadily holding hers. "No matter what you say, my loving you won't stop. Nothing will ever change the way I feel about you."

Gwen wasn't assured. Yet she did need to unburden herself to him. Perhaps, more than anything, that was why she had been unable to go on with her life. Maybe, subconsciously, she'd been wanting to wipe the slate clean, and free herself of her guilt. She sat down on the edge of the bed. Hands twisted together, she began. "I didn't discover that I was pregnant until several months after you'd left for school. It sounds incredibly naive—and I guess I was—but with my father dying so suddenly and you so far away, my being transported off to relatives in Ohio I hardly knew, I was very frightened. And more alone than I'd ever been in my life."

"And so you decided to give the baby up for adoption?" He spoke as if he understood that much.

She shook her head, remembering the pain that she'd incurred as she'd made that decision. "Not right away. I wanted to keep our baby. I never stopped wanting that. But, practically, I knew it wasn't possible. To do so would have been selfish and unfair to our child and, above all, I wanted to protect our baby."

"Why didn't you have an abortion?" he asked. He radiated an awareness of everything about her and a compassion for what she'd been through that she never dreamed he might possess.

Certainly, it would have been an easier way out. She gestured helplessly, palms upraised, tears blurring her vision. "It's against everything I believe. I can't speak for what other people do, but for myself it would have been unthinkable to destroy the life growing inside me." *The life they had created in love.* That much she did want him to understand.

"I'm glad." His hand covered her own, squeezed.

She knew she'd been right. He couldn't have forgiven her an abortion any more than she could have forgiven herself. A bond grew between them, strengthened by the resulting silence. How gratifying it was for her to know he understood—more, that he didn't hate her. At least not yet.

She traced the masculine hand clenched tightly over her right hand. "It was a very bad time for me, Dan." Gwen sighed raggedly. She'd been in such a precarious emotional state. "I don't like to think about it."

"I wish you hadn't gone through it alone. I would have helped you."

She didn't dispute the fact he could have, if he'd been there. But it was a moot point. "You were engaged to that heiress at the time."

"I didn't love her." Wordlessly, he opened his arms to her. She fell into them, letting him hold her close, new tears burning her eyes. His arms tightened around her, increasing in tension until her bout of weeping had drawn to an end.

"I didn't know that," she whispered, feeling as tortured as she had before. And yet oddly comforted, consoled. He loved her now. He loved her. Tears of a different sort spilled down her cheeks.

He wiped them away, held her close. "I'm sorry," he whispered, "so very sorry to have ever hurt you. My God, you must know—" His voice broke. He couldn't go on. He didn't need to. They had both made mistakes, errors in judgment, that they would pay for the rest of their lives. They did not need to punish each other or themselves any more. They needed only to go on.

"Gwen?" She looked up and saw love and compassion etched on his face. "Can you forgive me?" he asked hoarsely.

"I never blamed you. I blamed fate, myself, but mostly just...fate."

It had been a roll of the dice that allowed her to get pregnant. Her actions afterward had been much more deliberate. And from then on she'd taken no chances. She'd made love to no man. But now she needed Daniel as never before, and with the burden of deception removed from her heart, finally felt free to love him in return.

"I want to make love to you," he whispered, gazing down at her in the old, intense way, his hands slowly bringing her close.

"I want that, too," she whispered back. "So much."

The dark familiarity of her bedroom proved the perfect place to explore anew the depth of feeling that bonded them. His palms slid up the length of her spine to splay expectantly between her shoulder blades. He kissed her leisurely, then drew back, his look as sweetly compelling as his tender caress. She drew a heavy, shuddering breath as his eyes traveled over her breasts, and then his palms moved slowly down to cup her buttocks. Desire flared between them, as swift and electrifyingly potent as a bolt of lightning. The ache inside her was deep and vibrant, yearning, the need to be with him again—joined heart and soul—overpowering. She needed the merging of bodies, the love expressed.

"Tell me you need this as much as I do," he murmured hoarsely, his lips trailing softly down her neck. He paused, and his hands trembled as he undressed her.

"I need this," she whispered back, touching her fingertips to the dark lines of his brow, the taut flesh stretched across his cheekbones and jaw. She stood on tiptoe, moving her lips back and forth across the softly parted surface of his mouth. "I need you."

Her fingers seemed no more capable than his had been as he struggled with the assortment of buttons and zipper, yet soon they were both delightfully naked, surrounded by a pile of clothing. They fell, arms entwined, onto the soft cotton comforter of her bed.

"You're beautiful," he whispered, brushing the hair from her brow. "So beautiful."

She felt a moment's anxiety. What if he found her lacking? Her body had changed since childbirth. "Dan..."

He seemed to read her fear. Voice lowering huskily, he said, "I love you. I've always loved you." Tenderly, his hands tangled in her hair, spreading the wild auburn curls from her face and eyes. He traced the slope of her collarbone, the shape of her breasts. His lips circled the coral tips, drew back, teased, engulfed. She arched against him wantonly, arms twined around his neck, fingers threading through the short layered silk of his hair.

"I love you." Nothing existed for Gwen but the reality of their affection, the deep raging need. Her fingertips splayed across his shoulders, moved, massaging, down either side of his back, relishing in the bunched muscles beneath the sleek skin. Her legs touched his tentatively and, finding acceptance, cuddled close. His knee nudged hers farther apart. He lifted her, his hands splayed demandingly beneath her hips, his ardor urgent against her. "Oh, Dan," she whispered, trembling.

Taking pleasure in her response, he urged her to slow down, to prolong the pleasure for them both. "There's no rush." As if to prove his words, his lips trailed over her arm lingeringly from shoulder to wrist. His hands cupped her waist as his tongue darted into her navel and lower. His fingertips threaded lightly through the triangle of auburn down—stroking, separating, finding her center with dismaying, debilitating ease. She arched against him, all white-hot flame, gasping, crying. And then his mouth was on hers, his thighs pressed against hers. She lifted her hips, softly whispering entreaty.

The resistance of her passion-hot flesh stunned them both. She was caught offguard by the sharp, piercing sensation, and a moan escaped her parted lips. He paused, still nestled against her. Supporting his weight on his elbows, he hovered above her. "Gwen?" His look seemed to say, "Tell me it's all right to go on."

She knew he could feel the heat and moistness of her

desire, slick against her skin and his. He'd felt her trembling climactic response. "I want you," she murmured, lacing her hands on the back of his neck, lowering his mouth to hers.

He hesitated a moment, his eyes dark, intent, before cautiously resuming the kiss. Slowly, she wedged forward. He remained still, waiting, continuing the slow lazy savoring of her mouth, his hands fluttering lightly across the pebbled tips of her breasts, her limp acquiescent thighs, her tense spine. By degrees, their bodies meshed, the sensation overpoweringly sweet. "Sweet...heaven," he whispered in her ear, his breath hot against her temple, and then all restraint was lost in the building climb to passion, the shatteringly slow descent. They lay entwined, breathing raggedly, reluctant to draw apart. "So good," he whispered.

"Yes." She'd missed him. She'd missed this, the intimacy that could be achieved in no other way, the pleasure.

"I want to stay the night."

"I want that, too." Giving him no more time to talk, Gwen drew his head down to hers. And they proved the depth of their passion again and again.

Later, spent and lying entwined, watching the hands of the clock speed heedlessly on toward dawn, Dan asked, "Did I hurt you?"

"No," she said quietly. "I haven't been with anyone since my pregnancy." She flushed and turned her head to the side. Hand beneath her chin, he drew her head back. And she knew then, from the understanding in his eyes, that she had nothing to hide from him, nothing of which to be ashamed. "It's difficult for a woman after the birth of a child."

He was stunned, silent, as the meaning of her words sunk in. "You've never been with anyone else."

With Dan, she had always been extraordinarily passionate. He leaned over her, propping himself up on his elbows, his body aligned warmly over hers. Reticently, she explained, "No one else has ever made me feel the way you do. I've never been compelled to become intimate just for the physical side of it." Which was not to say she had not kissed other men. She had. But their embraces had left her cold. To progress to lovemaking had been unthinkable.

He was too silent. After a moment he rolled away from her, sighing heavily. Hands folded behind his head, he stared wordlessly up at the ceiling.

"Confession time," Gwen prodded lightly, trying to hide her hurt, her fears that for him the past decade had been anything but lonely.

He rolled toward her. He traced the profile of her face lovingly while his palm cupped her chin. "I'm not quite as virtuous as you. There have been women. But they've never come close to me emotionally. And they've always eventually left. Saying I kept too much back. They were right. I did. Now, being with you again, knowing what it's like to make love to someone you're in love with, someone you care about deeply, I'm not sure I could make love to another woman. I kept thinking I was imagining how good it used to be between us. Now I know I didn't half remember. It's impossible to recall anything this bewitching and believe it's really so."

And as if to prove the validity of his words, his devotion to her, he drew her to him and pliantly made love to her again.

As WONDERFUL as their night together was, the next morning it was back to business as usual, and that meant, for Dan, returning home to his work for IDP and the routine feeding and watering chores on the farm, and, for Gwen, the clinic.

Once there, Gwen found Elyse waiting for her with an urgent message from Nicki Kaufman. "Sounds like Cade has the chicken pox to me. I told her you'd be right out."

Gwen nodded. They had made it standard practice to make house calls on children with highly contagious illnesses, rather than chance infecting a whole waiting room full of patients. "How high is Cade's fever?"

"She doesn't know, according to the neighbor who called in on the C.B. They still haven't been able to get a phone installed. They don't have a thermometer, either, so you'd better take everything you need with you. Sounds like her medical supplies are limited. And her husband's already left for work on some temporary job."

Gwen thought of the impoverished but independent way the couple had been living. "You're right about that."

Driving out, Gwen realized she should have asked Dan about the possibility of Tim Kaufman's getting a permanent farming job with the Kingstons. She'd meant to. She frowned. Normally that wasn't something she'd forget. Had it been a deliberate slip on her part? Was she afraid that if the farm affairs were settled Dan would be all too quick to leave Kentucky again?

"Thank goodness you're here!" A distraught Nicki met Gwen at the door. Her house was little more than a one-room shack on the side of a hill. The inside was scrupulously clean; the furniture consisted of a bed, a crib, a table and mismatched chairs. What personal belongings they had were stacked neatly on the floor.

"How long has Cade been sick?" Gwen put her medical bag on the table. Cade's cheeks were flushed bright red. He looked hot and uncomfortable and sounded whiny.

"Just a few hours." Nicki lifted the baby's shirt to show Gwen a small water-filled blister on his abdomen. There were several more on his back.

"Chicken pox," Gwen confirmed. While Nicki held the baby she slipped a thermometer under his arm. The reading was nearly one hundred and four degrees. "We've got to get his temperature down," Gwen said.

Because there was no bathtub or indoor bathroom, it was decided to put Cade in the sink. He howled when he hit the tepid water, but Gwen held him fast. Nicki was nearly in tears, watching as Gwen gently bathed and spoke to the child. Fifteen minutes later, his body temperature had been reduced to a manageable level.

"You're probably going to have to do this for Cade every few hours. To help eliminate the itching, you can add a little baking soda to the water, too. I brought you an extra box."

"Thanks." Nicki swallowed.

"You can use baby powder on his skin. That will help keep him more comfortable, too. Right now I'd let him wear just a diaper. You can cover him very lightly when he sleeps."

"Okay." Nicki looked more relieved.

"In the meantime, you can give him acetaminophen for fever. Do not give him baby aspirin, because this is a virus and that might cause complications. Although he can't talk to tell us, he probably has a little head-ache, too, which is making him crabby. The acetamino-phen will help. I'll write down the dosage for him. You can give it three or four times a day. In a few days, the little blisters will break and form crusts. Cade will pick at them. They do itch. Try not to let him and, instead, whenever he gets uncomfortable, put him into a bath for a while. Powder him lightly when he gets out. He'll be highly contagious until all the lesions have dried up and formed crusts, so please keep him isolated from other children." She paused, remembering that Nicki was pregnant. "Have you and your husband both had chicken pox?"

Nicki nodded. "Tim has. I think I had it, too."

"But you're not sure."

"No."

"I'd better call Dr. Quarrick then. He'll probably want to give you a shot of hyperimmune serum or gamma globulin, just to be on the safe side, but we'll see."

"It won't hurt the new baby?" She looked worriedly down at her swelling tummy.

Gwen smiled. "The chance is so slight that you shouldn't even worry about it. However, you do need to try to get as much rest as possible. Are there any neighbors who could help out, someone who's already had the chicken pox and doesn't have children who might get infected?"

"The neighbor who notified you on the C.B."

"Okay. Look." Gwen glanced at her watch. "I've got several more calls to make. Why don't I stop back around noon, see how you're faring. By then I'll have had a chance to talk to Dr. Quarrick and if he deems it necessary to give you a shot—and he probably will because he usually does as a precaution—then I'll stop back and give it to you."

"You can't do it now?" Nicki asked.

"Not without Dr. Quarrick's permission. I'm not licensed to prescribe solo to pregnant ladies."

Nicki smiled. "Okay. I'll see you then. And thanks for coming out, Gwen."

"You're welcome." Gwen bent to pat baby Cade on the shoulder. His skin felt soft as down and only slightly warm now. "You get better for your mama, you hear?"

Cade just gurgled in response.

"I THINK I MAY HAVE FOUND the solution to your problems in reference to hiring help for your dad's farm," Gwen said the next morning as they dressed and then together descended the stairs to jointly prepare and enjoy a quick breakfast before going their separate ways.

"What do you mean?" Dan asked, adeptly buttering the toast while she scrambled the eggs.

Gwen told him about Tim Kaufman. "Doc gave him a temporary job doing jobs out at his place in Caldwell County, and Buddy has generously agreed to let him work as a jack-of-all-trades on one of his construction crews if he's still unable to find work once his stint with Doc is up. So at least they can buy groceries, pay rent and get the electricity turned on now. But what Tim Kaufman really wants to do is farm, full-time."

Dan looked intrigued, and sadly she noted, very relieved that he would soon be let off the hook himself if everything panned out. Dan brought their plates to the table while she poured the juice. "If Tim Kaufman's as dependable as you think, he's got himself a job. Have him come over for an interview."

"Great."

Despite their busy schedules, in the days that followed Gwen and Dan managed to be together every evening. Gwen had never been so happy in her life.

Unfortunately, the same was not true for the sparring Daltons. "I've had it with Buddy," Elyse fumed, stacking clean towels in an examining room.

Gwen followed her into the adjacent storeroom as together they began the once-a-month Saturday morning task of taking inventory of supplies. She felt so aglow with love herself it was hard to let anything penetrate her romantic cocoon of well-being. "Why? What's happened now?" Besides their stalemate, that was.

Oblivious to Gwen's newfound happiness, Elyse stormed, "He hasn't been home one night this week."

"How do you know that?" With effort, Gwen pulled herself away from the sensual memories swirling delightfully around in her mind. Obediently, she noted that they were short of tongue depressors and sterile gauze.

Elyse stated they were also short of isopropyl alcohol. "I called him, or tried to, that is."

Gwen glanced up from her clipboard, amazed at the fierce note of possessiveness in Elyse's voice. Perhaps there was hope for the warring couple after all. Gwen shrugged. "Maybe he's not answering his phone." Despite her friend's suspicions, Gwen couldn't accept the premise Buddy had found a new woman. He wasn't the type to fool around.

"No. He's not there." Blushing at the depth of her knowledge, Elyse nonetheless related, "One night I went over to the construction company trailer where he's been staying. His pickup was gone. All the lights were out. It didn't look as if anyone had been home all day. When we were together he was always at home and in bed by ten."

"So?" Gwen prompted.

"So, he's up to something, that's what!"

Gwen sighed her exasperation and shook her head. "Have you asked him what he's doing lately?" Maybe he liked to play poker. Maybe he was just out carousing with the boys.

"Are you crazy?" Elyse nearly shouted. "And have him think I'm checking up on him!"

Gwen couldn't help it. She laughed "Aren't you?"

"Gwen, you are not being of any help here," Elyse reprimanded sternly.

"Sorry." Gwen raised both palms in surrender. "I can't help it." She trusted Buddy.

Elyse sighed and thumbed through the various sizes of Band-Aids. "Just because you and Dan are happy again—" She stopped and bit her lip. Although Gwen was always ready to lend an ear and listen to someone's problems, she never discussed any of her own, particularly anything that personal.

"Go ahead and say it." Gwen smiled, for once not minding a public dissection of her private life. "The past week has been blissful." She and Dan had been together every night. He always left before dawn, but stayed long enough every evening to talk and make love and then hold her in his arms. It was the closest she'd ever come to heaven. And she knew it showed.

"But enough about my life, now that it's finally going well. What are you going to do about Buddy?" Gwen faced her friend.

"I'll tell you what I'm not going to do, and that's sit around waiting for him to apologize and beg my forgiveness," Elyse said determinedly. "I'm going out with Walt Fowler tonight. We're going to the ice cream social down at the church."

The evening was being sponsored to raise money for the addition to the Dawson Springs Clinic. "Oh, Elyse, you know Buddy's going to be there." The burly construction worker would go through the roof if he saw his estranged wife with a known womanizer like Walt

"Exactly my point," Elyse said stubbornly, her mind clearly made up. "Maybe if Buddy sees me with someone else he'll come to his senses."

"Or give up hope altogether," Gwen corrected dryly "Darn it, Elyse, you know what a lecher Walt is. And he can't ever resist provoking another man." At thirty, the affable but ragged-looking ex-soldier had a reputation for loving and leaving women, and for carousing for days when the spirit moved him. "All I know is that I can't go on like this," Elyse said. She pursed her lips tightly. "I want Buddy to know it, too."

Gwen swallowed tremulously. Although a gifted mechanic and the owner of the only garage in Dawson Springs, Walt could be a handful. "I hope this plan doesn't backfire on you," Gwen warned.

"It won't," Elyse assured.

Unfortunately, Gwen's prediction turned out to be grimly prophetic.

"Looks like trouble brewing," Dan observed later that evening on the church lawn.

Picnic tables had been set up beneath the trees. Home-churned ice cream of every flavor imaginable was offered up for public consumption, as well as large coolers of lemonade and tea. The whole town had been invited, as well as select members of the general medical and business community in Dawson Springs and the surrounding area. Buddy had arrived dressed to the nines in another new polo shirt and slacks. As formerly he'd worn only plaid lumberjack shirts, T-shirts and heavy jeans, it was quite a switch.

"Elyse is overdoing it." Gwen sighed, tasting the sweet strawberry ice cream. "The bodice of that dress is about three inches lower than it should be for a casual date." And to make matters worse she'd worn a push-up bra beneath it that only emphasized the lush fullness of her breasts and made her visual game for every man there. And most of them were looking, to Buddy's obvious discomfiture and fast-growing anger.

"She's certainly doing nothing to discourage Walt." Dan was disapproving, but in this instance Gwen couldn't blame him. Elyse was asking for trouble. And, seconds later, she got it as Buddy and Walt at last came face to face.

"Well, old pal," Walt drawled, apparently unable to resist the temptation to taunt one of the town's richest and most successful, sincerely benevolent men. "I don't see your date here."

Buddy glared at Elyse, his gaze moving pointedly to the ripe swell of her breasts above the clinging low-cut red dress. "I didn't bring one." The words were ground out. "Maybe I should have."

Dan stepped between the two men, intent on breaking up the potentially explosive situation. "Buddy, I just talked to Simon Chandler. He's standing next to Doc Quarrick. He's willing to donate some lumber for the clinic and whatever time he can spare. Why don't you go talk to him, see what you can work out in the way of timing and delivery and so forth." During the course of the evening, Dan had also recruited donations from an accountant, a pharmaceutical company salesman and an equipment supply outfit.

"Thanks, maybe I will." Buddy cast another warning look at Walt. Too much of one, evidently. Walt's hand slipped around Elyse's waist and then dropped caressingly low across her derriere. Before a white-faced Elyse had time to gasp her shocked indignation, Buddy had stepped forward. "That does it, Fowler," Buddy growled irascibly, and slammed a fist into Walt's face.

Walt went down like a bowling pin in a strike, but came up to grab at Buddy's knees just as quickly. Buddy struck back and then both men were down in the dirt, scuffling and punching like two kids. It took both Dan and Doc Quarrick to pull them apart. Once released, they went for each other again.

"Damn it, fellas, enough's enough!" Doc chided furiously as he and Dan broke it up again.

Tension laced the air as the men regarded one another silently. One more word from the mechanic and Gwen knew Buddy would go at him again.

"Buddy, you're hurt," Elyse stepped forward, looking genuinely shaken and sorry.

Buddy touched a finger to his bleeding upper lip and simultaneously blocked with his arm his estranged wife's attempt to blot it dry. "Thanks, but no thanks." Buddy scowled. To Walt Fowler, he decreed, "You want her that badly? You can have her." Buddy cast Elyse another scathing look of disgust. "I don't want her. Not anymore."

Buddy turned on his heel and left. Elyse burst into tears and fled in the other direction.

Fowler walked off toward the church entrance, where he promptly picked up an aghast teenage girl intent on nursing the slight abrasion on his cheek. "Hell, can't a man even take a joke anymore?" Walt mumbled loudly in a mock rueful tone.

Dan started after Walt, his mouth set grimly. Gwen caught Dan's arm. Another brawl they did not need. "One more word and I'm decking him, regardless," Dan decreed.

Gwen sighed. She couldn't say Walt hadn't asked for it. "You know Walt only carries on that way when he feels threatened."

"Seems to me that's most of the time," Dan stated implacably, but his spine had grown slightly less rigid.

"Only when he's around you and Buddy. He's envious of you," Gwen said softly. "You're an executive with an internationally based company. Buddy owns his own successful business. Walt's just got his garage, and because of the haphazard way he runs the place—taking off whenever he feels like going fishing or carousing—he's almost lost that several times."

"That's hardly my fault," Dan shot back irritably.

"Agreed. And I know the two of you never did get along, but Walt's his own worst enemy, Dan. He doesn't need any more. And he's helped me out with my Jeep more times than I can count."

"I guess you're right," Dan relented. Gwen knew, despite the conciliatory note in her beau's voice, that if there was one more remark from Walt, Dan would still deck him. So be it.

"IT SEEMS INCREDIBLE that in all the years we dated we never did this," Dan remarked early the next afternoon as they picked black raspberries from prickly green bushes.

Gwen faced him wryly. "It's not as if you were never asked," she said relishing the lazy Sunday they were spending together. "You just wouldn't go. Something about it being too sissy?"

Dan paused to rub ruefully at his jaw. "I was a macho type, wasn't I?"

"All he-man and high school jock." Hands on her hips, she gave him a squint-eyed appraisal. "But you've mellowed."

His brows rose in objection. But laughter glimmered in the jade of his eyes. "You make me sound like an aging hippie."

She pretended not to notice his censuring tone. "Matured, then."

"Better."

They paused for a lengthy kiss. He tasted like sweet berries. And Dan. "You've been eating more berries than picking them," she chastised, her index finger raised and stabbing the warm air.

"Can't help it." With facetious derision, she peered down into his barely lined bucket. "If you want freshly churned black raspberry ice cream for supper, you're going to have to do better than that."

His mouth quirked spasmodically as he suppressed the laughter welling up in his chest. "Yes, ma'am." He favored her with a mock salute.

They worked in silence for a while. The sweet scent of the berries lingered in the air.

"Where were you when you had the child?"

His tone should have warned her of the intensity of his need to know. Despite the heat she felt a glacial tremor run the length of her spine. She'd been expecting this for days. She was only surprised, in retrospect, that it had taken him so long. But then, she supposed, vaguely troubled, that he would have wanted to regain her trust.

"Why?" *What did it matter now?*

Dan shrugged. "I just wondered."

After a moment, she decided to answer. "I stayed in a home for unwed mothers, took most of my senior studies there," she said quietly.

"What was the name of the place?" he asked, pausing to empty another low bush of delectably ripe fruit. "Was it in Cincinnati?"

"Why do you want to know this?" Her composure fled. Some of the berries spilled out over the ground. Blushing, she bent to retrieve the fruit she had spilled.

Dan knelt to help her. "I want to know what it was like for you. I want to know more about the actual birth."

Gwen considered carefully before answering. She didn't want him to be more upset than he already was, yet he had a right to know what she had gone through. "I asked to be put under general anesthesia during the birth. I never held the baby while I was in the hospital, never saw it." Anticipating his next question, she said, "They didn't tell me if it was a girl or a boy and I was in no shape to ask at the time." *But you know now,* a small voice inside of her argued, dismayed at all she was still keeping from Dan. Her work at the Welby Home for Unwed Mothers had enabled her to find out.

"Don't you ever wonder if the child's happy, if he or she is being taken care of?"

She gestured helplessly. *What good would any of this do?* But at the same time she understood why he had to ask. The questions had haunted her, too.

Swallowing, glancing away from his penetrating gaze, she said, "The adoptive parents were very fine people. The social worker assured me of that." But she, too, had been compelled to search out the answers, discover what had happened to her child. The answer had stymied her and then, eventually, brought remarkable calm. But only because she had accepted the child's fate and decided that her child's happiness did lie with her adoptive family. And until Dan had come back into her life, she'd had no qualms about making that decision. Now, however, she was privy to the same desires as he. She wanted to recapture the past. She wanted to pretend she'd never borne a child out of wedlock—but she had, and wishing the trauma away wouldn't make it so.

Tears started in her eyes. Dan took her into his arms. "I'm sorry. I didn't mean to upset you," he said softly, stroking her hair. He was so warm, so solid, so giving. And she so deceiving. Still. If he knew would he ever forgive her? Would she ever forgive herself if her duplicity marred their relationship again?

EVENING FOUND THEM back in her kitchen, churning ice cream. As Dan had predicted, the wild raspberries added to the basic vanilla recipe proved delicious.

"Was it worth all the scratches and mosquito bites

you received today?'' she asked. After they got home, her nursing skills had been called into play to tend his many battle scars from the afternoon's events. Then, in turn, he had tended to hers.

"I'd do it again in a minute." He leaned forward to kiss away a bit of ice cream on her chin. His eyes said that he was remembering what they had discussed. "There are times, like right now, when if I could lock out the entire world, I would. If for nothing else than to show you how good it can be between us, under any circumstances, no matter how close or how trying. We're good together, Gwen. In your heart, you know that."

He was working up to a proposal. She yearned to be with him, but her duplicity weighed on her.

"Tell me you need me, too," he whispered.

"I need you." Tears blurred her eyes. His fingers threaded through her hair, cupping the back of her neck, as he held her mouth still for his. She turned toward him fully, on fire with the wellspring of his desire, taking pleasure from his pleasure, her arms moving up to wrap around his back. He used his hold on her to draw her nearer. "I need you. Don't tell me no."

She needed him, more than he would ever know. "I want you, too."

Velvet kisses followed. Together they ascended the stairs, drifted down onto the bed. Sensation swept through her, leaving her teetering on the edge of ecstasy when he withdrew, only to blaze questingly inward again. She closed her eyes helplessly under the maelstrom of pleasure and heard a purring sound of shocked pleasure emerge from her throat as her world exploded in a halo of fiery desire.

"I love you, Gwen," he whispered later, holding her tight.

"I love you, too." He kissed her lingeringly again.

Her eyes blurred with sudden sweet tears. *I have found everything in this man,* she thought. *Everything. If only he'll allow us to move into the future and forget the past once and for all.* But she suspected in her heart that it wasn't to be. Nothing had been simple when they parted years before. Nothing was simple now.

MILES AND BETTY RETURNED from Richmond early the next week, looking tanned and relaxed. They had souvenirs for everyone and many stories to tell. Gwen exclaimed over the pictures and postcards of the resort-style clinic and the tales of the "graduation" party they had attended in their honor last night.

"How is the new hired hand working out?" Gwen asked curiously.

Betty glanced fondly out the kitchen window to watch her husband walking through his garden, Tim Kaufman at his side. At barely nineteen, tall and lanky, with short-cropped black hair and deep-set brown eyes, the young man had a nervous energy that kept him moving constantly. He also wanted desperately to please.

"Oh, Miles and he get along famously already. And it's such a relief to Dan to be able to come and go now as he pleases." Betty sighed. "I can't thank you enough for finding him."

"I'm glad it all worked out," Gwen murmured. When she'd told Dan about the Kaufmans' plight and Tim's urgent desire for work, Dan had immediately set up an interview and hired him shortly thereafter.

"I understand he has a wife and child," Betty recounted, getting up to serve them more tea.

"Nicki and Cade and another baby on the way." Gwen paused. "We're getting a collection of infant clothes together to lend to the children. If you have any old linens or furniture just sitting in the attic, I'm sure they'd appreciate the use of them temporarily. Their place is meagerly furnished. And it will be a while before they can do much themselves on that score, even with the salary Tim's earning here."

"I understand," Betty said. "And they're welcome to whatever we have." She paused. "But perhaps there's a more tactful way of doing this."

Gwen sent her a mystified glance.

"Right now, they are living several counties away. Perhaps we could arrange for them to move into some place nearby, someplace furnished, so he'd be able to get to the farm more quickly when and if Miles needed him after Daniel leaves to go back to Chicago next month."

It was a solution that hadn't occurred to Gwen. And would, in a roundabout way, alleviate the insult to the Kaufmans' pride a direct handout might prompt, especially one of the velocity the young couple needed.

"When do you think that can be arranged?" Gwen asked.

Betty lifted her shoulders, already thinking ahead. "I'll talk to our neighbors this evening. They own the empty house up the road a mile or so. I'll find out if they're willing to lease it and what they want for rent. By the way, I want to thank you for the canning that you and Dan did!" Betty exclaimed.

"Oh, you're welcome." Gwen had been glad to help out.

"It must have taken you days," Betty observed slyly.

"All of one weekend," Gwen confirmed. "And, later, part of another." The rest of the produce they had frozen, which was much easier. "But we enjoyed it." She flushed. "I guess you heard about the air conditioner." As well as all the time Dan had been spending at her house.

"Yes." Betty smiled. "In fact, every time we called from Richmond, Dan had something to say about you."

Footsteps sounded on the stairs. Dan came down, a suitcase in one hand, a briefcase in the other. Shock rendered Gwen temporarily speechless. He noticed, but after casting her a brief reassuring glance, spoke first to his mother. "I've got to go in to Lexington for a few days." He turned back to Gwen and a slow smile spread over his face. She blushed, aware of Betty's eyes upon them both. But Dan seemed to have eyes only for her. "Hi," he said softly. "I didn't know you were here." He'd been in the shower when she arrived.

"I just stopped in to say hi to your folks." To her dismay, she felt herself blush again.

"And pick up her souvenir," Betty added. Of Dan, she asked, "How long will you be gone?"

He shrugged. "A few days. I've got to meet the rest of the task force I was telling you about and go over the modifications reference to the new system of business controls." He looked at Gwen. "Walk me to my car?"

"Sure."

He waited until they were outside before he spoke. "I was going to stop by before I left."

It had been a shock to see him in business attire
again. For the past couple of weeks she'd been used to
seeing him in shirts and jeans. And though she knew,
aside from overseeing the farm, he had been working
daily on the computer he'd installed upstairs, she'd put
the life he led elsewhere out of her mind. Now that she
was reminded, there was no way to avoid the resulting
depression and her fears that someday this Camelot
they'd found again would end for one reason or
another.

"I'll be around if your parents need anything."
Watching him pile his suitcases in his car reminded her
of the first time he had left her. Just the memory of it
hurt her unbearably.

"I'd appreciate it if you'd keep in daily contact with
them," Dan said, "by phone or whatever. I'll call you
every night while I'm gone and I'll be back as fast as I
can. I could commute, but then it would just take
longer."

"Do what you have to do." Gwen forced a smile.

Unmindful of his dad's presence yards away, Dan
pulled her to him and gave her a long ardent kiss.
"Take care," he said softly.

"I will."

WHEN GWEN GOT BACK to the clinic, Elyse met her at
the door.

"Dr. Quarrick's daughter has had an accident and is
going to need stitches. His wife just brought her in.
He's going to need you to assist. They're in treatment
room three. I'll handle the rest of the clinic patients
until he's through."

Robyn lay on an examining-room table, her arm

wrapped in a towel. Although she'd stopped crying, her eyes were still very red. She looked pale and drawn beneath her summer tan. Doc was standing beside her, talking soothingly as he prepared to give her a shot to numb the affected area.

"She accidentally threw her football through the living-room window," Phyllis explained. "The glass caught her in several places." Phyllis's eyes glistened as she acknowledged her guilt. In coordinated shorts and top, she looked lovely, if shaken. She wore no lipstick; her hair was badly rumpled by the wind.

Over his shoulder, Doc said, "Gwen, can you give me a hand?"

"Sure."

Standing next to him, she handed him instruments as they were needed. The cut was jagged, zigzagging across Robyn's wrist, up her arm, past her elbow. Gwen saw immediately that it wasn't as bad as it seemed. None of the cuts went that deep. But looking down again, Phyllis swayed. Elyse appeared in the doorway, taking Andrew from Phyllis's arms. Gwen caught Phyllis around the waist.

"Take her into my office. Have her lie down on the couch," Doc said, without turning away from his daughter. "It's going to be all right, honey," he informed his daughter gently. Robyn whimpered as he painstakingly removed bits of glass from her forearm, though by now Gwen was sure the child couldn't feel much of anything. "Everything is going to be fine." Apparently, Doc was well aware of his wife's inability to handle the sight of blood.

"Oh, God, I feel so responsible," Phyllis sobbed as soon as they were out of earshot of her daughter.

"Accidents happen all the time," Gwen soothed, anxious to get back to the doctor and also to see how Robyn was faring and if there was any way she could help.

"But you don't understand. If I had just gotten there sooner, or been able to prevent her from reaching for that ball once it had gone through the glass..."

The "what if's" were always endless.

"If you hadn't been there, think of where Robyn would be now. Stop torturing yourself," Gwen said softly. "She's going to be fine. Just relax."

Phyllis looked even whiter. Gwen placed a pillow beneath her feet so that the woman's head and shoulders were level and better able to get a fresh supply of oxygenated blood.

"Andrew—" Phyllis protested weakly.

"Elyse will see to him."

Doc was cleansing his daughter's arm when Gwen slipped back into the room. Robyn was lying quietly on the examining table, sniffling now and then. She was very pale, obviously still in some pain, but otherwise appeared to be much calmer. It had never been easy for Gwen to treat a traumatically injured child. But over the years she'd developed an emotional armor, one that allowed her professionally to shut off everything except what needed to be done, without losing sight of the emotional needs of the child. Without warning it deserted her. For a moment she was motionless, blinking back tears herself. Doc shot her a curious, probing look, wondering openly at the depth of her reaction. His concern snapped her out of it and galvanized her into action. Once again, she was the seasoned nurse, assisting competently and wordlessly. As Doc worked he kept up a low, steady stream of chatter, eliciting responses from Robyn, teasing her into a smile now and then. Gwen's admiration for the gentle, competent physician increased tenfold.

"I'm going to need to suture two of these cuts," Doc said over his shoulder to Gwen. "Thank goodness there was no nerve damage." He turned to his daughter sternly. "It could have been a lot worse. Don't ever—ever—put your hand through a broken window again, young lady, no matter how large the hole looks."

"Yes, Daddy," she murmured. Her lower lip quavered.

Doc patted Robyn's uninjured knee. "I'm not mad at you. Just scared thinking about what could have happened."

"Me, too," Robyn admitted.

Father and daughter exchanged a glance. Doc smiled. After a moment Robyn grinned, rolled her eyes heavenward and then emotionally sobbed some more. But these were tears of relief, not fear. Gwen, watching, fought back a new wave of empathetic tears.

Doc turned back to Gwen, accepting the numbing injection she had prepared. "Did Phyllis faint?"

"We managed to make it to the sofa."

"Thank heaven for that. She never could stand the sight of blood." He shook his head fondly.

Gwen sent him a wry glance, feeling abruptly ready to defend the poor woman. "Not many mothers with injured children can."

"True."

Although Doc had asked Gwen to assist him, he ended up doing most of the work himself, including the securing of the bandages. Which was just as well,

Gwen thought. She was feeling a little light-headed. She told herself it was from too little food earlier in the day.

Phyllis was sitting up on the sofa in Doc's office when Gwen went in to tell her Doc was almost through. "He's letting Robyn select a soft drink from the refrigerator. Can I get you something to drink?"

Andrew played nearby with his mother's car keys. "No," Phyllis answered with a sigh. "I think I'll be fine now. I feel like such a fool."

"Because you almost fainted?" Gwen leaned against the edge of Doc's desk. "Listen, under the circumstances you did remarkably well."

Phyllis didn't think so. She sighed heavily and raked a hand through her dark hair. "The past couple of years have been so hectic, especially since Andrew was born. There never seems to be enough time for either child. And because Andrew's so small, it's been Robyn who's getting less attention."

"I'm sure that's true in every family," Gwen soothed.

"Yes, but I'm just not sure I'm coping as well as I should."

"You're doing fine," Doc said, coming in to the office. He tousled his son's hair and picked him up in his arms. "And besides that, Robyn is old enough to know better."

There was no arguing that.

"Look, I've got three more patients to see. Do you feel well enough to drive? Or do you want to wait and all go home together?"

"Let's go home together," Phyllis said gratefully, apparently needing the reassurance that came with having all family members together, intact, after a trauma.

He smiled. "I was hoping you'd say that."

Gwen watched them depart. She'd never felt such envy, despite the trauma that had just enveloped the Quarricks. She wished abruptly that she had her own daughter to raise. She wished she'd married Dan when she had the chance, whether he'd wanted to marry or not. She wished she could recapture the past.

Chapter Nine

Buddy dropped by late Friday afternoon with the blue-prints for the extension on the Dawson Springs Clinic. While he was waiting for Doc to finish returning phone calls to patients, he shared a cup of coffee with Gwen in the staff lounge.

"So, when's Dan due back in town?" Buddy asked.

Though Elyse had seen her estranged husband come into the clinic, she had not spoken to him once. Instead, she'd glared at him pointedly, then announced stiffly to Gwen that she was leaving for the day. Buddy had made no attempt to stop or speak to Elyse, either. There was so much tension between them that Gwen had almost given up hope the Daltons would ever get back together.

"This evening," Gwen said.

Buddy sipped his coffee, watching her over the rim of the earthenware mug. "Are you going to see him?"

Unable to suppress a joyful smile, Gwen replied, "He said he'd come over first thing." Her heart soared at the prospect of being with him again.

Lounging against the wall, Buddy shook his head in awe. In dusty construction-worker clothes, he looked more like himself than he had in weeks. "You know, I still can't get over the two of you. It's as though the past decade had never taken place, the way you look at each other."

In many respects it felt that way to Gwen, too. She stirred cream into her coffee. "He's very special to me," she admitted quietly, feeling the heat of a blush.

"And you are to him, too," Buddy shot back, with a touch of envy. He shook his head in wonderment, relating, "You know, he's even asked me questions about what you were doing the year he left. He wants to know everything about you."

A chill of unease prickled down her spine. "What do you mean?" Gwen straightened up, the coffee burning in her throat. Her heart had started pounding. She could feel perspiration coating her palms.

"Oh, you know." Buddy gestured effusively with his free hand. "He wanted to know how you were after your dad died. How you got through the tragedy. More about your relatives, where you went to stay after that, if they were good to you, and so on."

"But you don't know anything about that, not really." Gwen stared at him, hurt and puzzlement lacing her voice. Why hadn't Dan asked her?

"I know." Buddy shrugged off the odd behavior.

Doc joined them good-naturedly. "Who's to explain the unpredictability of a man in love?" Doc favored her with a teasing wink. "He's asked me questions, too, though, Gwen. He wanted to know where you went to high school your senior year, if I knew—if I had seen your records, what your favorite flower was, things like that. Said he was planning some big celebration that would commemorate all your years together and apart. Wouldn't tell me anything more." Doc sent Buddy a quelling look. "Though I got the impression, at least, that it was supposed to be a surprise for Gwen."

"Oh, yeah," Buddy murmured, turning a dull shade of red. "Hell, Gwen, I'm sorry. I've had my mind so much on Elyse."

"It's all right," she soothed reflexively, her mind still wondering what Dan could be up to, if his delving into her past were really as innocent as both Buddy and Doc had been led to believe.

"Gwen can act surprised," Doc soothed.

She smiled in an effort to allay Buddy's guilty discomfiture. "Sure I can. I'll be up for an Academy Award before you know it." She paused for comic affect, narrowing her eyes. "Just in case, though, what did you tell him?" Her stomach lurched at the possibility that her beau's queries were anything but innocent.

Buddy shrugged. "Nothing much I could tell him. You weren't living here until a couple years ago."

Relief swept through Gwen. "Doc?" She forced a teasingly reproachful demeanor, trying with all her might to appear to be interested merely for vanity's sake.

Doc thoughtfully stroked his red beard. "That you attended University of Cincinnati and, later, Ohio State. I didn't know about high school. As for flowers, I guessed red roses, but that was all it was, a guess." Obviously he recalled the time Gwen had admired the rosebushes Phyllis Quarrick had planted around their white stone farmhouse.

"And that's all you told him, both of you," Gwen pressed. Both admitted it was.

"Maybe he's planning a weekend trip to your alma mater," Buddy shrugged, setting his coffee cup aside and reaching for the blueprints he'd brought with him.

Doc admitted, "It would be one way to recapture all those years together the two of you missed." He stared contemplatively at the coffee maker, as if surmising the romantic implications and creativity of the idea.

But Gwen knew that wasn't what Dan was after. "Well, I'll leave you two men to discuss the blueprints," she said lightly, hiding the faint tremors that had started beneath her skin. "I've got a date tonight." And it looked as if it was going to be an uncomfortably hot encounter. One that was liable to burn much more than Dan Kingston had ever anticipated.

DAN SHOWED UP PROMPTLY at seven-thirty, exquisitely dressed in dark suit, white shirt and tie, a ribbon-wrapped florist's box in his left hand, a bottle of her favorite Burgundy in his right. Though he'd asked her to go out to dinner with him, she'd insisted on staying home, preparing a meal for them both. She'd wanted to be alone with him, rather than in public, if it came to the confrontation she suspected they were going to have. And in that mood, knowing that it was essential that her self-confidence be at an all-time high, she had dressed in her best emerald-green dress.

As he entered her home, Dan sniffed appreciatively at the aroma of simmering beef Stroganoff. His smile deepened even more appreciatively as his gaze roamed the summery scoop-neck, belted waist and softly flowing skirt. His obvious delight in being with her made the deception between them all the more painful.

Doc had been right about the roses. Dan had brought

her one long-stemmed red beauty for every year they
had known each other. He also had something for
every year they were apart, including the years he'd
spent abroad and at Harvard, and a photo album to
catch her up on every major event of his life she had
missed. Peppered throughout were cutout hearts and
little signs that said he had never stopped loving or
wanting her.

"I measured every girl I ever met to you," he said
softly. "No one ever came close."

"Not even the heiress?"

"Not even her. I thought of you every holiday.
Every birthday. Every stormy or starry night."

Tears of joy glimmered in her eyes. "I thought of
you often, too."

"Let's not be fools anymore." He regarded her seriously.

"I don't want to be." Despite the armor she had
erected around her heart, she was moved by everything
he had disclosed, by his willingness to be vulnerable to
her.

"But?" he prompted tenderly when she didn't go
on.

"I can't help it. I'm still wary, afraid of my impulsive
nature where you're concerned. You know what they
say about fools rushing in where angels fear to tread. I
think of our future together and visualize only joy. Past
experience makes me *expect* to experience pain."

He nodded his understanding as he captured her
hand between the two of his and rubbed the icy ap-
pendage until it felt cozy and warm once again. "We'll
work hard to make it better this time, Gwen. I promise."

Naive or not, she believed him.

"Now that you know all about me, I want to know all about you," he said as they finished the last of the wine. "But I can wait until you're ready."

She told him stories about her days in nursing school, but said nothing about the child. She was weakening toward telling him what he wanted to know. He sensed it.

They ate by candlelight. "The dinner was delicious," he said at last, pushing back his plate.

"Thank you." She paused, unable to wait any longer. She studied her hands, knitted together on her lap. "I want to talk to you. It's important." Her head lifted. She fixed him with a searching look. "Have you been asking questions about me?"

For a moment he seemed to freeze. He reached for a crust of bread and buttered it idly. He didn't meet her gaze directly. It was one of the few times he had failed to do so. She took that as a further sign of guilt. "What do you mean?" he asked quietly.

Her heart was thumping painfully against her ribs. Somehow, she kept her voice steady. "To people around town. Your parents, Buddy, Doc Quarrick."

"Maybe." His jaw set implacably. He set the crust of bread down on the edge of his plate. Not surprisingly, he refused to volunteer anything more, just waited for her to recount her suspicions.

"To what purpose?" she asked softly. She wanted him to tell her it was innocently done.

Finally he said, "It was all a part of the surprise I was planning for you."

"This evening."

"Yes."

She sensed that when cornered he would not lie. Neither, though, would he volunteer more about his duplicity. And he knew, she could tell, that she was on to him, at least partially.

"What else were you planning for me, Dan?" She knew from the look on his face that he was embroiled in something else, something he didn't want her to find out about if he could help it. And she knew then in her heart what it was. Because if the situation between them had been reversed, she knew only too well what she would have done. "What else were you planning?" she asked. "To regain custody of the child we lost?"

He thrust his napkin down beside his plate. "It had occurred to me, yes."

Her lungs contracted painfully, as did her throat. Her voice was hoarse when she spoke. "Dan, you promised me you wouldn't."

He shot her an accusing look beneath fiercely lowered brows that said they wouldn't be in this situation if she had just been honest with him from the first. "I said I wouldn't discuss it with you further," he corrected icily, pushing back his chair. With restless anger he paced the room, then paused to shoot her a scathingly direct look as he recounted in a very low voice, "I never said I wouldn't look. Damn it, Gwen, the child was mine, too!"

She stood up, too, following him about the room, her legs feeling as if any second they would give way. Never in her life had she wanted more to faint. But even as the thought came, she knew she would never give in to the weakness. Not when the stakes were so high. "We lost all right to our baby years ago!"

He glided closer, radiating tension like a live wire. "I

never signed away my rights to anything," he said in a rough, possessive undertone.

But he had. The minute he'd walked out on her and broken off their affair. For him to try to turn back the clock now was pointlessly cruel to them all. "I'll never forgive you if you continue with this." Tears sparkled in her eyes, clinging to her lashes, spilling onto her cheeks.

For a moment he looked as if he were going to take her into his arms, hold her and soothingly tell her that everything would be all right. The moment passed and he did not. He stared down at her, his eyes luminous but hard. Deep in her soul she felt his desire to possess her.

"So be it." He muttered the pronouncement grimly, then turned on his heel and slammed out the door.

She followed him, feeling as though her heart were breaking. "Where are you going?"

He was in no state of mind to be driving. Neither was he in any condition to stay. She watched as he circled around the sleek black car and jerked open the door on the driver's side.

"To get drunk," he said, pulling off his tie and undoing the buttons at his neck. His suit coat hung open, giving him an elegant, disheveled look. "At this point, Gwen, it's the only thing in my life that makes any sense."

DESULTORILY, SHE DID THE DISHES, changed into casual clothes, in the faint hope that he would change his mind and come back at some point to talk. While she waited she again flipped through the photo albums he had left her. Yes, his life was all painstakingly chronicled, she noted. But missing were any real signs of pleasure. Had he omitted the lighter moments deliberately, she wondered. Or had they just not been there, not truly, not times he felt absolute joy in his heart? Knowing how it had been for her and knowing how genuinely glad he had seemed to have her back in his life, she guessed the truth lay in the latter. Considering how they had just parted, it was small consolation.

Gwen worried about Dan all evening. When the call from the bar came at 2:00 A.M., it was no surprise. Gwen had half suspected Dan would try to close down whatever dive he was in. What was unnerving was the fact that she was supposed to pick up Buddy Dalton, too. Had the two of them been into mischief? Gritting her teeth in irritation she drove over to Princeton to get them.

The bar, a notorious singles' place known for its ability to attract college students and young professionals, was empty except for the two of them and the custodial people cleaning up. Arms around each other's shoulders, feet propped up drunkenly on nearby chairs, the two men were singing their former high school fighting song. The slurred recitation brought back poignant memories of other happier times, and Gwen had to fight back tears of sheer exasperation. How had she and Dan gotten to this place in their lives? What did the future hold for them? What did it hold for Buddy and Elyse?

"Are you two scoundrels ready to go?" Gwen faced them, car keys in hand. Only the knowledge that she was partially responsible for Dan's behavior had prompted her to answer their summons.

Buddy raised his index finger in a conditional gesture. "Just one more minute." He raised his mug of beer and downed it swiftly, then wiped the excess from his chin and, with effort, stood up, weaving slightly, blinking exaggeratedly. "Ready."

Dan exhaled and stood. His command was much better than that of his friend. But he, too, was in no condition to drive. She was suddenly glad they had asked the bartender to call her. To Dan, she said stiffly when Buddy stumbled haphazardly, "Can you help me here?" Clearly, Dalton wouldn't make it on his own power.

"Sure."

Arms around Buddy's middle, they guided him out to her Jeep and half pushed and half shoved him into the backseat of her Renegade. Gwen fastened the seat belt around his middle. When she was settled in the driver's seat, Dan climbed into the passenger seat beside her. She waited as he fastened his shoulder strap before igniting the motor.

"You men ought to be ashamed of yourselves," she reproached in a deceptively mild tone as she maneuvered the quiet city streets.

"Wha's wrong with gettin' a little drunk?" Buddy smiled, sliding sideways down into the seat. He cradled his head on his hand.

Recalling Elyse's suspicions regarding another woman as the explanation for all the time he had been spending in Princeton, Gwen wondered if it hadn't been the bars he had been hitting instead. Yet, he'd looked too physically fit for that to have been the case—not the least bit hung over. "You've been coming into Princeton a lot, haven't you, Buddy?" she asked, turning the radio on low. Wind blew coolly in the windows, caressing her face, whipping her hair around her head. Dan relaxed in the seat beside her, watching her with a quiet intensity that she found unnerving.

"Yep." With effort, Buddy pushed himself to a sitting position. Arms extended in a muscle-man pose, he flexed both biceps proudly. "I've been getting into shape. Joined a health spa here, one that opens at dawn and stays open until 11:00 P.M. six days a week."

Gwen cast him a quick look in her rearview mirror. "Is that the reason for all the new clothes, the new haircut?"

Buddy shrugged and rubbed his jaw. "I figured maybe I was too country-looking for her. Figured I needed a new image to go along with my new physique." He snorted derisively. "For all the good it did me—she's running around with Walt Fowler."

"There's nothing between Elyse and Walt," Gwen said quickly, ignoring Dan's provokingly skeptical glance. "She just did that to make you jealous."

"Yeah? Well, it sure worked." Buddy yawned sleepily and rubbed his eyes. After a pause, he admitted, the liquor making him honest, "God, I love that woman so much." He sighed. "There isn't anything I wouldn't do for her. And how do I get repaid?"

"You walked out on her," Gwen reminded.

"Only so she'd come to her senses," he shot back belligerently, straightening his spine.

"Well, maybe you both ought to do more giving," Gwen said, turning her Jeep into Dawson Springs.

"That could be said for all of us," Dan said quietly. His words were like a live wire acting on her already battered senses.

Gwen said nothing more until they turned into the

site housing Buddy's construction company trailer. "Can you help me get him into the house?" Gwen asked, when Buddy couldn't even get his seat belt off by himself.

"I'll give it a try." Dan climbed agilely out of his seat and directed Buddy out of the backseat. Together, Dan and Gwen got him into his trailer and onto the couch. While Gwen opened several windows, Dan took off Buddy's shoes and covered him with a blanket. "You're going to have one hell of a headache come morning, friend," Dan said.

"Yeah, and you, too, pal," Buddy retorted. With another yawn he shut his eyes. In a moment he was sound asleep. Gwen and Dan retreated to her Jeep.

"What were you drinking?" she asked as she started her motor up again.

He shrugged as if it hardly mattered. "A few shots of tequila, then mostly beer." His jaw was clenched defiantly.

"It's a wonder you didn't get sick."

He laughed at her reproach. "Buddy did. Once. That didn't stop him."

She rolled her eyes in disgust, then swiveled to face him, one hand resting idly on the back of his seat. "Do you want me to drive you home?"

"I'd rather sack out on the couch at your place."

She shot him an astonished glance. He qualified quietly, "I'd rather not wake my parents if you don't mind."

"Right." If there was one thing Miles and Betty didn't need it was their son arriving home in an inebriated state.

"I'd like to talk to you, Gwen," he said softly. His efforts to remain furious with her failed. "Unless we work this out between us, neither of us will ever have any peace."

He was right about that much. "All right." She bowed her head from his assessing gaze, then concentrated on her driving. Neither spoke again.

It was nearly two-thirty by the time they walked into her house. Dan was still weaving slightly.

"I'll put some coffee on," Gwen offered. "Maybe then we can come to some sort of understanding."

He sighed. Catching her wrist, he held her before him. Abruptly, he was in no mood to compromise. Not on the fate of his child. "You want me to say I won't press or search further. I can't. I could no more do that than amputate one of my limbs. But that doesn't mean I don't love you or that I've stopped caring. On the contrary, my feelings for you are deeper than ever." The only course he was uncertain of was where they went from here.

The stench of the bar clung to his skin, marring the fresh scent she knew and remembered so well.

He seemed equally uncomfortable with his uncustomary dishabille. He threaded his fingers through his hair. "Mind if I use your shower?" he said softly, releasing his grip. "Maybe it will clear the cobwebs."

Silently, she gave her assent.

Though he'd had ample time to absorb the situation, Dan realized as he stepped into her shower, he was still in shock. The intellectual part of him could hardly comprehend the knowledge that he had a child. The emotional part of him had already accepted the news joyously; he wanted to exercise his claim on their child more desperately than he had ever wanted anything in his life. He wanted Gwen to need that, too.

Was it possible that Gwen had not realized how much the child would mean to him? Did she not know, either then or now, that he would have given any-thing—his education, his job—for the child and her? Or had she known and realized, or perhaps presumed in the long run, that marriage in their teens would have been the wrong choice, leading only to personal disas-ter—disaster that involved not only them but the tender, helpless feelings of a child?

It was hard to recall what it had been like for him then. Even glancing through his scrapbooks he could hardly recall how he'd felt about even major political issues, much less personal ones. He knew he'd been young then, but he felt sure he could have handled the responsibility of caring for a child if only she'd given him the chance. So could Gwen. Or could she have? Losing her mother, then her father, while still in her teens. Having no one to lean on, herself little more than a child, with no education, no way to support her-self should anything have happened to him. He knew she loved children. They flocked to her. Had she made the right choice giving their baby away? *Now they would never know. Or would they? Was it possible somehow to trace... ?*

Damn it, Dan thought, stepping out of the shower. He felt cheated and hurt. And most of all, sad. As though a part of himself and of her—perhaps the best part—had been lost, never to be regained.

After silently toweling and shrugging into a robe, he combed his hair and started solemnly downstairs. When he paused at the entrance of the room and saw the tortured look on Gwen's face, his resentment of her faded, to be replaced by feelings of compassion for all she had suffered. Right or wrong, she was still the only woman in his life, the only one there would ever be. He was determined to make their lives right again. And whether she liked it or not, that meant going back.

GWEN TURNED. It was obvious by the comtemplative look on his face that Dan had been watching her for some time. She wished she could read in his heart or his mind what he was feeling and hence know how to proceed. But all she could see now was the physical. His hair was glistening damply; he was clad in the robe he had left there the first week of their renewed affair. She noticed he'd shaved. His eyes were clear, but weariness etched in the lines surrounding his mouth. Without preamble, he came up behind her. She was prowling the room restlessly, her high-heeled boots digging into the carpet as she stared out the window into the darkness of the night. She jumped as he touched her, unable to help her jittery response. Part of her wanted him; part of her didn't.

"Would you like some coffee now?" she asked.

Overtaking her easily, he stretched out his arm and blocked her attempted escape into the kitchen. "Coffee's not what I need, Gwen," he said in a voice that was ominously quiet. "I think you know that." Panic curled inside her, making her tremble. "I want our child. I want you."

She shook her head, but deep inside she understood what he was feeling. Once she had yearned for the happily-ever-after, too. "There isn't any way that will ever happen, Dan. Face it. Stop living in the past. Oh, I know what you're thinking. You look back with the knowledge of what you now know the world holds for you. Then you were so restless, frustrated, aching to get out and experience more of life. You never would have been happy spending your life in Kentucky, Dan. You thrive on change, on the excitement of the city and big business. As for raising the child, I know you regret not having had the chance to do that. So do I, more than you could ever possibly know."

He was silent. "We could have reared our child, Gwen. I know it would have been hard then. It would be hard now. But we both still could have gotten our education."

Tears blurred her eyes. Her jaw set defiantly. "You would have grown to hate me."

"No, only to love." He tried to take her in his arms, but she refused.

"It's so easy for you to say all this now, looking back."

"I would have loved you regardless. In your heart you know that's true," he said, very low.

"But at what cost? To us and, especially to the child?" There was silence. Again, she was unsure. "I wanted our child to have the best of everything, not emotional insecurity or strife. Was that so wrong? I felt that our baby deserved both parents, if not us, then someone who would—could—care for the baby. Someone who was equipped to meet the child's every need." She waved her arms in despair, pacing, upset. "I know it seems simple now, Dan. Then, it wasn't. I was so depressed at the time, still recovering from my father's death, your engagement. I felt that I was falling apart from the inside out. Whether you had been there or not, I was in no emotional shape to care for the child. Every child deserves a good, attentive mother I couldn't have been that, no matter what." She swallowed hard. "Yes, I could have farmed the baby out for a while until I got back on my feet—put it in a foster home, given it to your parents to raise temporarily. But whose interests would I have been catering to then? Certainly not the baby's. You can't yank a child around like that, Dan, especially not so early in life. Believe me, in some of the free clinics and even in the upper-class families, I've seen the results of such parental selfishness. They're not good."

Remorse tautened the lines of his face. "I'm sorry I wasn't here for you."

His response was genuine, but it didn't help. "What's done is done," she said glumly, feeling treacherously close to sobbing uncontrollably, for once the tears started flowing, she knew she wouldn't be able to control them.

Was it? His eyes held the question, but sensing the depth of her distress, he said nothing more.

"And as for us," she continued emotionally sensing that he was about to try to make love to her again, "once, you took all I had to give." He would do it again now, given the chance. "If I'm not enough," she said bluntly, "if you have to recover the child, too..."

"You're more than love enough for me," he said softly, his hands coming up gently to frame her face. "But I want you to be happy, too. And until we can reconcile what we've lost..." His voice trailed off.

This time she let him hold her, needing his strength, his warmth. For the first time, she felt he understood how torn she felt.

"I know I've hurt you badly. Let me give something back to you," he urged hoarsely, his eyes never leaving hers as he evocatively closed the scant inches left between them, held her comfortingly close. "I want to make love to you."

"Just like that. You leave me to go out and get drunk and then come back here and expect—"

He gave her no room for denial. His hand cupped the back of her neck, tilting her head back and holding it still under his. The pressure of his mouth forced her lips open to the passionate taste and warmth of his. Desire surged through her, making her sway unsteadily. He lazily unlaced the belted tie of his robe.

In the end it was pointless to think of anything but surrender—to him, to the dictates of her heart. She was naked, her arms laced around his neck when he danced her into the living room by slow, swirling degrees. With a litheness of limbs, his body followed hers down onto the couch, his weight all solid warmth. His fingers found her, then his mouth. She arched against him, the moan of need echoing deep in her heart. And then he was above her, pausing as he took precautions against pregnancy, precautions he had never lost sight of from the renewal of their affair.

She found his concern for her touching and disturbing, unsure as to whether he was trying to renew the depth of their commitment in every way he knew how, or simply to avoid making a new one. She did want a child, she realized; she wanted to keep part of him. But she wouldn't commit herself to beginning a new life unless it was what he wanted, too, and it apparently still was not.

And then he was moving deep inside her, his strokes long and sure and deliberately sustained, his hands touching her everywhere, coaxing, caressing. When she whimpered her frustration, her passion, he murmured her name. His palms spread beneath her, arching her against his hard, prone length, cupping her close. Their lips met more fervently, rhythmically, paralleling the more intimate invasion. She yielded completely, craving the final burst of fire. He penetrated her so completely, so deeply, that she cried out.

The pressure of his mouth over hers stole her final climactic gasp of pleasure. Their breaths blended, trembling, unnerved, every ounce of their love exposed to each other's perusal. He held her to him possessively, tenderly whispering her name. They drifted drowsily—replete, exhausted. limbs tangled together—only minutes later to begin again at his ardent insistence.

"You're all I've ever really wanted," he whispered, his mouth at the nape of her neck, his hands teasing, then kneading, demanding.

She found she was capable of so much more love than she'd thought, physical and emotional, and that his feelings of contraceptive responsibility had not ended the first time or the second or the third. She wanted to ask him why. She couldn't. Not when everything still was so tenuous and uncertain between them.

HE WAS GONE when she awakened hours later. He'd left a note that said simply:

> Called Buddy. He's taking me over to get my car before it gets towed away.
>
> > Dan

There was no love in the signature, nothing. She wondered again how he really felt about her, now that he was sober and their night of fevered passion was over. She knew that he had feelings of affection for her, that much could not be faked. She didn't know how he felt about having her a real part of his future, or if he would ever really forgive her for robbing him of his child.

As per her usual routine, Gwen showered and dressed and then went over to the clinic. Saturday mornings were spent catching up on paperwork and seeing patients who needed to be seen before Doc Quarrick left the office for the weekend break.

Taking on the unaccustomed role of matchmaker, Gwen cornered Elyse and told her briefly what had happened the night before in the Princeton bar.

Elyse stared at her in astonishment. "But Buddy never drinks to excess!" she exclaimed, upset.

"Well, he certainly did last night."

"Is he all right?" an ashen Elyse asked.

"This morning I imagine he has a headache the size of Mount Rushmore. But Dan did mention in the note he left me that he was taking him over to Princeton to pick up Dan's car."

At the mention of the neighboring town, Elyse's expression soured. She reached for a packet of chips and a calorie-laden cola. "No doubt he's looking up his latest girl friend, too."

"I rather doubt it," Gwen informed her dryly. "He's joined a health spa, Elyse. That's where he's been all these nights. Working out. And the new clothes? Those were bought in order to impress you, you dimwit."

Elyse's chin dropped nearly to her collarbone. "You're kidding."

"He also expressed his undying love for you last night many times. Not that he's gotten over his anger at seeing you with Walt Fowler, you understand. That is going to take some soothing over."

"But he left me—"

"He said he only wanted you to come to your senses. Frankly, I think he's been sorry from day one, just hasn't known how to say it."

Tears glimmered in Elyse's eyes. She pushed aside the junk food in her hand that she'd been absently consuming and stared wordlessly down at the floor. "I love him, too, you know."

"Then do something about it!" Gwen roared.

"Amen to that," Doc Quarrick said, sticking his head into the doorway of the staff lounge. "It's about time we got the emotional climate around here back to normal. If it's all right with you ladies, I'm going to head on home now. Phyllis just called. She said the scout troop is coming over for a picnic and she needs my help."

"Good luck!" Elyse and Gwen said in unison.

"Knowing the talent of that troop for their collective ability to eat everything in sight, I'm going to need it." Waving his good-bye cheerfully, Doc left.

Gwen turned back to Elyse. "If you want to check out the spa story—"

"No, I believe him." Standing straight, she touched a hand to her hair. "The big question is, what am I going to wear?"

"Something chaste," Gwen suggested, remembering her come-hither look of the night of the ice cream social.

"You're probably right." Elyse left, plotting what color to do her nails.

Gwen smiled, finishing up the last of her notations on the medical records of the patients they'd just seen. For the first time in weeks, it looked hopeful that the quarreling Daltons would work out their problems.

Her spirits were further lifted when Dan called later in the afternoon to ask her to have supper with his family. At Dan's insistence and with Betty's expert advice and recipes, they grilled fish fillets out on the brick barbecue in the yard, Dan acting as chef, Gwen as his culinary assistant.

Afterward they all sat on the front porch as the sun set, companionably discussing the latest local events. Dan told stories about his work at IDP.

"When will you be going back to work?" Betty asked. Now that Miles had resumed roughly half of his normal activities and had hired Tim Kaufman to assist with the farm work, it was no longer imperative that Dan stay on in Dawson Springs. Yet, surprisingly, he had not rushed back to Chicago as Gwen would have half suspected he might weeks ago, but was instead being very closemouthed about his future plans.

"I've set my return date as September first," Dan offered reluctantly after a minute. "There's a position opening up in Chicago compatible with my skills and experience and management level with the company." He cast Gwen a worried glance, as if fearing she might freeze up. When she didn't react outwardly, he turned to his folks, explaining casually, "I want to spend more time with both of you before I return, make sure the farm is running smoothly. When I do resume work at

IDP, my life will necessarily be very hectic for the first few months, as it would be with any new job. I probably won't be able to make it back until Christmas, if then."

Betty and Miles nodded agreeably, long used to the demands of their son's hectic career.

Christmas, Gwen thought, a chill running apprehensively down her spine. Could she survive not seeing him for three or four months?

"Guess who I saw together on my way into town to pick Gwen up?" Dan interjected, abruptly recalling. "Buddy and Elyse."

"Have they reconciled?" Gwen asked hopefully. Seated next to Dan on the chain-hung wooden porch swing, she was aware of his thigh nudging hers, the arm he had placed on the back of the swing, touching her shoulders, and the gentle rocking and warm evening breeze. For the first time in years she was blessed with the sense of belonging, of family. It wasn't a sensation that would be easy for her to give up, she knew. But her comfort had to do with more than just her love for Dan and her being with him. It was like going home again in her heart to the place where she knew she truly belonged.

"I don't know, but they were sitting close together in the car."

Miles observed Gwen's pleased smile. Though given to occasional complaints about his new low-sodium, low-cholesterol diet, Miles was looking extremely well, tanned, relaxed. As a bonus he'd also lost weight, some fifteen or twenty pounds. His daily workouts had added a new muscularity to his frame. "Quite a romantic, aren't you?"

"I just think they belong together," she said. Marriage was a commitment that in her opinion should never be just thrown away.

Betty interjected, above the needlework in her lap, "We might say the same about the two of you!"

Miles tossed in his two cents' worth of advice. "Better not let that gal get away, son. Good women are hard to find and Gwen is one in a million. Oh, I know how it is for you young folks," he said, before either Gwen or Dan could protest. "You like to wait until everything is perfect before tying the knot, and I guess there are some advantages to that. But sometimes you can wait too long, if you know what I mean. Betty and I, we didn't have any money when we got married. We were both too young. But we managed and we grew together and we love each other more than ever now. If you and Daniel set your mind to it, Gwen, you could have the same."

Dan patted Gwen on the knee, the openly affectionate gesture making her blush. "Not to worry, folks." He grinned, showing a slash of white teeth. "I have no intention of letting her slip away again."

"Well, if you all don't mind, I think it's about time we turned in." Miles yawned and Betty made a great show of gathering up her needlework.

Dan turned to Gwen. "Game for a stroll around the property?"

She glanced at him, unable to read his intentions as he drew her to her feet. "Sure."

"Wait here and I'll get a Coleman lantern from the barn."

Miles admonished them both to be careful. Betty countered with a suggestion that her husband hush.

Minutes later, Dan and Gwen were walking slowly,

hand in hand, toward the mountains. "Where are we going?" she asked.

"To find some wild flowers to lace through your hair." He was in a buoyant, enigmatic mood.

Gwen whirled toward him, a smile dancing on her face. "There are no wild flowers left this late in June!"

"That's where you're wrong." As he'd promised, higher up on the stream, at the very edge of the Kingston property, was a haven of color. "Mom told me she'd scattered some seeds around here last spring. She'd never had time to come back and see what had bloomed. She sent me here to check it out the other day." Dan sank down in the grass.

"They're beautiful," Gwen said, watching him sift through the riot of color with his fingertips.

"So are you."

She watched, mesmerized, as he broke off several long-stemmed violets, delicate strands of columbine and mountain laurel and fashioned the multicolored blossoms into a fragrant lacy wreath. Gently he placed the crown on her head. Time faded away, and all that was left between them was the love they had shared. Hands entwined, they walked back toward the clearing next to the pond. Once there, Dan set down the lantern and turned the flame down to the barest sliver of unintrusive light. Gradually their eyes adjusted to the new level of darkness.

"I've wanted to ask you to swim here with me again ever since I've been back," Dan said. A shudder whispered through her at his low, intimate tone. "Will you now?"

Chapter Ten

A clear, starry night sky glimmered like dark velvet overhead. A warm breeze wafted down through the trees; the only other sound between them was the soft gurgling whoosh of the mountain stream.

"There's no danger," he reminded her, watching as she removed the crowning wreath of flowers and stood awkwardly cradling the gift in her hands. "The pool is only five feet deep." Dan wanted her more than she knew.

"I don't have a suit," she said finally.

His heart slamming painfully against his ribs, he closed the distance between them smoothly. Her face tipped back beneath his. She looked incredibly vulnerable, standing half in the shadows. He wondered how he would ever leave her again. How he ever had. Never had he been more conscious of his ability to hurt her. He didn't want that, not again.

"Neither do I." Dan wanted to swim naked with her. He wanted to hold her, her lustrous skin smooth and wet like silk against him. But that wasn't all he wanted. He wanted her to trust him. And she didn't, not yet, not entirely. He saw it in her eyes every time she glanced his way for longer than a moment or two.

"I'll wade across, that's all," she decided finally, unable to completely refuse his imploring look.

For the moment, Dan guessed, that would have to do. He watched, slowly removing his own socks and shoes, as she kicked off her sandals and, hiking up her cotton skirt above her knees, started, shivering, across the stream. His eyes roamed the mussed auburn curls framing her face, the slender lines of her back, the curve of her thighs as they disappeared into the dark luminescence of the stream. Laughing softly, looking as if she felt ridiculous, she turned back toward him. Her breasts swayed temptingly against the soft cotton of her scoop-necked T-shirt. Abruptly, she looked younger and more carefree than he could ever remember. He wanted to capture that moment in time and hold on to it. He wanted to use it to his advantage.

She was nearly to the other shore when he stood up and began unbuttoning his shirt. Gwen started, surveying him as he searched her face. Her mouth was dry as he unabashedly stripped off his clothing and dropped his pants onto the ground. The stones were smooth and slippery beneath his bare feet.

Clad only in dark bikini briefs, he started toward her, closing the distance between them effortlessly. She could not take her eyes from his exquisite form, but as he neared her, the water swirling up around his knees, panic and trembling excitement set in. It was reminiscent of the first time they had made love and yet infinitely more explicit. Where, before, his moves had been fumbling and boyishly earnest, he was now deliberately erotic. More, he knew how to arouse her to fever pitch.

Gwen groped for something to say that would stop him or bring her back sharply to her senses. She found nothing. His hands curved lightly on her shoulders as he backed her by degrees down the sloping edge into the pool. His lips ghosted lightly across hers, deliberately, evocatively, keeping the contact from deepening. Her lips parted helplessly as she sought the warmth and sweeping sweetness of his tongue. He allowed her entry into his mouth, but did not counter with a foray of his own. Rather, his hands swept across her shoulder blades to her spine, lingered at the back button-fastening of her skirt.

"I want you, Gwen," he said softly. Reading her fears accurately, he promised, "No one will disturb us."

"This is extravagantly indiscreet," she breathed. *When they could go back to her home almost as easily.*

"Yes." He took both her hands in his and paused to kiss the inside of her wrist. Another shiver of arousal sped through her like liquid nitrogen. "It is."

His eyes darkened. Before she could express her feelings, he'd undone her skirt and was lifting the material away from her hips, whisking it over her head. Seconds later, it floated across to the opposite bank.

"MARRY ME, GWEN," he said softly as they dressed. She whirled to face him, unsure of anything except the liquid need on his face, a need that until just now had been expressed physically or not at all.

He's feeling sentimental, she thought, *letting what his father said about finding me again and not losing me affect him.* "Because it's what your parents want?" She knew it would make both Miles and Betty happy. But she didn't want to enter into a union for that reason.

He shook his head, and she knew then that the Kingstons had nothing to do with it. "Because of me." He walked forward to take her once again into his arms. He touched her cheek with his palm. "Because my life has never been the same since I loved you. I hadn't realized how austere it was until you came back into it. I need you, Gwen, now more than ever. I've never stopped loving you."

"I love you, too."

"Then the answer is yes?"

"Yes, yes, one hundred times yes."

GWEN THOUGHT LATER that it was both fortunate and disastrous that they so swiftly cemented their plans, once the initial proposal and acceptance had been issued. But in reality they had no choice. Dan had to return to his job in Chicago within a month. And they wanted to get the legalities out of the way before going to Illinois. Hence, they were married the following Friday evening in the community church.

"You were beautiful." Robyn Quarrick sighed admiringly in the reception line.

On impulse, Gwen plucked a gardenia from her bouquet and placed it in Robyn's hair. "Thank you, sweetheart." She bent lower, so they could speak more confidentially. "How's your arm?" She wasn't due to get the stitches out for another two days, but the bandages were covered by the long, lacy sleeve of her floor-length dress.

"Better." Robyn grinned. She leaned forward conspiratorially, treating Gwen to a devilish wink, "No more football in the yard, though. They took my ball away for a while."

The ten-year-old didn't look that unhappy about it, Gwen noted. "How've you been otherwise?" Gwen asked. "Have you and the other girls in your troop been practicing your figure-eight bandages?"

Robyn nodded seriously. "I've already earned my first-aid badge. I'm working on cooking now. There's not much else to do since I can't go swimming again until the stitches come out."

"Are you looking forward to school?" Gwen asked.

Robyn rolled her eyes heavenward in exasperation. "Not really." Catching sight of one of her playmates, she said good-bye and dashed out the door and down the cement church steps. Gwen watched her go fondly, glad to see her looking so healthy and happy again. What she wouldn't give sometimes to be that age!

Bernie Quarrick ended his conversation with Dan and stepped up to offer his best wishes to the bride. "I'm going to miss having you at the clinic, Gwen."

Gwen laughed at his sympathy-provoking tone, looking up at her red-bearded boss. "Don't start—you'll make me cry." She could just see the mascara running down onto the collar of her dress. Dan slanted her a mild glance. Seriously, Gwen added, "I am working on lining up replacement candidates for you to interview." In the meantime, because of her responsibilities to the people in the area, she had agreed to continue working.

Doc nodded. "But it will never run as smoothly without you. I don't want to make you feel guilty, Gwen. Just loved and appreciated. And the fact of the matter is, you will be missed dearly."

"I agree." Phyllis said, holding a squirming Andrew in her arms. Dressed in a blue velvet suit, he looked charming, too. "Gwen, you look lovely."

"Thank you."

They paused for a moment to talk about Phyllis's scout troop and the many who had earned their first-aid badges. The Quarricks moved off, the perfect family of four. Gwen watched them for a moment. For the first time in years, she had no envy in her heart for the sense of family they possessed. She had hope that she and Dan would have the same.

Colored paper bags of rice were surreptitiously handed out as Gwen and Dan received the rest of their guests. When they headed down the stone church steps, they were hit with a storm of white rice and laughter and good wishes.

As they ducked into the limousine Gwen exclaimed with a jubilant laugh, "We're never going to get rid of all this rice! We should have commissioned Robyn and some of her friends to take off with the cache."

Dan chuckled and brushed the white kernels from his shoulders and hair. "At least you've got a veil to run interference for you."

In the front of the car Buddy was watching Elyse, as if momentarily forgetting his role as driver. It was plain to see that the couple was deeply affected by the ceremony and, barring further momentous complications, well on their way to reconciling. Dan noisily cleared his throat. Buddy started, then threw his pal a glance over his shoulder. "I'll get there eventually. Hold your horses."

The reception was held in the grange hall. The meeting hall had been decked out with garlands and baskets of flowers. A five-piece orchestra had been hired to play. Caterers had served a buffet. A six-tiered cake sat in the center of one linen-covered folding table. Gifts were displayed on another.

Hours later Dan carried her over from the car to the front porch of her house. "My only regret is my inability to give you a proper honeymoon now." Dan set her down gently while searching his pockets for the key.

About that, Gwen really could not have cared less, as she had assured him many times. "We'll do it later when we have the time to do it right, and Doc's found a replacement to take over, and we've had the time to peruse travel brochures and figure out where we want to go." At the moment all that mattered to her was being alone with him. She grinned impishly as he swung open the door and then prepared to pick her up again. She laced her arms around his neck. Her breath caught in her throat. "Besides, I trust you to make it special."

She hadn't anticipated the flowers everywhere, the chilled champagne and hors d'oeuvres. Every surface sparkled. When she'd left it hours earlier to go to the church, and dress, the domain had been a disaster. "More of your mother's handiwork?" she asked.

"No, all mine." He removed her veil, taking out the pins in her hair one by one, and letting her hair fall to her shoulders. "I figured you'd be too busy having a good time at the reception to eat or drink much. And I knew *I'd* be starved." His gaze drifted over her sensually. "For everything."

They sat down on the sofa, kicked off their shoes and opened the bottle of champagne. "To us," he toasted quietly.

"To us."

They kissed, sharing another intimate moment. He caressed her with fingers that trembled slightly. His eyes swept her lovingly from head to toe, then returned to her face, where they stayed, mesmerizing for a long time. Gwen felt as if she had been given the ultimate in love and affection, and for the first time she could remember, she was emotionally replete. Only the abrupt growling of her stomach broke the spell.

"You haven't had anything to eat all day, have you?" he asked.

"Except for the cake—which you mostly put on my chin—and a sip of champagne, nothing. I was too nervous," she confessed.

"We'll remedy the lack of fuel for your body now," he murmured, gently caressing the inside of her wrist. "The lovemaking can and will come later." The suppressed urgency in his voice made her tremble.

At Dan's exhortation, they dug into the food, laughing and talking all the while, exchanging impressions of the ceremony, the good time apparently had by all. It was more than an hour before they finished. Relaxed and content, Gwen gazed deep into his eyes. She struggled reflexively against the appeal his face held for her, wanting to draw out every second to infinity, wanting it never to be over, wanting their marriage to begin, knowing that, even as she played savoring games within herself, it already had. Nothing could compare with the topsy-turvy feeling inside her when he looked at her that way, she thought. Wordlessly, he took her hand and they walked up the stairs to her bedroom. This much she had taken care of. Fresh sheets adorned the bed. The covers were drawn invitingly back. She stopped when she saw the ribbon-

wrapped box on her bed, then gazed up at him inquir-
ingly again.

"I know you didn't have much time to shop for a
trousseau," he said, looking unusually shy.

The negligee was gorgeous, all ice-blue satin and
lace, the neckline plunging almost to the waist, the
back draping with similar immodesty down her spine.
The skirt was full and swirled luxuriantly to the hem.
"I love it." She smiled her gratitude, holding the gown
to her breast. "I have something for you, too." Gwen
went to her closet and came back with a small jeweler's
box. She hadn't intended to give it to him yet, rather
had been saving it for their actual honeymoon.

His fingers were clumsy as he unwrapped the ribbon
from the lid and opened the clasp to reveal a beautifully
engraved Swiss watch. "It's my way of saying I intend
to make every moment count," she said softly.

"Thank you. I couldn't have asked for a better gift."
He placed it on his wrist, then held out his forearm to
admire the gleaming gold against his hair-roughened
skin. He smiled, then turned back to her more seriously. "I want to make up for all the time we were
apart. The heartache you went through." He closed the
space between them and folded her close to his chest.
His voice lowered tensely as his eyes searched her face.
"I want us to be happy without the past and what might
have been clouding our thoughts."

"You have made it up to me," she said emotionally.

Mouth set grimly, he shook his head. "No I haven't,"
he said with self-censure, "but I will Gwen, I will."

He kissed her passionately, tempering his desire to
her needs. Breathing hard, erratically, she clung to him,
the tension knotting in the lower section of her body.

She shifted closer to him, needing his strength, relishing the hard proof of his desire, the sinewy tensility of his thighs. He moaned, cupping her close. "And what better time to start than right now."

He made love to her unhurriedly, sensually. In her heart she was as nervous as she had been the very first time they had made love. But there were differences, aside from age, and those differences, along with his loving regard, soon put her at ease. Where he'd been clumsy before, now he was sure and skilled. Her response to him had deepened, as had his to her. They were able to draw out each moment, linger and appreciate, savor and love. Married love, Gwen noted early the next morning as Dan slept cradled beside her, was inherently more satisfying, not less.

The next two weeks of August passed easily as they adjusted to the many entanglements of being man and wife. Insurance policies had to be changed. Gwen had to notify her bank and the drivers' license bureau of her change of name. But other than the few technical problems, she was surprised, really, at how very easily their lives meshed. It was only when he began to look to the past again that the trouble began.

"I want to hire a private detective to find our child," Dan said one night at dinner.

The fear that had haunted her for the last decade returned full force. Somewhere deep inside she was afraid that maybe this was why he had married her. It, more than anything else including their mutual job complications, was the reason she had allowed him to talk her into the hasty wedding. She'd been afraid that to wait would be to analyze too much, to wonder again and again what might have been if only they'd come together as a family, as man and wife, sooner. She put down her fork. "Dan, I promised we wouldn't interfere when I gave the child away."

He pushed his chair back from the table and stood, eyeing her contemplatively. "That's just it, Gwen," he said in a low, distractingly reasonable tone. "*You* promised, not me." Obviously, he'd been giving the matter considerable thought. "There's a chance we could have our child back or at least gain visitation rights to him or her. I've talked to a lawyer who's an expert on such cases, Gwen. He thinks we may have a case."

Fear was a wrenching pain in her stomach. "Because of your lack of knowledge of the adoption procedures?" Her limbs could have been chiseled in ice. She felt barely capable of speech.

Dan nodded. Never had she seen him look more intensely committed. Not to her, not to anything. Not even his father's illness had prompted such an incredible protective, possessive stance. They were talking about his child, she realized—his child, too. A child he never would have voluntarily relinquished.

"Yes. Fathers' rights are new in these cases. But it is a valid issue," Dan continued. One he felt strongly about.

For a moment Gwen allowed herself to entertain a brief ray of hope. Then reality came crashing in. She would not destroy her child's entire world, not for her own happiness. "Dan, we can't. It would be selfish." She stood, too. They circled restlessly, like boxers squaring off in the ring.

Her reluctance to open up the Pandora's box he had expected. His voice soothingly low, he consoled, "All I need is the name of the institution where you had your child, Gwen, a statement from you detailing your mental and emotional state at the time and your permission to proceed. You wouldn't have to go back if you find it upsetting, at least not initially. We could handle everything quietly, privately, through our lawyers. I hope it would need never become public, with the exception of the dealings between us, our child and his or her adoptive parents." Reading the open rejection on her face, he pointed out in the same methodical tone, "You were under a lot of strain, Gwen, in no condition to make a decision like that." He was deadly earnest, obviously convinced that he was taking the right course. His sense of responsibility wasn't surprising.

"At that time in my life I was in no condition to raise a child, either." Her voice broke with emotion. "It's the only time in my life I have ever been completely selfless, Dan. Don't force me to give that up, too."

He didn't want to. Neither could he live with himself, knowing he had a child. "My point is, if you'd had proper counseling you might have taken another route. You might have notified me of your pregnancy or placed the child in the care of my parents or some other suitable home temporarily, had you been thinking straight." In his opinion, she would have done anything except give up her child.

Maybe he was right, Gwen thought. And maybe he wasn't. At any rate, was it fair to hurt the child now because their hindsight had suddenly gotten better? Yet in her heart she knew how Dan must feel. She'd agonized over the decision for months before finally relinquishing her child for adoption. He'd never had the chance to make the decision or do what he felt was the right thing for the child.

"The courts and the lawyers will take it from there," he persuaded softly. "I know what you're thinking," he concluded. "Before we were married the outcome of such an action was questionable. But now..."

Another icier chill encompassed her heart. "Was that the only reason you married me?" Tears were thick in her throat.

"I married you because I love you." He tried to take her in his arms. She resisted, and he stepped back, his mouth tightening. His tone was less soothing as he continued, more aggressively determined, "It's for the same reasons I want our child. You can't tell me you haven't wished for the same, the opportunity to have a second chance, to regain the child. I've watched you with other children, Gwen. You're envious."

Tell him now, she thought. *Tell him now how you broke into the Welby Home for Unwed Mothers and looked at their records. Tell him you know firsthand the child we created is all right.* But when she tried, the words wouldn't come. In her heart she was too afraid. Afraid he would see the knowledge she harbored but had not shared as even further betrayal. She was afraid he would use that knowledge to obtain his own desires, and in the process inadvertently hurt so many innocent others.

"Why can't we just let it go?" she said softly, ignoring for a moment that she did know full well how he felt; at one point in her life she had been driven to resolve the same vital issues. "We could have our own child now, Dan," she pointed out persuasively. "One we could nurture from birth." Yet never once had he mentioned the possibility. Instead, even after the ceremony, he had taken precautions to make sure she was protected from pregnancy. "I want to have your baby."

He hesitated. Something in her died as she read the reluctant rejection in his eyes. "I want that, too. But...not now." His jaw tautened. "Not until we discover that our firstborn is all right." He wouldn't behave irresponsibly again. In a softer tone of voice, Dan continued, "I'll never be able to rest until I do know that for a fact."

But would he be satisfied with that, Gwen wondered. No, chances were he'd want more. And she couldn't risk the hurt their child might endure. It was too vulnerable a time for Dan. He wasn't thinking clearly.

"I can't do this," she said, refusing to meet his probing look. And then, more emphatically, she added, "I won't."

He studied her for long moments, then seeing the force of feeling behind her decision, exhaled raggedly. Abruptly, unexpectedly, the argument was closed. "All right," he said heavily. Both of his palms raised in acknowledgment of defeat. "Peace?"

Relief surged through her. "Peace."

They did the dinner dishes in uneasy silence. Together they mounted the stairs to their bedroom. For the first time since their marriage he did not make love to her, but turned his back. She knew he was hurting badly, but she was powerless to do anything about it. At only one other time in her life had she known such despair. She'd lost her child then; she didn't want to lose him, too.

Chapter Eleven

"Gwen, it is so sweet of you to do this for me," Phyllis Quarrick said, helping Robyn braid her long red-brown hair.

The chicken pox epidemic that had been slowly working its way across several counties had finally come to the Quarrick home. Robyn was immune, due to exposure several years previously, but Andrew was not. And unfortunately, he'd been subject to a very difficult case with high fever, sleeplessness and itching. Phyllis patted her daughter's shoulder affectionately, then stooped slightly to encompass her in a warm maternal hug.

"This poor darling has been wonderful since Andrew's been sick, but everyone deserves time out."

"Really, I don't mind," Gwen assured. "Especially since Dan's gone out of town for a few days to finish up the project he's been working on at the Lexington IDP complex." But when Phyllis had first called with the request that Gwen take Robyn to the new Disney movie in nearby Princeton, she had suffered her doubts. Was it wise for her to spend time with Robyn alone? And yet, knowing how busy they all were with work on the extension of the Dawson Springs Clinic, especially Doc, how could she refuse? And the truth of the matter was, she didn't have anything planned. Gwen glanced up at Phyllis with a purposeful smile. "You do look exhausted."

Andrew was covered with a liberal powdering of cornstarch and an assortment of sores, some healing, some not. To everyone's relief, his fever had finally waned the previous afternoon. Phyllis had her fingers crossed that he would begin sleeping normally soon.

"I've been going out of my mind trying to keep him from scratching," Phyllis said.

"He takes three baking soda baths a day," Robyn chimed in authoritatively.

Phyllis sent Robyn an affectionate glance. "And this little girl has been the most generous helper a mommy could want." She ruffled her daughter's hair. "You be good and mind Gwen, now."

The involuntary envy that had disappeared the day of her wedding was now back full force. Gwen blamed it on her distance from Dan, the fact he did not want to have a child now. "Will it be all right if we stop off for a quick ice cream before coming home?" Gwen asked hopefully. "There's a Dairy Queen on the way."

"If it's not too much trouble," Phyllis cautioned as a delighted Robyn jumped up and down in glee, clasping her hands together in mute appeal.

Gwen laughed. "None at all. And frankly, I'd be delighted with the ironclad excuse to splurge."

Elyse's habit of eating when depressed was beginning to rub off. Only now Elyse had lost her additional weight. Gwen, though holding steady, could easily be in danger of tipping the scales upward if she weren't careful. Which, after the interlude this evening, she intended to be.

"Do you diet all the time?" Robyn asked as they climbed into Gwen's Renegade and fastened their seat belts.

Gwen laughed. "More often than I'd care to admit. Why? Do you?" She shot the little girl a teasing glance. In a yellow-and-white shorts outfit, she looked very pretty. Her excitement showed as color shone in her cheeks.

"No. But my mom does. She says she hates it, too, but we all have to pay a price if we want to be beautiful."

"We sure do."

The movie comprised mostly slapstick, and Gwen found herself giggling right along with Robyn. Polite, well-mannered, responsible and shy, Robyn was any mother's delight. As promised, they went for ice cream after the show. Both had huge banana splits garnished with three kinds of sauce, whipped cream, nuts and cherries. They sat in Gwen's Jeep and ate, for lack of indoor facilities. "So you're going to be in what—fifth, sixth grade next year?" Gwen asked.

"Sixth," Robyn replied, licking chocolate syrup from the back of the spoon. "After that I go to junior high."

"Do you like school?"

"Oh, yes. I take piano lessons, too. Did Mom and Dad tell you?" When Gwen nodded her head, Robyn confided with a mock terrified glance, her wrist thrown dramatically across her forehead, "We have a recital every spring." Straightening in her seat, she continued more seriously, "Maybe you can come to it next time."

"I'd like that. How do you like having a baby brother?"

"Oh, sometimes Andrew's a real pain. He tears up my Barbies and gets into my stuff. And he colored on the wall of my room. But I love him a lot. He's really cute. And he's been so sick this week."

"I know." Empathy swelling in her heart, Gwen looked at the tears in Robyn's eyes. "You're happy, aren't you, living here in Dawson Springs?" Gwen's heart was pounding in her chest. But she had to know. This once, however casually, she had to ask.

Robyn shot her an odd look. "Sure. Why wouldn't I be?"

Gwen caught herself just in time. She shrugged her shoulders lazily, waving her hand—with effort, keeping it from trembling. "Oh, I don't know." She laughed, venting her nervousness with the recollection, "Sometimes when I was a kid I used to fantasize that I lived in Hollywood or New York City or Washington, D.C."

"Oh, yeah, I do that, too." Robyn let out a riotous giggle. "Most of all I'd like to live in Florida, though, so I could visit Disney World and Epcot Center every day."

Their chatter was similarly inane the rest of the evening. Gwen dropped Robyn off, then drove home to discover Dan's car parked in the driveway. Surprised, and sorry that she hadn't been home to greet him when he first arrived, she walked into the house. "Dan?" She called up the stairs, then stopped, seeing the sheaf of papers spread out over the dining-room table. Along with her college record and employment history, there was a detailed report of her volunteer work for the Welby Home in Cincinnati, as well as a report of her stay there and a copy of a birth certificate dated May first, eleven years priorly.

Ashen-faced, Gwen looked up to see Dan standing in the shadows by the stairs. He was studying her face, waiting, watching. When she issued no immediate denial, he said quietly, "You've known all along where our daughter is, haven't you? And just watched me suffer." He saw her hoarding of the knowledge as further betrayal.

Somehow she found her voice, desperate to explain. "I was afraid of what you'd do." Afraid of what she had almost done herself earlier that evening.

There was no quarter in his eyes as he slowly descended the stairs and, fists clenched tautly at his side, approached her. She'd never seen him looking so angry. Her heartbeat accelerated triple-time. It was suddenly difficult to swallow.

"Do Doctor and Phyllis Quarrick know they've adopted our child?" he asked icily at last, his look registering well the depth of betrayal he felt.

Tears clogged Gwen's throat. "No."

She hadn't known either, not at first. But he wasn't interested in hearing any of her explanations. She watched as he strode past her toward the front door. She pivoted and followed him, each breath feeling as if it were being forcibly wrenched from her chest.

"Where are you going?" Her voice was tearful and unsteady. Her whole world was disintegrating.

He pivoted sharply to face her, a muscle twitching convulsively in his jaw. "Does it matter?" He seemed to be daring her to try to claim that it did.

Aware that there was no reasoning with or placating him in his present mood, she remained silent.

"I can't stay here," he said finally. "I don't trust myself to be civil." His mouth thinned even more as he tensely related, "Nor can I go to my folks or a local hotel without a big explanation." He shot her a chill look.

She could understand his leaving. Maybe it was wise. But if it were to be for good...no, her heart wouldn't accept that. "When will you be back?" They had to talk, but only after he had calmed down enough to really absorb what she had to say.

He threw back his head, the bitterness welling up from his throat in a short exhalation of breath. "Let's put it this way, Gwen. Don't wait up!" The door slammed behind him.

She was furious with him, and yet she understood his hurt. But when the hours passed one after another and he didn't return home, her anger increased.

Nor did he return the next day or the next. More humiliating was the call she received from his mother. Gwen took it the third afternoon, in her cubbyhole at the Clinic. "Hi, Betty, what can I do for you?"

"I thought you might be lonely, with Dan out of town," her mother-in-law said pleasantly. "I wondered if there was anything I could do."

Not unless you can turn back the clock, Gwen thought. *Not unless you can change the events of the past.* What had Dan told her, Gwen wondered, chagrined. "A bit lonely," she answered lightly, wishing Betty would get to the point before she gave herself away. "How's Miles?"

"He's fine. Delighted with his new employee. Anyway, the other reason I called you, dear, is that Dan promised to bring his father a special new strain of plant seed when he returns from Chicago tomorrow. I know he'll go home first—and well he should—but do you think you could ask him to stop by as soon as possible the next morning? Miles is anxious to get his fall plants in the ground."

"I'll tell Dan," Gwen promised, hoping she would see him, that he would eventually call her or come home, and that this wasn't the end of their marriage. "Is there anything else I can do? Anything I could bring you from town?" Heaven knew she had plenty of time on her hands.

"No, darling, just take care of yourself and give my son a kiss."

"I will."

Steamed, Gwen hung up the phone. How could Dan do that to her? Leave her in such an embarrassing position! Damn him anyway! Again, that evening there was no word from Dan. On impulse she got his phone number in Chicago from information and dialed that number. Again, there was no answer.

She refused to let herself speculate where he might be and with whom. Still, sleep wouldn't come. Midnight passed with her wide awake, then one o'clock, two o'clock. Around three-thirty she heard his car in the driveway. Stiffening, Gwen waited. His steps moved across the porch. She had pulled on a robe and was at the top of the stairs when he walked in the front door, looking grim but sober.

He was dressed in a dark business suit and tie, looking every bit as distant and untouchable as he had that first day he'd learned the identity of their daughter. She had the feeling that they'd lost all the ground they'd recouped the past couple of months. She hated the distance between them. But her pride and her anger refused to make it easy for him. Not after he had walked out on her again for the second time in his life. *Did he think she would willingly be a doormat on which he could wipe his feet?*

"Your mother called." Stiffly, she repeated Betty's message. "Do you have any idea how I felt, hearing your whereabouts from her?"

"Probably the same way I did, discovering we had a child you'd given up for adoption." Dan paused. He sent her a level look. His jaw was clenched. "Did she know we were fighting?"

"No, at least I don't think so." Gwen was relieved to know their embarrassment about that was mutual. She did not want their personal troubles broadcast to their acquaintances. He nodded, as if that much of what she had done met his approval. She stiffened even more. His eyes caught immediately on the stacked blanket and pillows she had tossed down to the foot of the stairs just seconds before.

His mouth twisted. "Planning to keep me from your bed as well?" He looked her up and down laconically.

"I don't want another ugly scene." She turned on her heel and fled. The door slammed behind her, and the lock caught. Her fingers shook as badly as her knees.

The sound of his footsteps sounded heavily on the stairs. Her pulse pounded as he halted outside her door. "It's not going to work, Gwen. We're married, remember? To have and to hold from this day forward?"

She'd assumed he would demand she open the portal, would try to jiggle the lock. He kicked open the bedroom door, stood framed in the shadowy light of the hall, his hands on his hips.

She hated more than anything the complacency on his face. "You are not sleeping with me tonight!" she said between gritted teeth.

He stepped forward, his presence forcing her involuntarily back. The door shut behind him.

Her chin shot up as the lock clicked softly closed. *He's testing you, trying to scare you, to see how you'll react. Wait it out.* She did nothing. He stepped forward, one arm outstretched. Her tenuous composure fled. She twisted away from him, her arms hugging her breasts. "No!" Her breathing was as labored as if she had run several miles.

His mouth tightened. His eyes focused on her breasts, taking in the open summer robe, the thin lawn shift, the nipples peaking visibly beneath the cloth. He swallowed a lungful of oxygen, but his coldness matched hers in tone and vehemence. "Oh, yes, Gwen, tonight, and every other. You may have shut me out of all the details about the child, but you're not shutting me out of here."

Her head held high, she strode past him with as much dignity as she was able to muster. He let her get past him to the door. "Okay, then *I'll* sleep on the sofa," she said, her hand on the knob. She could feel his eyes slicing into her, could hear him turn toward her, his polished shoes moving on the bare parquet floor

He caught her by the shoulder and wrested her around. "No one sleeps on the sofa. Not tonight or any other." The grip on her shoulders intensified, his body hard as stone with the control on his temper that he was exerting. Lower, he said, "I spent half my life in love and away from you. I'll be damned if I'm going to spend the other half that way, too."

Unexpectedly, tears misted her vision. They were destroying each other by inches. "You just spent three days in Chicago without me."

"I had business to conduct, funds that needed to be raised for the clinic. I saw some friends there, people with money who might be willing to contribute. As it happened, some did. I felt we needed the time apart, to think."

She couldn't argue that. "You could have called me."

He shrugged uncaringly. "I could have. I didn't. I didn't want to."

He didn't have to be that bluntly honest. "And I'm supposed to accept that and welcome you with open arms?" Her tone was saccharinely sarcastic.

There was a pause. His grip relaxed to the former gentleness she had known. "Maybe we both have some forgiving to do," he said roughly, but inexplicably there was a new, more familiar tenderness in his gaze.

They were both human and they had made mistakes. She felt her resistance weakening. She didn't want to give in to him, yet she felt powerless to turn the tides of what she was feeling. She raked her hands through her hair, pushing it away from her face. "You don't understand anything about me," she said. She couldn't hold on to a single thought except how it would be to get close to him again.

He reached over to extinguish the single lamp burning dimly by her bedside. There was a click, then darkness, another tingling moment as their eyes adjusted to the blackness, as his hand reached up to loosen, then discard his tie and his suit coat and unfasten the first buttons on his shirt. She stood paralyzed—watching, waiting, knowing that she wanted him to continue, that she would die if he didn't.

"Then show me what you feel," Dan counseled softly, taking her once again into his arms. This time his touch was thoroughly gentle. His voice was exhausted, subdued. He, too, was tired of fighting, weary to his bones, needing only to hold and to be held by her in return. She realized in that instant how very much she'd hurt him. "I need to know you want me, Gwen," he whispered, his mouth trailing over the nape of her neck. His hands found her breasts, the heart of his palms the tender, engorged nipples. Her flesh swelled, grew vibrant beneath his searching caress. "Not just physically, but as part of your life, your soul." He captured her face between his palms, the heat of his skin searing her to her soul. "There's so much I don't know about what you're feeling, hoping, dreaming," he said. The heels of his hands dropped across her shoulders, splayed across her collarbone to rest on her breasts. A warmth flowed through her, vibrant, as assuaging as his voice. He folded her near, his breath stirring her hair. "So much I want to discover, if only you'd let me."

"I never meant to hurt you," she said. And she knew then that he'd never really meant to hurt her. Tears blurred her vision. She needed to forgive as much as she needed to be forgiven.

He kissed her gently. "Promise me you won't disrupt Robyn Quarrick's life," Gwen said.

"She's our flesh and blood, Gwen."

"If we were to interfere now, we'd ruin Robyn's life. I can't do that to her. Can you?"

Gwen had had ten years to wrestle with the problem, he just a few days. "I don't know," he said softly. "I can promise you this. I won't act hastily. I won't do anything this week, this month, maybe not even this year." He sighed heavily, honestly meeting her gaze. "But beyond that, I don't know. I'm just not sure I'll ever be able to give up the idea of having her with us, of somehow being a part of her life."

SUNDAY AFTERNOON FOUND THEM having dinner with his parents at their farm with a host of other guests. The occasion was Betty and Miles's thirty-fifth wedding anniversary.

"I'm glad we've had this time together this summer," Dan's father admitted as they strolled along the lawn. Dan leaned back against the base of an oak, loosening his tie.

"Then you're not upset that I'm headed back to work at IDP?"

Miles shook his head, reaching into his pocket for the after-dinner mints he now savored in lieu of a cigarette. "No. I admit to having had thoughts in that direction after my heart trouble in June. I realize now, after working with Tim Kaufman, seeing his passionate desire to farm, that I just wanted to pass on my expertise. To someone young, someone who felt the same." Miles grinned, offering Dan a mint. "As much as I've enjoyed having you here with me, son, I have no desire to chain you to the yoke like some recalcitrant ox. It's a hard world out there, Dan. It looks as though you've found your niche. My advice is to go for it." Miles grinned again, clapping him on the back, "Just make sure you take that pretty wife of yours with you."

Finding Gwen proved nearly impossible, though, particularly since the last time he'd really had sight of her was during the noon meal. Since then they had gone separate ways, mingling with guests and friends. He knew that she was still upset with him about his attitude toward their child. But there was no helping it, and he wouldn't lie to her about how he felt. There'd been too much dishonesty between them in the past. Hands in his pockets, Dan strolled the yard. Children of all ages and sizes, dressed in their Sunday best, were scattered over the premises in rowdy bands. He smiled, watching them play.

Robyn approached, busily blowing bubbles from one of the plastic kits his mother had thoughtfully provided for their entertainment. "I'm glad your parents are having this party," she said gaily, agitatedly waving her small pink plastic wand in the air. She watched the silvery coils sparkle in the afternoon sun. "These bubbles are fun! And the food was terrific, especially that chocolate coconut cake!"

"I'm glad to hear that," Dan said. He had no complaints about how the Quarricks had raised her. She was a thoroughly engaging child. Remembering her fondness for her own black-and-white cat, Buttons, he said, "Would you like to see the kittens that were born last week? They're around the side of the house, beside the porch."

"Oh, yes." She glanced with momentary trepidation at her dress. "That is, if we won't get dirty. My mother will kill me if I ruin this dress!"

Dan laughed at her mockingly aghast tone and tomboy nature. "I promise you we'll both stay clean as a whistle, scout's honor."

Several other children accompanied them. They found the kittens sleeping in a flannel-lined wicker basket, curled up next to the black-and-white mother cat.

Observing the litter raptly, Robyn was the last to leave. She glanced up at Dan. "How come your cats are all different colors?"

"A neighbor of ours had a litter. The mother cat died, so we brought the kittens over to nurse with our mother cat."

"So she adopted them," Robyn observed, delighted.

"Yes."

Robyn ran a hand through her tousled red-brown hair, her fingers brushing the bangs from her forehead impatiently. It was a gesture Gwen used often. He found the similarity disturbing. "I'm adopted, did you know that?" Robyn said more seriously as they walked back to join the others.

Slowly, Dan gave his head a negative shake. *Give me the strength and wisdom to get through this,* he prayed.

"Andrew's not," Robyn continued importantly. "My mom said it doesn't make any difference, though, she loves us both the same." Her mouth curled thoughtfully. Clearly she was untroubled by the admission. And Phyllis did love her children equally.

Dan nodded to show he was listening. As if knowing she had a sympathetic audience, Robyn mused, explaining further, "My biological mother was too young and couldn't take care of me, so she made the biggest sacrifice a mother can make, and gave me to Mom and Dad." She was quiet for about one second. Dan had time to realize just how much of a sacrifice his wife had made, and that she truly had done it out of love. Knowing Gwen, knowing her inherently giving nature, it had to have been immensely painful. But, as always, she'd put the needs of others—in this case their child, a child she still loved from afar—ahead of her own. He couldn't help but admire her for that. He wasn't sure he would ever have possessed such unselfish strength.

Jubilantly, Robyn informed him, "Naturally, Mom and Dad were so happy they couldn't stop smiling for days!"

Dan grinned. "If someone could package your exuberance we'd all be rich!"

"What does that mean?" she asked, flushing to demonstrate that she knew she'd received a compliment.

"It means you're fun to be around. Don't ever change."

Robyn rolled her eyes in a clownish gesture, then eyed him shyly for a long moment. Dan's heart was near to bursting. He knew now why Gwen had wanted to be near their daughter. Seeing her didn't make up for all they had lost, but it made him feel a hell of a lot better about giving her up, knowing she was happy, almost dauntlessly so.

"I've got to go now. Thanks for taking me to see the kittens." Robyn dashed off to join the other children lining up to play Red Rover.

Dan glanced up to see Gwen staring down at him from the front porch. Obviously, she had misinterpreted what had gone on between the two of them. Before he could close the distance between them, she was disappearing back into the house. His father, meanwhile, stopped Dan to have him repeat the latest series of company jokes for the other men's benefit. It was nearly half an hour before he was free to look for Gwen again.

He found her in the dining room, surrounded by many of the same relatives and friends who had attended their wedding only weeks before. She was bending her head, listening animatedly to something Nicki Kaufman had to say, while holding their baby boy in her arms. When she glanced down at the infant, Gwen smiled, looking so blissful and content and maternal that it was incredible. Abruptly, he knew what he had to do, perhaps what they should have done all along. Winding his way to Gwen's side, he drew her off and spoke quietly.

"We need to talk."

She turned toward him, vaguely accusing, afraid. It irritated him to see that she still mistrusted him so. Yet, to be honest, he knew he hadn't given her much reason not to where Robyn Quarrick was concerned.

"Not here," she said quietly, smiling across the room at someone else. At the touch of his hand on her elbow she disengaged herself from the group and started toward the front door.

"No," he agreed. And not in her house, either. He wanted to be somewhere neutral, somewhere with no past or present to intrude.

They left his parents' farm with the first crush of people. As he drove, he filled her in on his plans for the next twelve hours. "You're sure you don't mind?" he asked minutes later as they shrugged out of their dressy attire and into more casual clothes. He knew peripherally that his decision to camp out might seem odd to her. But he didn't want to explain fully, not yet. He'd rather that waited until they were alone and the time was right.

"I want to be with you," she said simply. "If you feel you need to get away that badly—"

"I do." It was settled, then.

What Gwen didn't have at home, they stopped and bought. He drove her Jeep to a ranger station at the Pennyrile Forest State Resort Park and registered at the information center. They hiked toward a deserted area where camping was allowed. They stopped shortly before dusk on a hilly site next to a stream. It was the end of summer; there was no one else around. The mountain air was clean and fresh, and as the sun set and Dan knelt to light their small Sterno-fueled stove, it was distinctly cool.

While Dan set up the pup tent and rolled out their sleeping bags, she heated water for coffee and sliced some cheese and bread. As both had eaten a heavy noon meal, neither professed to be very hungry. He watched her quietly, noting the strain on her face. With the hike it had lessened but was still there. "I've put you through a lot lately, haven't I?" he observed softly.

Gwen grinned ruefully. Her arms and back were aching from the long trek with the heavy pack. Noticing, he came over to massage her shoulders with the firm but gentle touch she cherished. "I've wanted to be with you. I haven't wanted to force you to stay, even temporarily," she said. And she knew that for the last month or so his presence in Kentucky had been at least as much for her sake as for his dad's.

His intent look telegraphed his love. "You didn't force me to do anything, Gwen. I needed to be with you again."

"But you resented the fact that I forced you to do that here." Because she wouldn't return to Chicago with him as his live-in companion or lover or friend.

"Maybe initially. But it was more complicated than that, Gwen." The massage stopped. The coffee was hot and fragrant. Wordlessly, Dan leaned forward to pour them each a cup, then looked out at the dark night sky, relishing the simple quiet, the sounds of the wind whistling through the trees, the fresh mountain air, the hard feel of the ground beneath him as he stretched out alongside her.

Casually he related his earlier conversation with his dad, what Miles had said about Dan not belonging on the farm. "I don't think I've ever loved him more than I did today." He took Gwen's hands in his and rubbed his fingertips lightly over her knuckles, delighting in the warmth and the smoothness of her skin. "I always knew Dad was there for me, of course, no matter what. When I got myself into the scrape with the local police for hanging toilet paper in the school yard trees, he bailed me out. Never said a word. But one look let me know how he felt. Later, when I wanted to go to an Ivy League school, he urged me on, even though I know in his heart he and Mom both would have preferred to have me at a college much closer to home. The same was true when I took a job at IDP. They knew I needed to be challenged professionally to be happy. And they supported my decision to go after success with every fiber of my being." He sighed. "That's why I was so upset earlier in the summer. I knew Dad had never asked me for anything. So how could I refuse his request to stay on and manage the farm, just until he recovered? But at the same time I knew how he felt, about wanting me to live closer to home, about wanting to pass on the farm to someone who cared. What was worse, I realized I'd disappointed him by not carrying on in the same tradition, sharing his hopes, his dreams, his way of life.''

"You can't fabricate that," Gwen counseled softly. "No matter how much you love him. You are what you are."

"I know that now. But then, all I felt was guilty. And I vented some of my anger on you. I'm sorry."

"We were both difficult in the beginning." *For reasons far more complex.* She paused. "Dan, I saw you talking to Robyn earlier today." Despite herself she was unable to keep the worry out of her tone. She knew how that felt—to want to tell the child for reasons that were purely selfish.

He nodded. "She told me she was adopted." Gwen's breath stalled in her chest. She could hear her heart thudding mercilessly; her hands were damp. "I didn't say anything to her," Dan assured levelly. Relief poured through Gwen. "I love her too much to put her happiness in jeopardy," he explained.

"That's the way I feel, too." Gwen said quietly.

He studied her closely. "There isn't going to be any storybook ending for us, no happily-ever-after?" Though he hated to give up on the dream of their someday all being together, he saw now more and more that it was patently unrealistic. Like Gwen, sooner or later he was going to have to make a choice. And it wasn't going to be any easier for him than it had been for her years before. If anything, it was tougher. Because if he did let her go, and later Robyn found out who he was and why he had not acknowledged her, she might never forgive him. Yet if he did interfere, if he tried to take her away from her adoptive father, she would probably never forgive him, either. Either way, it seemed to him, he would lose.

He rose and said, "All my life I've walked the straight and narrow, Gwen. I thought I had my priorities straight. I put work and responsibility first. Discovering that I'd sired a child threw me. All these years I'd thought basically you had turned your back on me, not the other way around, when you refused to wait for me, to continue our relationship after I was away at school. Finding out that wasn't so was a shock. I knew I'd let you down badly. I wanted to erase those years of hurt. All I could think was that Robyn was our flesh and blood, that we should raise her or at least play a major role in her life. Today, spending time with her changed my mind. If she'd been unhappy or neglected it would have been easy to disrupt her life. But to hurt a happy child—I couldn't do it."

"I know. I felt the same."

He came back to sit beside her. He watched her steadily. After a moment, he said, "You're sure you're not going to mind leaving Dawson Springs?" Dan lifted her hand to his mouth and caressed the skin with his lips. He slanted a glance down toward her. She felt vulnerable beside him and yet so strong. He looked at her steadily. He was talking about leaving Robyn, she knew.

"I think it's for the best. I am glad we're keeping the house, though, for a weekend retreat." It would enable them to see the Quarricks and his family from time to time.

"I am, too. I want us to have a child, Gwen."

Gwen paused. It was what she had waited and prayed for, and yet she was filled with a terrible sense of disquiet. She'd seen what happened to Buddy and Elyse's marriage when he tried to pressure her into having his child before she felt ready. "You know I want that more than anything," she began, "but I don't want you doing this just to make up to me for what we lost." She didn't want to trap or force him into anything. And he hadn't been ready just weeks before.

"I'm very sure I want your child," he said, taking her into his arms. "And what better place to make a child than on a bed of Kentucky bluegrass and fallen leaves, the stars overhead, the breeze stirring the air."

She laughed, loving the reassuring quality of his touch. "You make it sound so romantic," she said, tracing the lines of his face.

"That's because it is." He followed her down to the ground, kissing her upturned lips. "Every time I'm with you I feel as if I've been blessed with my heart's desire."

DAN AND GWEN ATTENDED the white sale and fundraiser for the clinic on Saturday evening. It was the last time they would see all their Dawson Springs friends before leaving for Chicago, and they circulated freely, talking and laughing.

"We're sure going to miss having the two of you around," Buddy said, wrapping his arm around Elyse. Since the two of them had reconciled, they had the glow of honeymooners. And, though, according to

Elyse, no decision had been made as to when to have a child, they had at least agreed that both did eventually want a family and were discussing the timing at length, with eventual compromise as to timing, in mind.

"We'll miss seeing you, too," Gwen said.

"But we'll keep in touch," Dan promised.

"You'd better!" Buddy and Elyse said in unison, laughing.

"How much longer until the new addition to the clinic opens?" Dan asked his friend. Buddy's construction company had done a first-rate job.

"Assuming the weather holds and we have no major construction problems, the end of October," Buddy theorized.

In the distance, Robyn Quarrick was playing with a group of children. Gwen drifted that way. After a moment, Dan followed her. "She's a beautiful child, isn't she?" he said softly, his breath brushing her earlobe.

At that moment, Robyn dashed forward. She stopped just short of Dan's feet and, out of breath, gazed up at his towering form. "My dad says you guys are leaving tomorrow!" she reported with her customary vivaciousness. In that respect she was more than ever like her adoptive mom.

Dan nodded. "That's right."

Robyn's face fell, mirroring her disappointment, but after a second she perked up. "You're going to be coming back, though, aren't you?" She narrowed her glance contemplatively, as if trying to come up with a way that would allow their friendship to continue.

"You bet," Gwen said.

"Great. And you'll come to see me when you do?" Robyn made them promise.

"Sure."

"All right!" Robyn made a forward cheering motion with her upraised fist. "Be sure and write!" she urged.

"I will," Gwen said softly. "You can write us, too, if you like."

"That'd be neat!" Robyn exclaimed. "See you later." With a last parting smile, Robyn raced gleefully back to join her crowd. Dan's hand meshed with Gwen's. His grip tightened. They both knew that they were doing the right thing.

Without warning, Phyllis Quarrick joined them. "We have to talk," she said quietly.

Dan and Gwen exchanged a glance. There was something knowing in Phyllis's glance, too knowing. It hadn't been there previously. Nor had Gwen ever seen her look so worried.

Doc joined his wife. Above his beard his eyes were tense with anxiety. "In the clinic," Doc specified.

The Quarricks waited until they were alone with Dan and Gwen before Doc spoke. "I wouldn't ask you this unless I were fairly certain, Gwen. But I need to know the truth, for our own peace of mind." He paused, biting his lip. Without warning, his glance drifted to a photo of Robyn on his desk. Gwen knew then what it was all about.

"Are you . . . ?" Phyllis asked. Her voice broke emotionally. She was unable to go on.

Gwen had an empathy for what they were going through. "I'm Robyn's biological mother," Gwen affirmed.

Chapter Twelve

"How did you find out?" Gwen continued calmly, when the gravity of the situation permeated her shock. She wondered how long they'd known.

Doc sighed, running a palm worriedly across his beard. Phyllis stood next to him, anguish showing on her face. "More than anything, it was an accumulation of facts, though not until Dan arrived on the scene, and we noticed the resemblance of the three of you, did we begin to put it together," Doc admitted. "Add to that your pale reaction when Robyn was brought in for stitches and your attempt to show no unusual interest in either of our children; yet we know for a fact how much you love children, Gwen, and how naturally they seem to gravitate to you, as was evidenced by your popularity with the girls at the first-aid session for the scouts. I've also wondered for a long time at the coincidence that brought you to us. You see, when I initially phoned one of your nursing supervisors in Cincinnati for a more complete reference, she was so gung ho in selling your skills to me that she even mentioned the fact that you had donated time at the Welby Home for Unwed Mothers, counseling girls. I wondered why you didn't mention it on your application when you applied to come and work here, but knowing how reluctant you are to proclaim your own worth, I thought nothing of it. Later, I began to wonder if there wasn't a more personal reason for your devotion."

Phyllis interjected, "An adoptive parent's greatest fear is the reappearance of the biological parents. We knew from the case history the agency provided at the time that there was the possibility that the unwed mother involved could probably, if she so chose, later claim duress. The counselors there assured us you were not likely to take such action, that you were very emotionally stable. But you were, after all, very young at the time. Your father had just died."

"I never meant to deceive you." Gwen sighed. "I didn't want to interfere."

Phyllis returned her graciousness, admitting softly, "We didn't want a lawsuit, nor did we want to confront you, particularly when we knew you were leaving Dawson Springs, but if there was one, we wanted to be prepared. And I guess maybe in our hearts we were hoping you would be satisfied just knowing Robyn was well cared for."

"When did you find out?" Dan asked.

"Only a few days ago. I talked to the adoption agency officials and explained. Fearing a lawsuit, they gave me Gwen's name in the hope any ugliness could be averted."

Dan and Gwen both assured the Quarricks that they wanted only the best for Robyn, and that meant having Robyn remain in the Quarricks' care. Phyllis and Doc both looked inordinately relieved. Gwen knew from their caring reaction that she was doing what was best for Robyn. "If you were afraid we were Robyn's parents, why did you let me take her to the movie?" Gwen asked curiously at length.

"I know what it is to love a child. I couldn't bear to give either of my children up. But I also know what it is to love a child, nurture it within you for nine months." She knew in her heart what a sacrifice Gwen had made. Phyllis shrugged, wiping tears away with the back of her palm. "I realized I was being selfish. And love isn't about holding someone back or keeping her all to yourself. Love is about letting go. And with Andrew sick, I realized I couldn't do it all. And you were so helpful when she was hurt. I felt I owed you the chance to get to know your daughter. And maybe, too, maybe I wanted to test you, to see if you would put her feelings first in this difficult situation." Gwen always had.

Tears seemed to be glistening all around. Doc and Dan cleared their throats.

"She is a very sweet girl," Gwen admitted. "And in a way much more yours than mine because you have raised her day-to-day. But I had to come to Dawson Springs to find that out. Now that I have, I know I can go on, at peace with myself and with what's happened to her."

Dan said quietly, "We've already decided not to disrupt your family." He and Gwen exchanged a look.

Gwen said, "Our decision hasn't changed. We want Robyn to be happy. That's all that counts." It was all that ever had, no matter how much hurt it caused to her and Dan. The child's needs came first. There was no other way.

The Quarricks looked extremely relieved. "We're grateful to you both. We think that would be best for

Robyn. At least for now. If and when there comes a time when she expresses curiosity about her natural parents..." Doc said conditionally.

"We'll be there for her," Dan promised. Gwen nodded her agreement.

Phyllis walked over to embrace Gwen. "In the meantime, you can see her whenever you like. We'll write and keep you posted on her development."

"That would mean a lot to us both," Dan said, clasping Gwen's hand.

It was much more than Gwen and Dan had ever hoped for. They left Dawson Springs, happiness flowing from them, the deception that had been weighing so heavily upon their hearts finally put to rest.

"WHAT HAVE YOU GOT THERE?" Dan asked several months later, looking up from the stack of parenting books on his lap.

Gwen smiled, handing him a stack of color photographs. "Another letter from the Quarricks. They sent pictures of the kids sledding." She smiled, opening a second envelope, addressed in a bold but childish scrawl. "There's also a letter from Robyn, thanking us for the gifts we gave her and Andrew for Christmas."

They'd gone back to Kentucky for the holidays, taking gifts for all of their friends. Miles was once again in excellent health. Tim and Nicki Kaufman had leased a home closer to the Kingstons. When Nicki delivered her second child, Betty Kingston would take care of their son Cade. Thanks to a steady salary and a time-payment plan offered them by the hospital, the Kaufmans would be able to afford the proper medical care without relying on charity.

Gwen handed Dan the letter and sat next to him on the living-room sofa. Absently, she stroked his shoulder. Although they'd been living in Chicago for nearly six months, she hadn't lost her wonder at just being with him. Rather, it seemed to increase by the day. As did their interest in their own forthcoming child.

"It says here the Quarricks may visit early next summer, see the sights." He cupped an affectionate hand over her thigh. His eyes met hers. He smiled. "Robyn wants to help out with the new baby, since she's already a pro, in her own words."

Remembering the freeway-like tangle of Ace bandages that Robyn, Andrew and the kitten had created, Gwen laughed. "Maybe she'll earn another scout badge in the process." Gwen smiled. "One on infant care."

"Do you miss seeing her?" Dan asked.

Gwen paused, reflecting. "Now that I have you and the baby to look forward to, not so much. But I think there will always be a very special place for Robyn in my heart." But she was clearly the Quarricks' child.

"In mine, too."

Dan breathed deeply, stretched. Then, as if reminded, he cast her a sideways glance. "Did you do your Lamaze exercises today?"

She groaned. "I knew you wouldn't forget."

"You're right about that much." He got up and retrieved the stopwatch and pillow. When she was comfortably settled on the floor with him beside her, they went through the now-familiar routine.

"So what do you think?" Dan asked lazily, stretching out beside her as soon as they were through. "A girl or a boy?"

"I don't care," Gwen said honestly, curling against his body. Her head rested on his shoulder. She inhaled the familiar scent of his skin.

"Neither do I." He gave a satisfied smile. Then he slanted her another more curious glance. "Any names?"

She sat up. They never had been able to agree on a name. "Not Hortense!"

"If it's a boy I was thinking about John," he said softly.

"After my father?" Tears blurred her eyes.

"And Miles after mine," he said. "John Miles Kingston. If it's a girl, though, I like Daffodil or Dandelion, something faintly ethereal."

She knew he was teasing. Groaning, she pulled the pillow back over her face. "Spare me."

He chuckled low and deep in his throat. "Spare you?" he mocked lightly, and pulling the pillow from her hands and lifting her shoulders, he placed it back beneath her head. "Not a chance, sweetheart. You and this baby are both going to get all the love I can give."

"I think I can live with that," she said, happiness huskily tempering her low voice.

"You're positive?" he bent toward her, bestowing her with a tender kiss.

"Absolutely," she murmured, kissing him in return. Passionate minutes later, he paused, lifting his head. "I think, for comfort's sake, we'd better continue this in the bedroom."

"I think," she said, accepting his hand up and the possessive wrap of his arm around her waist, "that you're right."

"What do you think?" she asked, moments later,

undressing him in the dark, loving it as he undressed her in return. "Is our future heir going to like having a mother who works part-time?"

"She or he'd be crazy not to love a practicing N.P.," he murmured, sighing mischievously as his fingers played low over her spine, folding her close. Everywhere he touched he ignited a wildfire of desire. "And regardless of sex, he or she is going to be computer-oriented."

"Of course." Tenderly, she took renewed possession of his mouth. "Now if we could just agree on a girl's name..."

"Later," he said, following her down onto the cool, crisp sheets. He blanketed her body with warmth, supporting his weight on his elbows, then rolling so that they lay on their sides, facing each other, one of his thighs resting cozily alongside hers. Tender stroking motions accompanied the low husky sound of his voice. "First things first, and loving you is always going to take number-one priority in my life."

"Mine, too," Gwen agreed, raining kisses down the hollow of his throat, her hands skimming down the smooth hard muscles of his back. She knew that she would never tire of his infinite gentleness, his concern, or the tender affection in his gaze. "Always."

You're invited to accept 4 books and a surprise gift Free!

Acceptance Card

Mail to: **Harlequin Reader Service®**

In the U.S.
2504 West Southern Ave.
Tempe, AZ 85282

In Canada
P.O. Box 2800, Postal Station A
5170 Yonge Street
Willowdale, Ontario M2N 6J3

YES! Please send me 4 free Harlequin American Romance® novels and my free surprise gift. Then send me 4 brand new novels as they come off the presses. Bill me at the low price of $2.25 each —an 11% saving off the retail price. There are no shipping, handling or other hidden costs. There is no minimum number of books I must purchase. I can always return a shipment and cancel at any time. Even if I never buy another book from Harlequin, the 4 free novels and the surprise gift are mine to keep forever.

154 BPA-BPGE

Name	(PLEASE PRINT)	

Address		Apt. No.

City	State/Prov.	Zip/Postal Code

This offer is limited to one order per household and not valid to present subscribers. Price is subject to change.   ACAR-SUB-1

Readers rave about
Harlequin American Romance!

"...the best series of modern romances
I have read...great, exciting, stupendous,
wonderful."
— S.E.,* Coweta, Oklahoma

"...they are absolutely fantastic...going to be
a smash hit and hard to keep on the
bookshelves."
— P.D., Easton, Pennsylvania

"The American line is great. I've enjoyed
every one I've read so far."
— W.M.K., Lansing, Illinois

"...the best stories I have read in a long
time."
— R.H., Northport, New York

*Names available on request.

You're invited to accept 4 books and a surprise gift Free!

Acceptance Card

Mail to: **Harlequin Reader Service®**

In the U.S.
2504 West Southern Ave.
Tempe, AZ 85282

In Canada
P.O. Box 2800, Postal Station A
5170 Yonge Street
Willowdale, Ontario M2N 6J3

YES! Please send me 4 free Harlequin Presents® novels and my free surprise gift. Then send me 8 brand new novels every month as they come off the presses. Bill me at the low price of $1.75 each ($1.95 in Canada)—an 11% saving off the retail price. There are no shipping, handling or other hidden costs. There is no minimum number of books I must purchase. I can always return a shipment and cancel at any time. Even if I never buy another book from Harlequin, the 4 free novels and the surprise gift are mine to keep forever.   108 BPP-BPGE

Name	(PLEASE PRINT)

Address	Apt. No.

City	State/Prov.	Zip/Postal Code

This offer is limited to one order per household and not valid to present subscribers. Price is subject to change.   ACP-SUB-1